Part 4

HEAD GAMES

Melodrama Publishing
www.MelodramaPublishing.com

FOLLOW
NISA SANTIAGO

FACEBOOK.COM/NISASANTIAGO

INSTAGRAM.COM/NISA_SANTIAGO

TWITTER.COM/NISA_SANTIAGO

Order online at
bn.com, amazon.com, and
MelodramaPublishing.com

Cartier Cartel - Part 4: Head Games. Copyright © 2018 by Melodrama Publishing. All rights reserved. No part of this book may be used or re-produced in any manner whatsoever without written permission except in the case of brief quotations embodied in critical articles or reviews. For information, address info@melodramabooks.com.

www.melodramapublishing.com

Library of Congress Control Number:2018957232
ISBN-13: 978-1620780992

First Edition: March 2019

Printed in Canada

cartier Cartel
Part 4
HEAD GAMES

NISA SANTIAGO

1

The Gansevoort Hotel in the Meatpacking District of New York City was the epitome of luxury. With mind-blowing 360-degree panoramic views of the city and the sunset over the Hudson River, it offered guests a retreat from the urban commotion that surrounded the hotel via 24-hour room service, spa treatments, spacious rooms, and a well-appointed bar.

One of the guests taking advantage of the hotel amenities was a former inmate, recently released from prison. Henry "Head" Jackson lounged shirtless on the king size bed in his boxers, his tattoos and battle scars on full display. He held the remote control to the flat screen TV in one hand. His other hand held the hotel phone to his ear.

Head wanted to devour a steak, swallow potatoes whole, and throw back some chilled champagne. He wanted to fully indulge himself and celebrate his freedom. Head had given the state his time, paid his debt to society as they said, and now it was time to live again.

"Yeah, this room service?" he asked. "I want that rib eye steak cooked medium-rare with the buttered potatoes and some cabbage. You got that right? I need my food to come fast. How long is the wait?"

While on the phone with the hotel's kitchen, Head's eyes switched their focus from the NBA playoffs to the beautiful young woman coming out of the bathroom wearing the hotel's monogrammed bathrobe. She had just finished taking a shower, and Head would have preferred she come out naked.

Her name was Pebbles, and she was an Instagram influencer. She had the face, the body, the personality, and she had over a million followers. Companies were paying her a substantial fee to post things like teas to flatten stomachs, indie clothing lines, and hair products. Pebbles had gifted the overnight stay at the Gansevoort. She was playing the big shot, trying to impress Head. She thought the infamous gangster whose past had been aired on numerous networks had millions of dollars hidden.

Head was over her continually talking on her phone about upcoming business deals. She walked around the room name-dropping celebrities, and after Pebbles thought she had proven she was somebody important, she turned her attention toward him.

She smiled at him. He didn't smile back. He was on the phone trying to satiate his hunger.

"Okay and do y'all have Ace of Spade champagne?" he continued. "Cool. Bring us up a bottle of that on ice."

Head ended the call. He could now focus solely on Pebbles. He had been released from prison early this morning and his woman, Pebbles, was there to pick him up. She had greeted him at the gates of the jail with hugs and kisses, and she was a sight for weary eyes.

"Did you order something for me, baby?" Pebbles asked.

"I didn't know you were hungry."

"I am. Are you gonna share then?"

"I got champagne coming up too," was his response.

She smiled and replied, "That's nice."

Head quickly put the television on mute. "When you got in the shower and washed away your dirt, why didn't you wash it all away?"

The question stopped Pebbles in her tracks. "What do you mean?"

"That makeup on your face. Why you still got it on? Who you trying to impress?"

Cute, she thought. *He's jealous.* "I only have eyes for you, bae."

"I told you 'bout that makeup, though," he said. "I like my women natural."

Pebbles nodded and went back into the bathroom to wash it off. It wasn't that she was insecure; she knew she was pretty. But her false lashes and perfectly groomed and penciled eyebrows gave her that extra layer of confidence. She didn't want to think about it, but she was a little nervous. Tonight would be the first time she and Head fucked, and she wanted to feel her sexiest. She now looked like she was going to the gym.

Pebbles wasn't out of the bathroom for sixty seconds before she went to the dresser and picked up her smartphone to check her social media accounts. Her phone was always buzzing with alerts, and text messages, and updates, and replies.

Head watched her like a hawk from the bed. He didn't understand the thirst for all this exposure. People posting their every move—breakfast, yoga poses, videos of making smoothies, gym workouts—the whole nine yards. For some reason, strangers were interested—people watching other people live their lives from the Internet. *Where is the thrill in that?* he thought.

Head was old school. In his era, niggas needed anonymity. A real nigga—a real hustler— made moves in silence and stayed ahead in the game. But this was a new generation, one that craved exposure and notoriety by any means necessary. Everyone wanted to be seen and heard. Everyone wanted to feel and look important, so social media became either their platform for acceptance or an escape from their mundane lives.

While he was locked down, he read about the fools who'd murdered the rapper XXXTentacion and how they had gotten caught from posting their shit on social media—Instagram to be exact.

"Stupid muthafuckas," he had said to himself.

Pebbles' attention was on her smartphone. She seemed hypnotized by the activity happening on the small screen. Her fingers moved in a blur when she was texting.

Meanwhile, Head felt like he was being ignored. "How long you gonna be on your phone?" he asked her.

"Give me a few minutes, baby. I'm just trying to handle some business."

"You need to handle *my* business. You know I just got out, right?"

Without missing a beat, she grinned his way and said, "I got you, boo," and continued to text.

Head sighed. He was hungry and he was horny, two of the worst things to be at the same time.

His eyes went back to the TV, watching the Bulls try to make it past the first round in the playoffs. So far, it wasn't looking good for them. They were down two games against Miami, and it looked like his team was on their way to being swept.

His eyes shifted toward Pebbles again. She was a busybody. She was multitasking, working her phone, doing her hair, and going in and out of the bathroom.

Pebbles was the youngest sister of Head's former cellmate, Danny Boy. She was thirty, but she looked to be in her early twenties. She had two kids by two different fathers who lived with her mother. Head knew she was fucking with him for who he was and what he probably could do for her. Head was the enigma, and Pebbles wanted in. His reputation in the streets and in New York was legendary. Even if he wanted to start over, it would be difficult for him to live a low-key lifestyle. His life story had been aired on all the cable networks—BET, Bravo, and AMC had all featured his life of crime. They broadcasted reenactments of incidents from his life of crime, and Head remained relevant because he was cool with celebrities, top rappers, and a few R&B groups when he was in his prime.

But his relevance also came with a cost, and that cost was the feds. The FBI suspected that he had hundreds of millions buried somewhere. They still had him under covert investigation. What people didn't understand was that these stories created by the government had helped bolster the agents' status, and drug dealers played right into their hands. When interviewed for cable networks, individual agents would explain that Henry Jackson had made over a hundred million dollars pushing cocaine and heroin in the New York hoods and beyond, and he was one of the top suppliers of narcotics on the eastern seaboard. The FBI felt they had good reason to believe that the bulk of his money was buried or concealed somewhere.

Let the feds tell it, Head had nearly fifty rival drug dealers murdered. Head knew it was an exaggeration. The number was half that. Dealers with egos would have co-signed the embellished tales, but not Head. The alphabet boys had been recycling the same rumor about buried money since the eighties. It was once the infamous Pablo Escobar's real story. Escobar and his cartel had buried billions, but niggas in the hood weren't burying money. They didn't have the time to search for it and dig it up, and what about erosion? Head did amass several million, but he didn't blow through hundreds of millions, as the media reported.

Head watched the basketball game for a few minutes, but he couldn't stay focused on it for too long. There was a knock at the door. Head predicted that it was room service finally arriving, but he marched toward the door and took a look through the peephole. Being from the streets, he knew you could never be too careful.

"Cover up," he told Pebbles and then opened the door to allow the room service attendant to wheel in the cart of food.

Pebbles sat in a chair, crossed her legs, and folded her arms across her breasts. She made sure her goodies weren't peeking out through the thick robe.

The look in Head's eyes affirmed that her actions weren't good enough. "So you just gonna disregard my orders and sit there naked under that robe while a stranger enters our room? You think that's legit?"

The young man was taken aback. *Orders,* he thought. *This is different.* The female wasn't doing anything different from what most guests did, which was get their room service in a bathrobe. This was a hotel. He shrugged it off and assumed he had just walked into the middle of a lovers' quarrel.

Pebbles looked down and in a low voice replied, "He can't see anything, Henry."

Head looked at Pebbles with a cold, hard stare. He had practically been begging to get fucked for hours, and she was getting her rocks off giving peep shows to this little broke nigga.

The young man went on to do his job. The champagne was in a bucket of ice. He removed the lid to the tray to reveal the meal Head had ordered. The aroma hit Head, and his anger dissipated. He was ready to eat and drink.

"Is everything to your liking, sir?" the room service clerk asked.

"Yeah, everything is on point."

Head tipped him twenty dollars. The young man thanked him and pivoted and left the room.

Head sat by the bed and immediately attacked the steak with a knife and fork and his hands, tearing it apart like a predatory beast that hadn't eaten in days. It had been years since he'd had food this good. The buttery potatoes were immediately devoured.

Pebbles watched him with a side eye. "I guess I'm not hungry."

Head paused for a moment, "C'mon now, let's not ruin our night." He popped open the champagne and poured two glasses.

Satisfying his hunger and thirst, he was ready for something special next. He fixed his eyes on Pebbles, who now had her lips poked out.

"Yo, why you all in your feelings?"

Pebbles didn't know if she should speak up, but within a few hours Head had done a 180. Behind bars, the nigga was Romeo making her all type of promises. He was courteous, attentive, and complimentary. And her makeup wasn't ever an issue. Now, he seemed cold and selfish.

"I guess I'm wondering why food wasn't ordered for me too. It ain't like you paying for it."

"Pebbles, you think you doin' something with this low budget bullshit?" His voice was low, measured, and had a hint of amusement. "You could have easily squashed this—whatever *this* is—and picked up the phone and ordered your own meal, maybe handled your business like a woman."

Head walked to the phone and picked it up. Seeing this, Pebbles went to stop him.

"Nah, chill," he said. "I got this."

Head ordered up a buffet of entrees, and the whole time Pebbles was about to go into full-blown panic mode. When he hung up, she began apologizing profusely. "You're right, this is petty. I was childish. I'll make it up to you, baby. Let's not fight."

Head replied, "I don't fight women," before turning his attention back to the game.

Pebbles got her room service, and then Head got his. He removed his boxers and lay back against the bed. Pebbles reached for a Magnum and popped it in her mouth and lowered it on his throbbing mushroom tip like a porn star. She then straddled him nice and slow as his thick, long penis stretched her pussy to its limit. He grunted as he felt every inch of her wet walls and reached up and squeezed her tits. As she slowly rode him, she smiled down at him and said, "You know this pussy is yours, baby. It's all yours. I know you waited a long time for this."

Head was hungry for every sexy inch of her nakedness.

"Ohhhh baby, fuck me!" she moaned.

Pebbles bit her bottom lip as she pushed him farther in. His erection was solid and hard as it explored her. She rubbed his chest and stomach, as their bodies sexually entangled. Head's body was muscular and smooth, and his dick was the best she had ever had. Their mouths parted, and they kissed enthusiastically. Pebbles continued to grind on his lap. Rhythmically they were one, as he was bringing her close to an orgasm. She wanted to come with him—to explode with passion together.

"You're so fuckin' tight!" he cried out. "You 'bout to make me come!"

Head continued to moan, thrusting upward into her until he finally exploded.

After he nutted, Head was drained. Pebbles collapsed on top of his chest, and they both drifted off into a peaceful sleep.

The following morning, while Head was still asleep, Pebbles removed herself from the bed and sauntered into the bathroom. She took a quick shower, applied some foundation and lip gloss, and then styled her hair. She wanted to take a selfie for the 'gram with her new boo—her handsome man—and the caption was going to say: *I woke up like this.* She eased herself onto the bed next to a sleeping Head, and she angled her smartphone just right so that she could capture herself and Head in the background. She grinned and was ready to take the picture when she heard him say, "Yo, what the fuck you doing?"

His booming voice interrupted her moment. She stammered, "I just wanted to take a picture with you."

He angrily pushed her off the bed, and she went tumbling to the floor. He leaped up and scowled down at an embarrassed Pebbles. She looked like she wanted to cry.

"It's not that serious," she said.

"It *is* that serious. You trying to put me on blast or something? You know I don't fuck wit' that social media shit," he hollered. "Don't put me in your stupid fuckin' world."

Pebbles was devastated by the outburst and wondered if she had crossed the line. She reasoned that Head was still institutionalized and not used to social media. But she saw the future and knew he'd eventually come around to seeing things her way. The more followers you had, the more addictive it became.

"Don't ever do that sneaky shit again. You know those peoples be watching!"

She picked herself up off the floor. "Okay, Henry. I hear you, and I'm sorry. Let's order breakfast and enjoy our morning."

Head nodded. "You do that. I'll be back in a few."

He hurriedly got dressed in his sweat suit and his Yankees fitted and left the hotel room, slamming the door behind him. Downstairs at reception, he gave Pebbles a noon checkout, paid the bill in full, and bounced.

2

Cartier sat behind the wheel of her Bugatti Chiron and checked her image in the visor mirror. She looked picture perfect for her man. Her lip gloss was popping, eyebrows threaded, and her eyelashes were long and curled. The outfit she wore showed just enough leg and cleavage to capture attention, but it still left something to the imagination. Cartier was still that classy boss bitch, and she dressed the part.

The first thing she wanted to do was hug and deeply kiss Head. Cartier knew that once she wrapped her arms around him that she wasn't going to let him go this time. A lot of time had passed, and a lot of foul things were said and done between them. She was in love with him, and she wanted to put all that behind them and make love to him until the sun came up.

Sitting in her Bugatti, Cartier started to feel a bit nostalgic. She remembered the first time they had met, when he damn near ran her over in his black Porsche Cayenne with the music blaring. Cartier had come at him disrespectfully, looking for a heated confrontation with the driver, but Head's calm and smooth demeanor quickly shut her slick mouth. Right away, she knew there would be strong chemistry between them.

Cartier sighed and kept cool, but she was excited. Her past was in her rearview, and she wanted a new beginning with Head. Fuck running the streets. Fuck revenge. Fuck pushing dope and moving ki's.

Cartier Timmons was reformed and officially out of the game.

Her eyes narrowed and keenly observed every Rikers Island bus that came to a stop. She watched men and women get off each bus, anticipating when he would finally arrive. But she didn't see him.

Isn't this ironic? she asked herself. It wasn't so long ago that Head showed up at her front door hoping to take her away from Hector and she shitted on him. She had made a mistake. Truthfully, she had made lots of mistakes, but those were growing pains. Her poor judgment was what allowed her to decipher what and who she wanted.

As each inmate got off each bus, they gawked at the expensive vehicle and its occupant in awe. Cartier looked like a celebrity from a distance. Rihanna, Remy Ma, Cardi B., even Mary J. is what most thought, and she loved the attention. She was finally back. Those few licks with Apple and Kola in South Beach had put her back on her feet where she belonged. Cartier refused to ever fall off again. She looked at the wood grain, bucket leather seats, and premium technology and snorted at what her life was like just a few months ago. The thoughts seemed like an alternate universe now, as if she was in a deep sleep and had dreamt about her mundane life in Seattle.

Waiting on Head had her mind skipping over dumb shit like what Edward was doing now and if he got to marry his white trophy wife. The thought of him instantly put her in a sour mood, so she pushed those irritating thoughts out of her mind and clicked on the radio. Ella Mai was singing "Boo'd Up," and she made a mental note to download her full album.

Time was moving at a snail's pace, but dusk finally came. The next bus came to a screeching stop, people got off, and still, no Head. It was the last busload coming from Rikers Island.

Cartier had sat for hours in the jail parking lot knowing that Head was supposed to be on one of the buses, but there was no sign of him. Had she missed him somehow? She felt that something was wrong. She sighed heavily, pulled out her cell phone, and made a call to the jail to find out about his release. Previously Cartier called from South Beach and was told that today was his release date, so where was he?

"He's been what?" she shouted at the jail clerk.

"He's been released already—days ago."

"How is that possible? He was supposed to be released today," she said.

"Well, he's not in our custody anymore, ma'am, and there's nothing else I can tell you," she said. "Call him."

Cartier ended the call abruptly, and she became livid.

"Muthafucka!" she yelled.

She started her car and peeled out of the parking lot so fast that it took several minutes for the smoke to clear. She did a beeline for the nearest highway and raced back to Brooklyn.

The spring weather brought everyone out into the streets. There were pockets of hustlers in their expensive toys, the block huggers, and the cute girls strolling through the neighborhood in trendy outfits. Cartier cruised through the area in her flashy Bugatti, and all eyes were on her. As the block was watching her, Cartier's attention was on searching for Head. She knew he would be somewhere on some block in Brooklyn, either in East New York, Brownsville, or Bed-Stuy. She pulled up to a group of hustlers on the corner. Immediately, the young boys recognized her.

"Cartier, what's poppin'?" one of the young hustlers asked.

"Y'all saw Head around here?" she asked them.

"Nah. I ain't know the nigga was home. That's what up," he replied.

Cartier knew they were of no use to her.

"Hey, tell Head I said what's—"

Cartier drove away from him mid-sentence. She wasn't anyone's messenger.

In East New York and Bed-Stuy, she went to barbershops, community centers, gambling spots, and liquor stores, but to no avail. Head wasn't there. The more she looked for him, the angrier she grew.

Why am I out looking for him? The nigga got shit twisted, she thought. For Cartier, his release day had gone from joy to anger and nearly hatred. What upset her was that she didn't think he was serious in those letters. Foolishly, she felt she could win him back.

On a mission, Cartier raced to Brownsville seething. Brownsville was full of life from corner to corner on the warm spring night. Block to block, music was blaring and young boys were working their territory with the local fiends scattered through the hood like roaches—all over the place and hard to get rid of. The cops were patrolling the area with their judgmental gazes trained on the young black men and their activities. Cartier leisurely cruised through the streets and the projects, rolling up on certain goons and asking them if they had seen Head around. Many people didn't know that he was home, and those who did know had no idea where he was.

Growing impatient and restless, Cartier was ready to put her fist through the windshield. *This nigga is really feelin' himself!* she thought.

Just as she was about to give up her quest, she spotted a girl she knew named Drea coming out of a hair salon on Rockaway Avenue. Cartier immediately did a beeline her way. Drea was strutting in her heels toward her white-on-white Benz parked on the side street. She hit the alarm and unlock button to the vehicle, and before she could take another step, Cartier came to a sudden stop nearby.

Cartier hollered from the driver's seat, "Drea, what's good?"

Drea was caught off guard by the harsh approach. "Damn, Cartier, what's up? You got beef with me or something?"

"Nah. I wanted to ask if you've seen Head around."

Drea smiled. "Yeah. I have."

"Where is he?" Cartier barked. It was news she had been waiting for.

"Look, I don't wanna get involved."

Cartier quickly scowled. "Involved in what?"

"I mean," Drea swung open her driver's side door in case she had to make a quick getaway, "I'm not 5-0 or a snitch to be dropping dime on a nigga's whereabouts—"

"Where the fuck is he!" Cartier hollered. She put her car in park and began to take her seatbelt off. This dumb bitch thought she was funny. Drea and Cartier went way back, and Drea was a jealous-hearted, insecure chick. Cartier had never laid hands on Drea before, but she was ready to beat the brakes off her now, despite her sexy outfit and five-inch red bottoms. "You play too much!"

Drea wasn't a fighter but she was always kicking the hornet's nest, which had earned her numerous beatdowns. She couldn't help herself. There was something about getting under people's skin that excited her.

"Last I heard he was at Basil Bar in Williamsburg," Drea finally revealed.

"Basil Bar? What the fuck is he doing over there?" Cartier replied.

"He chilling, I guess."

Cartier knew the spot. It was family owned and operated by six brothers who loved to allude that they had mob ties. The brothers were buff with overly tanned skin from frequenting pricey tanning salons. They used hair gel to slick back their extra dark hair, sported pinky rings and Rolexes, and had thick, New York Italian accents that were indicative of something. One could only speculate what that something actually was.

Before Cartier left, she gave Drea some parting words. "Tonight I'ma let ya slick mouth slide, but I promise you one day I'ma lay these paws on you."

Drea feigned innocence. "What did I do?"

Cartier ignored her and raced to Williamsburg with a sick feeling.

She hoped that if Head was there with a bitch that they had already left. Cartier was looking too cute and didn't want to show out.

Cartier could see the Williamsburg Bridge just ahead. It was expansive and illuminated in the spring night. The area was newly trendy with lots of eateries and people strolling about, thanks to gentrification. Parking was tight, and no one seemed like they would be moving anytime soon. Cartier circled the block looking for Head, and she spotted him at an outside table at Basil Bar with some bitch—some bitch Cartier had seen around before. Her eyes zeroed in on them both, and she fumed. It was disrespectful.

She continued to circle the block, hoping that someone would move their vehicle. Each time she came around, she would see the two of them laughing and flirting with each other. Not only did she see Head with some dumb cunt, but Barkim and Chemo were sitting there too. Cartier felt betrayed. Barkim and Chemo knew how she felt about Head. They were supposed to be down with her.

Completely frustrated with not finding parking anywhere nearby, Cartier decided to double park her Bugatti. She thrust the door open and hopped out all gangsta-like. Cartier's walk was unmistakable. Her legs were slightly bowed, and she had a mean switch to her hips. She marched their way, ready to make a scene in her sexy dress, red bottoms, and a fresh haircut.

"What the fuck did I tell you, nigga!" she yelled. "Didn't I warn you?"

The unexpected outburst drew attention, and it was embarrassing to everyone at the table except Head, who didn't seem fazed by it at all. He calmly looked at Cartier, swatted her away, and said, "Yo, get the fuck away from us wit' that drama."

"Drama!" Cartier shouted. "You out free for days and you don't fuckin' tell me!"

"I'm just doin' me, Cartier."

"Doing you! Fuck you, nigga!" she screamed.

"Never again," he retorted.

"Wow, really?" His remark nearly leveled her. "After everything I did for you, you do me like this? I waited all fuckin' day for you to get out, and you're dining and wining wit' this bitch!"

It didn't take long for Cartier to turn her anger toward Pebbles. Seeing the pretty chick nearly glued to his side ate her up.

In his deep baritone voice, he chuckled. "You waited one day, she waited three years. Get lost, Cartier. I'm only going to tell you once."

"Or what?" She took a couple steps closer to the table, invading their space.

Pebbles watched the ghetto chick in action. She knew of Cartier well—all her antics, the past and present crews, the jail time. Cartier's whole resume was etched in her brain. Cartier was her competition, and right now she was studying. She was prettier than Pebbles remembered, and the matte lipstick was something she now wanted. What shade was it? Teal? Turquoise? Pebbles made a note to self to update her makeup collection.

Pebbles finally spoke. "Look, baby, you know I don't do these ghetto shenanigans. Let's just go. People are staring."

"Are you dumb, bitch? I will bash ya fuckin' teeth in!"

"Like I said, ghetto," Pebbles reiterated.

Cartier stood strong, hands on her hips. "Head, you better check that fuckin' bitch!"

"It's Henry now. Not Head, Henry."

Cartier sucked her teeth, befuddled. "Negro, please!"

A few patrons got up to complain about the ruckus, which brought over the waitress. "Is everything all right here?"

Head smiled. "Yes, we're good. Could you bring us the check? We were just leaving."

She nodded and hurried off.

Head said, "Cartier, you need to bounce. You and I are on two different frequencies."

There was something so dismissive and final in his tone. Coupled with the fact that he was leaving to go fuck someone else, it tore Cartier up inside. Was it really over? Did he not love her anymore? She felt like he was undermining what they had once shared by speaking to her this way in front of Barkim, Chemo—who, by the way, was quiet—and Pebbles. The only thing she could do was what she knew best. Set it off.

Pebbles didn't know what hit her. First, she was standing on two legs, and then she was on her back against the concrete trying to defend herself from the series of solid punches to her face and body. Each hit landed someplace more damaging than the last. Pebbles could feel knots on her head starting to form. *Where the fuck is Head?*

"What now, bitch, huh?" yelled Cartier.

At first, the men stood by, not wanting to get involved in that girlie shit. They figured it was a fair fight, but Cartier quickly mopped the floor with Pebbles.

When the manager lunged for Cartier and attempted to try and pull her off of Pebbles, Head reacted impulsively and knocked him out with one punch.

An all-out brawl ensued outside the bar. The brothers rushed out, and they, too, tried to break things up, along with several patrons who got the violent end of fists and feet. It was so chaotic that it seemed like everyone was fighting someone with chairs and objects being flung everywhere. Some patrons gawked in disbelief while others began recording. Some found it to be the perfect opportunity to dine and dash. During the melee, the gun that was subtly attached to Cartier's thigh fell to the ground, and sirens were heard blaring in the distance. A patron picked up the gun and let off a few shots in the air before tossing the pistol in the gutter.

Barkim and Chemo knew that it was time to go. They went for Head, trying to pull him off one of the brothers.

"Hen—Head, we need to fuckin' go!" Barkim shouted.

But Head was adamant that he wasn't leaving unless Cartier stopped beating on Pebbles. Head rushed toward their fight and angrily snatched Cartier into his clutches. He wanted to toss her into the street. He wanted to break her neck. He wanted her to chill out. But Cartier was stubborn. She was able to wiggle herself out of Head's grip and charge at Pebbles again. The poor girl looked like she'd had enough of Cartier.

Head tried to race behind her, but Barkim and Chemo hurriedly grabbed him from behind, and Chemo yelled, "Head, we need to go! You just got home, and five-oh coming."

They were close.

"Fuck!" Head cursed.

He knew Chemo was right. He couldn't be caught in the melee outside the bar. So he relented and retreated with Barkim and Chemo to the car while Cartier continued to pound on Pebbles.

The moment Head took off with Barkim and Chemo, the first cop car arrived onto the scene, and two officers went charging into the heated riot to try and break it up. More marked cars came, and soon there were nearly a dozen cops on the scene. It didn't take the officers long to break things up and bring order back to the establishment. Cartier's gun was found in the gutter, and right away, everyone was detained and ultimately arrested. The cops radioed in for a police van. As much as they wanted to, they couldn't pin the gun on any one person, so everyone had to go down to the precinct for questioning. From the looks of the Mafioso-looking men who owned the bar, the cops believed that it was one of theirs.

"You fuckin' cunt. Fuck you!" Cartier shouted at Pebbles.

"I'm going to sue you," Pebbles returned. "I'm going to take everything your ghetto ass has!"

Cartier snorted. "My food stamps!"

"You think I'm joking? Do you know how much my face fetches!"

Cartier wanted to reply, but she couldn't help but to burst out laughing. *Fetches?* Head done found a live one.

Pebbles continued, "That car—what is it? A Bugatti, huh? You drug dealer. Well, that's going to be mine soon. My lawyers will drain you! With all my connections, you're going down."

"Bitch, who you frontin' for? Who you trying to impress wit' that bougie facade like you didn't grow up where I did? Like you ain't run with hoodlums and fuck hustlers like I did. You have two talents—thief and whore!"

Even locked down at Central Booking, Cartier and Pebbles couldn't stop arguing. They had to be placed in two separate jail cells, yet they continued to sling insults from across the room.

Pebbles had done the last three years of Head's bid with him—driving long hours round trip to visit him, putting money on his books, and accepting his phone calls. They made plans for the future, and Head promised he was done with his ex, so it was quite a shock that Cartier had shown up so quickly. Oh, Pebbles expected her once he was released, but the turnaround was swift. Pebbles had just turned twenty-seven when she had committed herself to Head, and now at thirty, she was ready to break a leg to become Mrs. Jackson.

During their earlier visits in the upstate correctional facility, Head would go on and on about how Cartier did him wrong and chose another dude over him. He explained that she broke his heart and that he had never felt that kind of pain before. Pebbles was his anchor, his shoulder to cry on, the one he could confide in. She listened to him intently. He spoke distastefully about Cartier's stink attitude but omitted that it was one of the things he truly loved about her. Now they both were sitting in a jail cell bickering back and forth.

The cops had gotten wind that the girls were fighting over a man, and they decided to have a little fun at the girls' expense.

"Whoever he is, he ain't worth going to jail over, and that man is probably with his *real* girlfriend right now," one cop joked.

There was laughter, but the girls didn't find it funny.

"I bet you he an ugly fellow too," another cop joked. "It's always the ugly men that make the women go crazy."

More laughter erupted around them.

"I guess if I do girls dirty, then babes will fight over me too."

More laughter.

Their sarcastic remarks had stifled Cartier, and Pebbles too. Cartier sat there in silence, sulking to herself. They were right. She wondered when this life would stop. *I shouldn't be fighting over no nigga*, she thought. Despite warning Head that she would beat up any females he was messing with, she knew she should have just walked away. Yet, she found herself in a ghetto-ass brawl like she was some ghetto-ass chick. She went from anger to embarrassment, sharing the holding area with someone she felt was beneath her.

The cops stopped their teasing and the night was getting late. There was no denying it—Cartier was going to spend the night in jail.

A few women slept on the hard benches or the floors while others tried to pass the time by gossiping about this and that. There was one girl who tried to flirt with the guard to get bumped up on the call list, and then there were the ones who just sat there looking aloof—like it was their first time in lockup.

Cartier's scowl kept everyone at bay, but one particular girl caught Cartier's attention. She looked exactly like Cartier's deceased best friend, Monya—only shades darker. The young beauty sat across from her on one of the benches with her head lowered and her eyes glued to the floor. She hadn't moved the entire night, and Cartier swore she hadn't blinked either. The girl looked genuinely innocent. What on earth could she be in for? Cartier examined her features from where she sat, and the young girl had the smoothest and darkest skin. Although she was seated, Cartier could tell she was tall and she was model-pretty.

Cartier's curiosity about what the girl had been arrested for grew. Her wardrobe was decent and clean, and all night, the young girl had been hesitant to talk to anyone. The jail was a scary place, especially for first-timers.

As the night turned into dawn, more females were added to the already overpopulated holding cell. Arrestees were coming in quickly and were slow to go out. The hard benches became prime real estate. A husky woman with broad shoulders, battle scars across her face, and a few permanent gold teeth came barreling in. Her eyes quickly darted forth and back until they settled on the young girl. Her steps were heavy, measured, and deliberate as she made her way toward her prey.

Forcefully she tapped the young girl on her shoulder. "Get up!"

Wide eyed and fearful, the girl began to oblige. The only place for her would be the floor. As she put her body in motion, she heard another command.

"Nah, don't move," said Cartier. "Stay seated."

The husky woman quickly spun around to confront the loudmouth bitch. "And who the fuck is you!"

One word was all that needed to be said. "Cartier."

After a pregnant pause she asked, "Cartier from Brooklyn?"

"Facts."

"Oh, what's up, girl? You remember me. I'm Tracy—Rhonda's cousin?"

Cartier shook her head. "Nah, I don't."

"Tracy? They call me Big Tee. I used to live in Lafayette Gardens."

Cartier looked her up and down and cut her eyes. She didn't respond. Tracy's eyes darted around. "Anyway, you cosigning for everyone?"

"Do you."

Tracy turned toward the next female and commanded, "Get up," and she did.

Around 9am the holding cell began to thin out. The moment a seat next to Cartier was vacated, the young girl bolted to it. It had been nearly 14 hours she had spent in jail, and now Cartier was cranky. She no longer wanted to be bothered, but she made a conscious decision to not take it out on the girl.

In a low, feminine voice, she heard, "I just wanted to say thank you."

Cartier replied, "No problem."

"My name is Harlem."

"Harlem?" Cartier repeated. "Your parents actually named you Harlem?"

Harlem slightly giggled. "Yes."

"It's a cute name . . . different, but cute."

"Cartier is different too," Harlem concluded.

Cartier asked what she vowed she never would. "What you in here for?" The words tumbling out her mouth felt so lame.

Harlem looked away with a look of embarrassment on her pretty face.

"Look, I'm in here too, so I'm not here to judge you," Cartier added.

Harlem sighed. She shyly looked at Cartier and uttered, "I'm being accused of something that I didn't do. I'm innocent."

"And what's that?" Cartier asked again.

Harlem leaned in and whispered, "Prostitution."

Cartier was shocked. *Prostitution?* How could a pretty and innocent looking young woman like herself get caught up in something like that? It angered Cartier. She never understood how a woman could allow a man to dig so deeply into her mind that he could convince her to sell her body.

"I'm actually an escort," Harlem clarified. "I don't really sleep with men. I just keep them company."

"And they arrested you for the company you keep?" Cartier asked, her voice laced with sarcasm.

"It's complicated."

"In this day and age, what isn't?"

The two continued to whisper to each other on the bench, and it was helping the time go by quicker. Harlem opened up to Cartier about her life. Once she got started, it was hard to stop.

Harlem was nineteen years old, and her parents were born in Ethiopia. Kofi and Eden Williams moved to America before she was born. They embraced the American culture to fit in, gave their daughter the only name they could think of that represented where they were living at the time, and changed their last name to what Harlem considered a slave name. They had moved fifteen times since she was old enough to remember, so she had a hard time connecting with people. She hated her parents and blamed them for not having an identity and being confused about who she was.

"Your peoples are from Ethiopia, huh?" Cartier said.

Harlem nodded.

"I always wanted to see what it was like over there."

"I couldn't tell you," Harlem said.

"You've never been home?"

Harlem shrugged. "Africa is no more my home than yours. I was born here. This is my home. I love and celebrate my culture, but that's it. I'm American."

"True," Cartier agreed. There was an uncomfortable moment of silence and then, "So, arrested for being an escort, huh? That's your story you're sticking to?"

Harlem looked directly into Cartier's eyes searching for a connection. "It's true. They never touch me; we just hang out."

Cartier gave her the side-eye. "Selling ass is so wack. What's wrong wit' good ol' fashioned stripping?"

Harlem grinned. She liked Cartier's candidness and realized the jig was up.

"Two things. Tits and ass," and then she added, "and rhythm too."

"There are so many commodities that you could sell, especially living in Harlem. Coke, weed, clothes, fake bags, books, oils, incense, CD's. Explain to me how a young, pretty girl decides to sell her pussy and especially for a pimp."

Harlem shook her head rapidly. "He's a she. And no one says—" she looked around, "*pimp* anymore."

"A woman?"

"Her name is Esmeralda and she's deadly."

Cartier knew her well. So that bitch was still getting paid. "You're too smart to be exploited like this, spreading your legs for niggas out here for coins."

"I'm working off my parents' ten-thousand-dollar debt. That was the only way I could quickly come up with so much money."

"Oh." Cartier knew the game. "Sucks to be you."

3

artier stood in front of the judge the following morning and awaited her punishment. She knew it was going to be minimal damage. She hoped they wouldn't trace the gun back to her, and she felt there was no need to hire outside counsel. It had been a long couple of days, and the only thing she wanted to do was go home, take a shower, and get some sleep.

Cartier pled guilty to disorderly conduct, and if she didn't get into trouble in the next six months then the case would be dismissed. The judge was lenient. Cartier strutted out the courtroom a tired, but thankful bitch. With her record, things could have gone a lot worse.

Seeing the judge right after Cartier was Pebbles. Her face had lumped up, showing visible signs of the prior day's beatdown. She looked pitiful, really. Still, Pebbles held her head up high, refusing to show any hint of weakness. Cartier didn't want to see that bitch anytime soon, so she kept her eyes focused on her exit and left the building.

However, both ladies expected to see Head in the courtroom for their inconsequential arraignment, but he wasn't there. Noted. If the shoe were on the other foot, they would have been there for him.

At the bottom of the courthouse steps, Cartier lit a cigarette and took a needed drag. She wanted to go home, but there was one thing she wanted to do first. Harlem had been on her mind, and she didn't want to leave the young girl behind in case she needed bail money. Cartier felt strange. Her mind kept flashing back to Monya, all the good times they had, and then Harlem. It was as if Monya was telling her to look out for the young girl. Reluctantly, Cartier went back inside the courthouse and took a seat. She figured the young girl's charges for prostitution would be dropped to a minor infraction such as loitering, especially with this lenient judge and it being her first offense. She also assumed she would see Esmeralda in the courthouse on behalf of Harlem.

Two hours later Harlem Williams was arraigned, and the DA read off a litany of prostitution charges. Bail was promptly set at $15,000, and Harlem screamed and wailed for mercy. "I don't have any money," she cried. "Please, don't send me back . . . don't send me back!"

"Order! Order in the court! Bailiff, quiet this defendant!" the judge instructed as he banged his gavel.

Harlem was practically dragged back into a holding cell, shackled.

Cartier sighed. *Don't do the crime if you can't do the time,* she thought.

Cartier exited the courtroom, still not understanding why she had taken an interest in the little liar. But she had. She walked a couple blocks north and ended up at Freedom Fighters, Inc., a local bail bondsman. Ten percent was needed, and luckily for Harlem, Cartier had that and then some on her person when she got arrested.

Hours later, Harlem was finally released from Central Booking. Cartier waved her over, and the girl was shocked to see her outside.

She approached Cartier with a nervous smile. "Are you waiting for me?"

"Yes."

"Why?"

"Because I posted your bail," Cartier answered.

Harlem thought it was Esmeralda. She grinned and gave Cartier the tightest hug until being shoved off.

"Are you hungry?"

She nodded.

"C'mon, let's go get something to eat. But first, I need to go and get my car."

With Harlem by her side, Cartier flagged down a cab, and the two climbed into the backseat.

"I need to go to the Brooklyn Tow Pound," Cartier told the cab driver.

He nodded and drove off.

"What the fuck? Are y'all fuckin' serious?!" Cartier cursed while staring irately at her Bugatti Chiron, which now had a scratch and a noticeable dent on the side. "Y'all don't know how to take care of people's shit?!"

The tow yard worker named Benny shrugged. "File a claim," he said. "Sometimes accidents happen."

"Accident my ass! Ya'll fools were careless towing away my shit," Cartier corrected.

Cartier circled her car looking for more damage. Fortunately, there wasn't any.

"You know how much this car cost?"

"I know it's an expensive car," Benny replied indifferently.

"Very expensive—more than you'll ever make in your lifetime," Cartier snapped.

She was pissed off. It was bad enough that she had to spend the night in jail, now she had an ugly dent on the driver's side of her car and an obnoxious scratch. *Fuck me!* she said to herself. It was because of Head—his dumb ass, she believed. The only thing she could do was pay the fine, take pictures of the damage, and take it to the auto body shop the next day. It was going to cost her. Her Bugatti was her new baby, and she wanted to knock someone out for what she perceived as a deliberate act.

She huffed and slid behind the steering wheel and started the ignition. The car roared like a lion. *At least the interior is unscathed,* she thought. She turned to look at Harlem, who was still standing idly on the side. She was in awe that Cartier drove such an expensive vehicle. The woman now piqued Harlem's interest. Harlem was curious of two things. What did Cartier do for a living? And why was she locked up?

"Get in, Harlem," she said.

"We going to eat?"

"I'm taking you to my place first."

"I can't stay long. Maybe it's best I just go. I need to get back to the Bronx and see Esmeralda. I need to tell her what happened."

"Don't worry about her. I'll take care of that," Cartier replied.

Harlem looked reluctant. How was Cartier going to take care of her situation? But Cartier was adamant that she would handle things for her. Harlem climbed into the passenger seat of the Bugatti—never had she seen such a lovely interior to a car.

"Sexy!" Harlem squealed.

"Nice, right?"

"It is. One day I'm going to own one just like it."

"You fuck with me long enough, and you'll have something just like this soon." Cartier smiled and sped off, smoothly shifting gears to the Bugatti like she was a NASCAR driver. Harlem sat back and enjoyed the ride inside the luxury vehicle. It felt like she was riding on air.

Cartier steered her way through the Brooklyn streets and arrived at her apartment a few minutes away in Downtown Brooklyn. She pulled into the garage of her building and parked. Both ladies exited the car, and Cartier hit the alarm button. They stepped into the elevator and Cartier pushed for the sixth floor. They rode up in silence.

Harlem felt a bit uneasy. Cartier was nice, but why the hospitality? Why post her bail? And why take up for a stranger against a bully? Harlem knew that patience was a truth revealer, so she would just wait.

Cartier's home was a three-bedroom rental less than a mile from the Kings County Criminal Court in Brooklyn—the same one she had sat the night in. Her rent was $7,500 a month and that was considered cheap nowadays. Coming back from Seattle and Miami, she couldn't believe what Brooklyn had become. Rent in the hood, with bullets whizzing past folks' heads, cost two grand. It was outrageous. Anything considered decent was $3,500 or more.

Harlem walked into an empty apartment, and she was baffled. The only furnishing was an inflatable bed, some scattered clothes, shoes, and shopping bags, and there were some oranges on the kitchen countertop. Besides that, the apartment was spotless and bare.

"You live here? Where's the furniture?" she asked.

"I just moved in," Cartier explained. "I haven't had the time to nest."

"Oh. It's still a beautiful place. I could live here forever with a futon and bean bag."

"Yeah, it's expensive, but it's worth every cent. It feels good to be back on my old stomping grounds. I swear, the only way I'm leaving Brooklyn again is in a body bag. I will live and die here. Real talk."

Harlem felt the statement was a bit dramatic, but who was she to judge? Harlem shook her head. "I could never love anything, or anyone, let alone a crummy borough as you've described."

"Never say never."

"Maybe. Hey, would you mind if I take a shower?" Harlem asked, and then smelled under her arms. "Kinda funky."

Cartier laughed and dug in a Saks bag for some toiletries for Harlem to use. "The guest bathroom is down the hall, to your right. I'll put out some fresh linens for you."

Harlem smiled, thanked Cartier, and walked away to use the bathroom. She wasn't the only one who needed a shower. Cartier could not wait to wash the funk of that jail off her skin. While Harlem showered in the guest bathroom, Cartier did the same in her master bath. After her shower, Cartier joined Harlem in the guest bedroom with a new dress for her to try on.

"This should fit you," said Cartier.

"It's brand new—and expensive." Harlem eyed the four-hundred-dollar price tag on the Christian Siriano dress.

"It's too small for me. I haven't worn a size two in a while."

Harlem looked at Cartier's curvy shape. She had a flat stomach, plump ass, and thick thighs. "What size are you?"

"A four. Sometimes a six."

"Well if you have any more clothes that are a size two, just send them my way. I ain't too proud to beg."

"Hold up," Cartier said and walked to her room. She did in fact have a few more pieces. She came back and gave Harlem what she had.

Harlem eyed the clothes and fell in love with each outfit. "I love them."

"I knew you would. Now try them on," Cartier suggested.

Harlem was popping tags, grateful for this stranger's unexpected benevolence. But as she eyed her attractive image in the mirror, her mood shifted all of a sudden—something had dawned on her.

She turned to face Cartier with a look of apprehension and asked, "Am I gonna have to fuck for these clothes?"

"What?" Cartier responded. Did she hear her correctly?

"These expensive clothes—you know I don't have any money, so will I have to go down on you or something? Or do I have to fuck a friend of yours? Just keep it one-hundred."

Cartier was disgusted by the statement. "You got me fucked up right now. I'm strictly dickly and I'm not here to try and slut you out. Just take

36

my generosity with a thank-you and a smile."

"I'm just not used to people being nice to me unless they want something from me . . . usually pussy."

The young girl needed some work. Cartier knew that. She sighed. "Listen, if you don't add some self-worth to yourself, then someone will convince you that you're worth less than you are."

"It's complicated," Harlem admitted. "My parents taught me how to barter for everything. They explained that in Ethiopia if you wanted milk, then you'd trade rice. I was so confused between the American and Ethiopian culture that I got teased—bullied. You should have seen me. In second grade, I wanted a classmate's shoes. I had a pencil and asked for an exchange. The kids clowned me until I cried. We spent all our time in America begging until my father met a friend who was from Nigeria. He seemed nice. He would give us money for food, and my parents would exchange my mother until the price was too much for her. Last year my father borrowed money from Esmeralda and bought a huge shipment of fake Gucci bags. The wholesalers saw him coming. They gave him the easy-to-spot fakes, the ones the manufacturer should throw away. There was no way he'd make a profit. Esmeralda got wind that my father couldn't pay her back with interest, so she sent a hit squad to kill him. My father made the trade, and here we are. Basically, I am worth a fake Gucci bag."

"You're not!" Cartier refuted. "You can't believe that."

"Sometimes I do, sometimes I don't."

Cartier thought about her mother. "You know, most parents aren't perfect. My moms left me hungry numerous nights while she was out getting fucked. But Trina would have died before she sold my pussy. How can they sit back and watch you go through this—getting locked up and exploited?"

"They ran back to Ethiopia shortly thereafter and asked me to go too. But I refused to live in a country that I'd never been to, so here I am."

This was a lot to process. Cartier said to Harlem, "C'mon, we're leaving. Let's go eat."

Harlem followed Cartier out of the apartment wearing the dress Cartier gave her and the clutch purse she'd had when she was arrested. She worried how she was going to explain her long absence to Esmeralda.

The two of them exited the elevator into the parking garage and walked toward the car. Cartier immediately noticed something on her windshield, but Harlem grabbed it first. It was a white note card with a menacing black skull with hollow eyes, a sharp dagger, blood, and the letter *D*. The *D* was handwritten in block letter format—the format criminals use to disguise their handwriting.

She held it up to show Cartier, and it gave Cartier pause. *What the fuck is this?* she thought. She stood there for a moment inspecting the card, and Harlem could see some worry written across her face.

"What does it mean?" Harlem asked her.

"It's nothing . . . just someone playing a joke or something. Just toss it away," Cartier replied, brushing it off and climbing into the driver's seat of her Bugatti.

Harlem didn't toss the card. Instead, she quickly stuffed it into her purse and climbed into the passenger seat. Cartier drove out of the parking garage, refusing to be bothered by what she found on her windshield. She had some business to attend to, and she rebuffed any threats.

The blue-and-white Bugatti had jaws dropping to the ground as it drove by on the gritty South Bronx streets. For so many, this was a car they only saw in rap videos or in the movies. It slowly cruised by the onlookers, and it soon came to a stop in front of a towering housing project with the Manhattan skyline in the background in Soundview, Bronx.

Harlem instantly became worried. She stared at Cartier with uneasiness and said, "Thank you for everything."

"I want you to wait here," Cartier said.

"What? Wait, why?"

"Just wait here in the car and don't get out," Cartier demanded.

Harlem was baffled by the request, but she didn't protest.

Cartier reached into one of the compartments to the car and removed a .45 handgun and concealed it in her Gucci handbag. She climbed out of the vehicle, leaving Harlem inside, and marched toward the projects. She was bold enough to confront Esmeralda on her turf with no more than a .45 to hold her down. It was a risk, but Cartier was used to taking risks and coming out on top. It was the Bronx, but she was from Brooklyn—and like they say in Brownsville, "Never ran, and never will."

She strutted into the projects with everyone staring at her and wondering who this nicely dressed bitch was invading their turf. Cartier was attentive to her surroundings, but she remained undaunted and walked into the project lobby on a mission. She stepped into the pissy-smelling elevator and pushed for the tenth floor. Cartier looked stoic about her impromptu meeting with a dangerous female pimp as the elevator ascended.

Approaching the apartment, Cartier took a deep breath. She knew she had this shit under control. She was Cartier—once the leader of the Cartier Cartel, a ruthless organization that held shit down, made millions of dollars from the streets, and was respected everywhere. No Bronx pimp was going to intimidate her.

She banged hard on the door, and a shirtless thug soon answered it. He glared at the striking Cartier with her short bob haircut and growled, "Who you, bitch?"

She looked him dead in his eyes and said, "I'm here to see Esmeralda," with authority in her voice.

He continued to glare at her, blocking her entrance into the apartment. Cartier could clearly see that it was hectic inside, and the weed smell coming from the apartment was pungent.

"This is business," she added.

"Business?" he questioned with a raised eyebrow. "She knows you?"

"No. But I know she will want to get to know me when she sees this," Cartier said, opening her purse slightly to show him the ten stacks wrapped in a rubber band.

He stepped aside, and Cartier walked into the apartment filled with goons galore. The smell of weed was amplified, and there were a few girls lingering in the living room, looking like they were ready to turn tricks. All eyes were on Cartier. She knew she was on treacherous grounds. The Bronx was a grimy borough with some grimy people.

"Follow me," the thug at the door said to her.

He led her down a long hallway and knocked on the door to the master bedroom. Cartier stood behind him on alert, keeping her gun close and trying to ready herself for anything that came her way. She was deep in the lion's den.

"Come in," said a voice on the other side.

The door opened, and Cartier continued into the bedroom. Surprisingly, the place had been converted into a small office. The windows had been blacked out, and there was a large flat screen mounted on the wall, couches and a love seat, and a small desk. Seated behind the desk was Esmeralda. She was a well-dressed, petite, dark-skinned woman with long dreadlocks, and she carried a cold gaze.

"Who this bitch, Tony?" she asked the thug from the door.

"She says she got some business with you, Esmeralda," he replied.

Cartier boldly interrupted their conversation with, "You don't know me, and I don't know you, but we have someone in common."

"And who's that?" asked Esmeralda with some interest.

"Her name is Harlem."

A glimmer of shock passed through Esmeralda's eyes. "I've been looking everywhere for that fuckin' bitch."

"Well, right now she's with me," Cartier said.

"With you? And, once again, who the fuck is you?"

"I'm someone who's willing to take Harlem off your hands for a price," Cartier sternly replied.

Esmeralda laughed. "You got fuckin' balls bitch to come up in here and proposition me. And once again, who are you? And what makes you think we won't fuck you up right now and put your pussy up for sale?"

Cartier stepped closer to the desk, locking eyes with the woman and looking unworried by the threats she threw out. "You wanna know who I am? My name is Cartier Timmons, and you probably heard of my organization, the Cartier Cartel from Brooklyn. If so, then you already know I'm not somebody you want to fuck with."

Cartier tossed the ten stacks from her handbag onto Esmeralda's desk. Ten grand was light cash for Cartier—it wasn't shit with the amount of money she had from South Beach.

Cartier kept her stern stare aimed at Esmeralda. If it were anyone else, male or female, they would not have made it out of the office alive. Fortunately for Cartier, her name did ring out, even in the Bronx. Esmeralda had run with Kola back in the day, and they had prostituted girls back then. Also, Cartier's name was echoing heavy in the streets of New York from the work she had put in down in South Beach. She was lethal, and the streets knew it. Cartier was considered family to Apple and Kola, and although Esmeralda had a deadly and robust team, she didn't want any trouble with Apple, Kola, and Cartier. Especially not over a young bitch like Harlem.

Esmeralda stood up from her chair, and the mood in the room suddenly changed. "I've heard of you and definitely know what you're capable of. Do you want a drink?"

"Nah, I'm good."

"So, ten grand for Harlem," Esmeralda chuckled. "You like the bitch that much?"

"She somewhat grew on me," Cartier replied, being terse.

"She has that effect on people."

Esmeralda picked up the cash from her desk. Briefly, she wondered if she should give it back in good faith to get on Cartier's good side, but she knew it would make her look weak amongst her men.

"You can have the bitch, Cartier. Her debt is paid as far as I'm concerned."

Cartier slightly nodded. It was respect. "So we good?"

"Yeah. We good," Esmeralda assured her. "But I'm curious—what brought you back to New York from South Beach?"

It was her personal business, but Cartier didn't get offended. She replied, "My nigga."

"I can respect that," Esmeralda returned.

Cartier didn't want to prolong her business with Esmeralda. She had what she came for, and now it was time to leave. The two ladies gave each other a nod, and then Cartier turned around to leave.

"A word of advice," Esmeralda called out. Cartier paused, her back still to the pimpstress. "Don't trust her. She's a slick bitch."

Back in the driver's seat, Cartier stared at Harlem with a straight face. She couldn't reconcile her willingness to help this stranger, other than that it was in her DNA, buried deep under heartbreaks and heartaches. As a teenager, Cartier protected her cartel by any means necessary—even if that meant losing her own freedom when she copped to manslaughter. Cartier was an alpha female who protected—not preyed—on the weak. When Monya, Shanine, Lil Momma, or Bam needed her, she rescued them all time and time again. And now she found herself liberating this pitiful prostitute, this Monya-esque little liar.

Harlem didn't know what Cartier was thinking or what to expect from her. But she knew one thing for sure: Cartier had to be somebody special to leave Esmeralda's place unharmed.

Finally, Cartier said, "You don't have to worry about Esmeralda anymore."

Harlem was shocked. "What?"

"You're free."

"Bullshit. You actually did it?"

"Don't ever doubt me," Cartier said.

4

The gray Audi came to a stop in front of the two-family home on New Lots Avenue in East New York at two in the morning. Head killed the ignition. For a moment he stayed behind the wheel and watched the residence. It was dark and still, indicating that his great aunt was most likely asleep. Aunt Gloria was old and loving. He was paroled to her place and was trying to keep a low profile.

The home was for sale with a high asking price of just under a million dollars. Head stared at the *For Sale* sign and smirked. He couldn't believe that the dilapidated building with ancient linoleum floors, peeling paint, tiny rooms, and outdated fixtures could fetch that much. Every day there was a mouse caught in a trap, and there were too many roaches to count. He'd only been living at his great aunt's for a week, and he was grateful that she had taken him in. However, he didn't plan on being there long.

He had been driving around in Pebbles' gray Audi with no regard for whether she needed the vehicle or not—nor did he pick her up from Central Booking the previous week. He knew it was fucked up, but he felt nothing. She had been calling his phone repeatedly, filling up his voice messages and leaving multiple texts. He blocked her number for the moment. It wasn't anything permanent; he just wanted some space— some alone time—and Pebbles was becoming bothersome.

Head wanted some peace tonight to focus on putting together an operation out in Flint, Michigan. Inside the pen, Head met a lot of well-read men who opened his eyes to world views and self-awareness—influential men who preached not like Brother Malcolm or Dr. King, but more in the vein of Dr. Yosef Ben–Jochannan, AKA Dr. Ben.

Upon his release, a lot of Head's old friends came to see him and they had blessed him with ten stacks or better. It was respect. He still had lots of cash stashed away for a rainy day, which his Aunt Gloria held for him. The entire time he was locked away she never touched a dime. Gloria was one of those overly religious individuals who believed what she preached. There wasn't any way she was going to spend his drug money. Most hypocritical church folks would preach about greed and morals, but the moment a hustler tossed a stack of money their way, they couldn't spend it fast enough. But not Aunt Gloria. She didn't want anything to do with it. She did him that one favor, and that was it.

Head finally hopped out the car with some urgency to get what he needed and go inside. He walked to the trunk but then he stopped suddenly and gazed into the night. He eyed a car driving too slow for his comfort with its high beams blinding him. He was a thoroughbred hustler who knew to carry his pistol on him, even though he was on parole. Head would rather be caged for carrying a gun than dead for not. He reached for the gun tucked against the small of his back, but as he did so, several rapid shots rang out—*Pop! Pop! Pop! Pop! Pop!*

The gunshots echoed deafeningly. Head took cover behind Pebbles' Audi and managed to pull out his pistol and return gunfire at the vehicle. Six slugs tore into the Audi's exterior, but thankfully he wasn't hit. The lights were still blinding him, so it was difficult for him to shoot with accuracy. Finding his moment to flee, he took off running from his great aunt's home, not wanting to bring anymore heat there. She didn't deserve that kind of drama. He ran away like a track star, and to his benefit he wasn't being followed. But it was embarrassing that he had to run in the first place.

Four blocks later, he made it to a gas station. He was out of breath and sweaty. He kept the gun in his hand, knowing it was a risk to keep it. It would be worse to get caught without it if the same car was still lurking, though.

"Fuck!" he cursed at the top of his lungs.

His head was on a rotation. The early morning hour made it easy for him to keep track of things, with the traffic and activity being sparse. For several minutes, he stood at the gas station on alert, waiting for something that probably wasn't coming. Whoever it was, they took their shot and missed. Head puffed out his frustration and decided to call an Uber.

After twenty minutes of waiting at the gas station on high alert and keeping his gun close, his Uber finally arrived. Head was highly irritated. Veins were bulging near his temples and his jaw was tightly clenched. The Ford Taurus slowly pulled into the gas station with the female driver looking for her pick-up. Head noisily exhaled. He was relieved that it was a female driver. If it was a man, he would have kept his gun in his hand. Still, he didn't trust anyone. He coolly walked toward the Taurus.

"You my Uber, right?" he asked.

She nodded and asked, "Is your name Henry?"

"That's me."

"Okay. I'm Jennifer."

Head got into the backseat. The gun was tucked back into his waistband. He kept his eyes open as he scanned the dimly lit streets to see if they were being followed.

"So where are we going?"

"To my girl's place," he replied.

He gave her the address and she started to pull out of the gas station.

"Hang on. I need you to do me one favor first, though."

"What's that?" she asked, hitting the brakes and turning toward him.

"I just want to drive by my aunt's place to see if she's okay. I'll give you a nice tip for that."

"Sure, that's not a problem. We can do that."

As Jennifer pulled around to his Aunt Gloria's home, Head remained slouched in the backseat trying to stay out of sight in case his enemies were still lingering. The block was quiet, Pebbles' Audi was still parked out front, and Gloria's place seemed untouched. Head was pleased to see that. It took away a lot of worry. The last thing he wanted was for his aunt to get hurt, or worse.

Jennifer dropped Head at Pebbles' place, and he gave her a healthy tip for her help. She was thankful. He marched toward Pebbles' door and banged. It was early in the morning and sometimes Pebbles slept like a rock. Fortunately for him, she heard his steady banging at her door and finally answered it wearing a long white T-shirt.

"Damn, baby, what the fuck? Why you knockin' on my door like that?" she wanted to know.

Head pushed past her and walked straight to her bedroom.

Pebbles followed behind him like a concerned puppy. "What's wrong? What happened tonight?"

He spun around to look at her and slammed his fist into the palm of his hand. "Yo, some muthafuckas just tried to get at me!"

Pebbles' face went from worry to shock. "Wait—somebody tried to kill you?"

"They did, but they missed," he said, his eyes narrowing to slits. "Muthafuckas must got death wishes. Fuckin' roaches!"

Head had no idea who wanted to see him dead, but he strongly suspected that it was someone trying to make a name for themselves by murdering a street legend.

artier sat at the table in the kitchen drinking her coffee and watching Harlem try on numerous outfits. From her long legs to her perky tits, you could tell she loved herself. Harlem wanted Cartier's approval on which outfit complimented her most. Cartier was amused. Harlem was Monya reincarnated. Monya would wear the tightest jeans and flaunt her little bony body around proudly. You couldn't tell her that she wasn't the bomb-dot-com.

Harlem had been staying with her for a week now, and so far everything had been copasetic. Their conversations were easy, and Cartier was learning a lot about Ethiopia. Besides, Harlem was some help in taking her mind off of Head—or Henry—and his bullshit.

Cartier had her good days and her bad days. Today felt like it was going to be one of those bad days when she tried not to think about him but couldn't stop. She needed to unleash the rage inside her because Head wasn't cooperating with her; he wasn't giving their love a chance. The only thing that kept her going in Seattle and in Miami was that they would be together when he came home. Now, he was running around town with some new bitch. Cartier said to herself, *Not on my watch*—not while she sat around and let the streets tell their love story.

She came up with an idea. She didn't know why she thought of it, but doing the unthinkable would somehow placate her. She had a temper, and it was hard for her to control. Thinking about Head being with Pebbles set her off like a rocket. She didn't want to face the fact that she had lost him.

Cartier spent the entire day plotting something devious.

It was late evening when Cartier stirred Harlem from her sleep and said to her, "You down to do something stupid and reckless tonight?"

Harlem didn't know what to say, so she replied, "What is it?"

"Well, I need a favor," Cartier said.

"Okay." Harlem felt that she owed Cartier, so whatever favor she was asking for, it would be granted.

"I just need for you to drive for me tonight," said Cartier.

Harlem looked befuddled by the request. "A driver?"

"Yes. I wanna pay a visit to my man."

Harlem sighed. She wasn't down with relationship drama, but she agreed because she was living rent-free and Cartier had paid her debt.

"Hurry up and get dressed—preferably in all black," said Cartier.

Harlem got up and glanced at the time. It was only 10pm. Harlem didn't realize that she had gone to sleep so early. The one thing she hoped didn't happen tonight was that she would lose her freedom.

They exited the building, and Cartier tossed her the car keys. "You drive," and they got into a dark blue BMW. It wasn't as fancy as the Bugatti, but it was still a nice car to get around in. Cartier instructed her where to go. "Make a left here . . . turn onto this ramp . . . go a mile down."

Harlem did what she was told, and she didn't ask any questions. It felt like she was in a cheesy gangster movie, with the two of them dressed in black and cruising through the city at night looking for some trouble to get into.

The Brooklyn block was eerily quiet as a cool breeze chilled the spring air. The two ladies had set up on the block and were stalking a residence from a short distance. Cartier's eyes were on the property. She wanted to make a glaring statement to that nigga who had wronged her. There was a good chance he wouldn't show up tonight, but Cartier was willing to wait—even all night if she had to. If they had to pee, then they would squat down low near the car in between the doors.

"What now?" Harlem asked her.

"Now we just sit back and wait for him to show up."

"That could take all night."

Cartier cut her eyes at the young girl. "Do you got somewhere important to be?"

"No."

"Then we sit here and we wait. That's it."

Harlem didn't have a choice. She huffed and rolled her eyes.

"Are you serious? You wanna blow out your mouth and complain?"

"I'm fine."

"You sure?" Cartier barked.

"Yeah, I'm good."

"Then just fuckin' relax and have my back. That's all I want from you."

Harlem was starting to see another side to the woman. It was a side that was intimidating. She figured it was best to stay still and quiet, and not make any more complaints or annoying noises. She also learned that Cartier had patience. Most likely it wasn't her first time stalking someone.

A few hours later, there was still no sign of Head. Harlem was well past the point of impatient, but she didn't want to upset Cartier. It looked like their little caper was going to go into the morning. But then suddenly, things changed. Cartier noticed a pair of headlights turning onto the street and she kept her attention on the approaching car. Soon, a gray Audi drove right by them and she caught a glimpse of Head behind the wheel. It was about time.

"This is it," she said to Harlem.

She watched him park and eyed him lingering in the driver's seat for a moment. She wondered what he was waiting for. *Did he spot us? Is he plotting against us too?* Cartier's mind was spinning with all kinds of worries. This was supposed to be her sneak attack. He wasn't supposed to see her coming. *What if he comes charging our way blasting? Then what?* Cartier knew she wasn't ready to take Head straight on. He was a savage—a coldblooded killer when he needed to be.

The driver's door to the Audi opened and Head climbed out. Harlem started the ignition, threw on the high beams, and she slowly maneuvered the BMW his way, while Cartier donned a ski mask to cover her face and cocked back a Glock 19. Head was looking directly into their line of fire. Cartier leaned out the window clutching the gun, aimed, and fired several shots his way. She witnessed Head take cover behind the Audi. She could have killed him if that was her intent. She had him dead to rights. But she didn't want him dead. She wanted to scare him. It was petty, but it was payback.

What Cartier didn't expect was for Head to return fire so soon. Fortunately for them, the high beams threw off his shot, and he took off running. Seeing him run away, Cartier laughed. She found it hilarious. She said to Harlem, "Let's get the fuck outta here."

Harlem couldn't get away from the scene fast enough. She stared at Cartier with a look that said, *This bitch is crazy!*

The next morning Harlem woke up, threw on a T-shirt, and stepped out of the bedroom to find Cartier hanging out on her blow-up bed with a glass of cognac in her hand. Sensing someone was standing behind her, Cartier turned around to find Harlem there.

"I see you finally woke up," she said. "How did you sleep?"

"I slept fine," Harlem replied.

"Are you hungry?"

"A little bit."

"Cool. Get dressed and we'll get something nearby. I know a spot, and we need to talk," Cartier said.

Before lunch, Cartier made a detour to the furniture warehouse in Brooklyn Heights. It was time to decorate her place. She dropped nearly thirty grand on bedroom sets, a dining room table, a living room set, fashionable chairs, and some high-end décor. It all would be delivered the next day.

Leaving the furniture store, Cartier was feeling a little altruistic and decided to take Harlem shopping. For the rest of the afternoon, the ladies went in and out of boutiques from 5th to Madison. Since Harlem couldn't wrap her mind around Cartier's generosity, she began to feel as though she had earned all these perks. To Harlem, the universe owed her plenty, and Cartier was the vessel through which she would receive her rewards.

Never once did Cartier mention what had gone down the night before. Harlem didn't know if Cartier missed her man on purpose or not, but it wasn't her business. She did log the incident in her mind as a teachable moment. It would be a cold day in hell before Harlem would ever go ape shit over a man.

After their shopping spree, the ladies ended up at Rao's on 114th Street to finally eat. The atmosphere was lively, and it was reminiscent of those old Italian movies. Seated at the decorated table, they enjoyed mouthwatering meatballs and the famous marinara.

Sipping on her champagne, Cartier gazed at Harlem and now things were about to get serious. "Listen, after today, you need to start pulling your own weight around here," she started.

Harlem was listening, knowing Cartier was about to drop the bomb on her.

"What do you need me to do?" she asked.

"You either need to get a job or you need to go back to school."

Harlem was taken aback by the options Cartier threw at her. She was certain that she was going to be asked to do something illegal, maybe turn tricks for Cartier or set some niggas up to get robbed. But get a job or go to school? What was the catch?

"You want me to do either—why?"

"Why? Because I want you to win."

"Usually people try to take advantage of me," she said.

"Well, I'm not those people."

"I see that."

"So, which one?" Cartier asked.

"I'll get a job," she opted.

"All right then," said Cartier.

Harlem climbed out of the Lyft on 56th Street in Midtown Manhattan and looked at the building that most likely would become her new place of employment. It was nestled in the middle of the block, and it was a well-known nightclub called Escape. It was one of the top clubs in the city, and they were hiring young bottle service girls. Her outfit wasn't the usual interview wear, as Harlem entered the nightclub dressed in black coochie-cutter shorts, a sleeveless magenta blouse, and heels. Her flat-ironed hair was styled into a long ponytail, and her lips were popping in the new NARS Damned she had picked out on her shopping spree with Cartier.

The place was huge—bigger than she had expected. The afternoon hour made the club a ghost town, but tonight it would become an entirely different atmosphere with VIPs, blaring music, and pretty girls.

"You here for the position as a bottle service girl?" asked the woman behind the bar.

"Yes. I'm Harlem."

x

x

x

The woman signaled for her to come closer. Harlem walked to the bar and gaped at the woman's beauty. She was white with green eyes and long blond hair and she looked to be in her mid-thirties.

"I'm Michelle," she said. "Could you turn around for me so I can see what you're working with?"

Harlem did so, slowly turning around and showing Michelle her lovely figure.

"You're pretty, sexy, and exotic. Where are you from?" Michelle asked.

"I was born here, but my parents are from Ethiopia."

"It shows. Have you ever worked in a nightclub before?"

Harlem shook her head.

"It's a demanding task, and when it comes to my girls, I ask for three things—professionalism and courtesy when it comes to our guests; a pretty, smiling face at all times; and don't be late," Michelle said.

"Then I'm your girl."

Michelle stared at her for a moment, taking in everything about her. She would be an asset to the venue.

"The money can be great if you know how to handle yourself, and our VIP clientele can be huge tippers if you play your cards right. I don't mind the girls flirting with our clubbers and our high-profile customers, but don't fuck our clientele—mixing business and pleasure isn't good, and I don't allow it. One fuck and you're fired," Michelle warned. "You go by my rules and we'll be okay."

"I understand, and I'm ready to work."

"Good. You can start tonight."

Harlem smiled. She knew that only the prettiest girls landed the position because they got the best tips. It was well known that Jay-Z had once tipped a bottle service girl eleven grand, and another girl fifty thousand. Harlem was hyped and ready to make that money.

6

*H*ead drove the bullet-riddled Audi into the auto body shop on Ralph Avenue and hopped out to greet Ray, the owner of the place.

"My nigga! Long time no see," Ray said, giving Head dap and embracing him in a brotherly hug.

"I ain't been a nigger in a while," Head replied. "But what's up, though?"

"True. I hear you, black man."

"I hope so, 'cause we can't keep spreading propaganda to our youth. We gotta teach them that we're not niggers or niggas. Our history doesn't start at slavery—" Head puffed out his chest and adjusted his Yankees fitted—"As the original race, the black man has a duty to correct the infiltrated minds of our brothers and sisters. You feel me?"

Ray nodded. *Here we go*, he thought. He had watched this scene play out a thousand times. Dude comes home after doing a long bid in jail, and overnight he's the conscious, self-aware Asiatic black man. Ray gave Head ninety days outside before all this supreme wisdom wore off.

Ray looked at the car and asked, "Damn. What happened?"

"Some bullshit that I'm about to correct," Head replied.

"Just got home and you made some friends already," Ray joked.

"I'm not even in the joking mood right now. Muthafuckas tried to come at me outside my great aunt's place the other night," said Head. "This is what I'm talking about. Brothers are misguided!"

"Damn. For real?" Ray said and took another look at the botched vehicle. He whistled. "So how you gonna handle this situation? You gonna sit down and politick—shake hands and squash whatever this is like men? 'Cause this black-on-black violence ain't the move. I know you been locked down for a while, but nowadays the movement is Black Lives Matter. I know you're above all this material shit, and killing a black man over a car is unethical, right? I'm only asking so I'll know what to tell the youth."

Head had to use all his restraint not to put paws on Ray. He knew he was trying to undermine his teachings and play him out.

"Why you assuming that a brother is behind this attack? For all I know, the white devil has masterminded this very act to try to pull me out my character and grab my hammers so I could end up doing life in a cage. Those alphabet boys been on me hard for half my life. That's real talk."

Ray weighed whether he should mention that it was Head who implicated the black man in the shooting. He replied, "The feds shooting up cars now? Damn, Head—"

"It's Henry."

Ray smirked. "What?"

"My name. I don't go by Head anymore. That name represents my former self. My born name is Henry Jackson after my great-grandfather who owned businesses and was a pillar in the black community."

Ray erupted in laughter. His fat gut was heaving in and out rapidly as he struggled to talk. His voice rose to a feminine level. "Yoooo! Henry . . . Henry . . . nah, man, you gotta change that to something powerful like Muhammad or Khalid."

Head's cold stare zeroed in on Ray. "Are you done?"

"Yeah." Ray adjusted his clothes and got back into business mode.

"This is a huge inconvenience. Now I gotta hear shit from my lady about her car getting shot up," Head added. "But you got me? Can you take care of things?"

Ray moved closer to the car and did a minor inspection of it. He then looked at Head and said, "I got you. I can get this fixed and back to new in no time. You going through insurance?"

"Nah, so don't hurt my pockets."

"You're in good hands."

Head was grateful. He had a lot of making up to do to Pebbles. He had to kiss her ass because he couldn't go back to his aunt's place. Pebbles owned a condo in Battery Park in Lower Manhattan, and he felt it was safer for him to stay there.

"So, are you back in business?" Ray asked him.

Head smirked and patted Ray's chest and waist. "You wired up?"

"Come on, man. This me."

"Nah. Never again will I push poison to our people. I'm working on some different things, my brother," Head said.

"Different things, huh? Like what?"

"I'm on a different path—a path that's a lot more righteous and life affirming out in Michigan. You feel me?"

Ray had no idea what he was talking about, but still, he replied nonchalantly, "Yeah, I feel you."

"What's the estimate for the damage?" asked Head.

"Give me a day. I'll get back at you."

"Cool, do that. I appreciate it."

"No doubt. You know I got you," replied Ray.

The two dapped each other and embraced in another brotherly hug, and Head left the shop. To Ray, Head seemed like a carbon copy of one of those fraudulently woke niggas—nothing but a snake oil salesman hiding behind racist rhetoric and narcissistic ideals.

"Oh shit, I'm gonna come!" Head huffed.

Pebbles had been riding him for a moment and she soon had him about to explode.

"Come, baby . . .oooh, I want you to come for me, baby," she moaned as she felt his hard dick thrusting in and out of her, making her legs quiver.

It took a few more pumps inside of her before he finally exploded, releasing pent up energy. Head exhaled and he looked like a balloon deflating. Pebbles plopped down beside him, placing her head on his chest, and Head wrapped his arms around her. They cuddled. She wanted some pillow talk, but Head looked like he was ready to go to sleep on her already.

"Bae, wake up," she said, trying to stir him awake. "You gonna fuck me and go to sleep that fast?"

"It's been a long day," he said.

"So, talk to me."

"About what?"

"About anything."

Head sighed. He wasn't in the mood for Pebbles' emotions. He was holding her in his arms, wasn't that enough for tonight? But he guessed that she wanted to feel like his woman and she wanted to know what was going on in his life. Head was comfortable at Pebbles' place and things were going well. The sex was good, they had been cooking dinner together, and it felt like they were an actual couple. But to Head, something was missing. Pebbles was a sweet girl, and she was very territorial over him, but he felt that she was hiding something from him and he wanted to know what it was.

"So, is my car gonna be ready tomorrow?" she asked him.

"That's what Ray's telling me."

"And you have no idea who came at you?"

"You already know the answer to that," Head said.

"Well, you know this is your home, baby. I got you. You take care of me and I'm gonna always take care of you. I love you."

Head continued to caress her shoulders.

She expected to hear him say it, and his silence disappointed her. "You not gonna say 'I love you' back? Especially after I gave you some pussy?"

"Pebbles, I'm fuckin' tired, all right? And I'm not tryin' to argue with you right now," he griped.

She replied with an attitude, "You wasn't too tired to fuck me a moment ago," and then she angrily removed herself from the bed and stormed into the next room, slamming the door behind her.

Head didn't chase after her. He figured she needed some time to herself to calm down. No matter how upset Pebbles was with him, Head knew she wasn't going anywhere. She needed him more than he needed her.

The next day, Pebbles got dressed and told Head she was leaving to get her toes and nails done. It was like last night hadn't happened and she was no longer upset with him. Before she left, she passionately kissed him goodbye and promised that tonight was going to be another great night for them.

Head watched her leave. Once the front door closed, he uttered to himself, "What the fuck you hiding from me?"

Pebbles was going to be gone for a long time with her manicure and pedicure, so Head knew he had time to go snooping around her place. He started with the bedroom. He opened several drawers and went digging through her belongings. Pebbles wasn't the best when it came to keeping her personal business private. It didn't take long for him to find what he was looking for. He came across piles and piles of bills and past due notices.

He also saw that she was in serious debt and the bank was threatening to take her condominium.

"Fuck," he said with frustration.

You can get expensive manicures and pedicures, but you can't pay your fuckin' bills on time? All those big deals she talked about and all her bragging about being hired over one of the Kardashians to promote certain products, and yet she was $15,000 in debt.

He didn't want her to lose her place. He needed to stay there. He needed to regroup and rethink his situation, and laying low in lower Manhattan was convenient for him. He placed everything back the way he found it and booked a Lyft.

As Head was driven through the boroughs in the Lyft, he felt like a mogul. The iPhone was so advanced, everything was at his fingertips. You could move money through bank accounts, pay bills, book flights and hotels, shop online, make business and booty calls—the possibilities were endless. And Head used all the capabilities to help make his life easier. After booking a roundtrip Delta flight to Michigan and a hotel, he called his realtor.

"David, give me some good news."

"Hey, Henry!" Head could almost feel the agent's huge grin. "Did you get the pictures I sent you?"

"Nah. When did you send them?"

"It's been about an hour now."

"Hold on." Head went to his Gmail account and the email was there. He opened up the attachment and saw lots of properties. "Okay, cool. I got it. I'll look at them and hit you back later."

"We gotta act fast, though," David said, a touch of pushiness in his tone. "These properties won't be on the market for long. We should make an offer as soon as possible."

"If I like what I see, then I will."

"When?"

"When what, nigga!" Head didn't like to be pressured, nor did he like that this clown thought he could run game on him. His righteous persona was on pause for a moment.

"I just wanted to stress that Flint's real estate is on the rise and properties don't usually stay on the market for long. But take your time."

"I always take what I want! Money, lives, women, bitches, and my muthafuckin' time. Yo, don't ever try to play me again. You get one warning."

"Sure, Henry—"

"Mr. Jackson."

"No problem, Mr. Jackson. And again, forgive me. I'll just wait on your call. Have a good day and please note that I meant no disrespect."

Head deaded the call and then glared at the driver, whose eyes were shifting from the road to the rearview mirror. He was now terrified of the man who just moments earlier seemed like a respectable businessman. Head peeped the camera on the dashboard most likely recording.

Head thought quickly. "Pardon me, man. There's only so many hours in a day and I was running some lines with my producer."

"Producer? You in the industry?"

"I executive produce cable shows. *The Wire* opened a lot of doors."

"*The Wire?* I loved that show. What do you produce?"

"You heard of *Power*?"

"*Power!*" the driver nearly squealed his delight. "I love that show. Tommy is my favorite. Some people even say I look like him."

Head nodded. "Yeah, I see the resemblance."

"I can't believe this. I knew you were someone important when I picked you up. And I wasn't being nosy, but not many people can afford to take a Lyft through boroughs and make it a roundtrip."

"My lady has my driver and I have moves to make, so thanks for looking out and riding with me for the day."

"So back to *Power*. Did that argument have anything to do with it?"

"I was going over lines," he lied. "The writer was complaining that it wasn't authentic, so as the EP it all falls to me." Head exhaled his fake frustration.

The driver turned out not to have an off button. He drove Head to his bank where Head retrieved several bundles of cash, and then he drove him to Green Acres Mall so Head could buy some new kicks, jeans, and a couple more fitted caps. They also stopped by the Cheesecake Factory and finally headed back to Lower Manhattan, and Head didn't get a moment of silence.

When Head finally came back, Pebbles wasn't home. She was still busy dolling herself up with money she should have allocated toward her bills.

The following day, Head gave Pebbles $20,000, and she was completely shocked by it.

"You giving me twenty stacks? Really?" she asked.

"I just gave it to you."

"But for what?"

He didn't want to let on that he had snooped through her things. He believed that she was going to make the best of the twenty thousand and take care of her bills and her business.

"For you to do what you want with it. Go and handle your business," he said to her.

Pebbles grinned so hard and bright, it damn near took up the entire room. She leaped into his arms and thanked him with hugs and kisses.

"I love you. I love you. I love you. You're the best, baby!" she exclaimed.

"You know I got you."

"I know, and I definitely got you tonight," she replied. "What would I do without you?"

Find another hustler. Head laughed to himself.

He stared at Pebbles for a long moment, seeing how gracious she was for the large sum of money and he said to her out the blue, "You know if we don't arm ourselves, then we start to harm ourselves."

Where did that come from? she thought.

"What you mean?" she asked him.

"It's just something I learned when I was inside. You have to arm yourself with knowledge. Spiritual, financial, and historical knowledge. You understand me?"

She slightly nodded her head. "I understand."

"Educate yourself, baby, because if not, I won't be around you for long. You won't hold my attention. More bluntly, your pussy won't. I need a woman with substance. Truthfully, I don't know you. All those visits served their purpose, which was to have the prettiest woman sitting across from me for everyone to see. You did that. But now we gotta get our grown on. I don't give a fuck about Instagram. I don't give a fuck about who you think is hatin' on you. And I give no fucks about what brothers tried to holler at you. I want to know YOU. Do you believe in a creator? Are you agnostic? Atheist? Are you a proud black woman or are you consistently spewing those blends like you half African American, half Native American, half Latin American, half Caucasian? Why aren't you raising your kids? What's your credit score? What can you bring to my table?"

"What are you talking about?"

"I guess you're half deaf?"

Pebbles was now wide-eyed. This money was coming with what felt like an accusatory lecture. Her feelings were hurt and she had no idea why she was being verbally assaulted.

"Why are you saying this to me? Do you want this money back?"

"Do you want to give it back?"

"It's not cool to answer a question with a question, but no. I don't."

"Good. We're making progress. You're manipulative. Your question about the money was meant to tip the scale in your favor."

"That's not true!" she screamed. "I want this money, but only if you wanna give it to me! It's not that fuckin' serious! Damn!"

Head never raised his voice. "That money was yours when I gave it to you. I gave it to you because I wanted to. You hungry? I bought us some food."

Pebbles exhaled. "Yeah, I could eat."

7

*B*rooklyn wasn't big enough for Cartier and Head to not run into each other. With winter gone and spring in full swing, there were events and parties throughout the city, and people were out and about enjoying the beautiful weather. It was the season where everything was blossoming. The bright days and blue skies hinted at the summer to come.

The late afternoon sunshine percolated through Cartier's bedroom window, making the room glow with a heavenly radiance as she got dressed for a day party at Escape. Barkim and Chemo were coordinating the event, which would last from 5pm to 10pm. Harlem was working today doing bottle service, and Cartier had promised to come through and show her support. Harlem had been working at the club for two weeks now, and she had fallen in love with the job.

Cartier had a feeling that Head would be there, and she wanted to look her best. She wanted to have niggas' jaws dropping, including Head's. She also knew he would bring that bitch, and this time she wanted to maintain her composure and show him what he was missing out on.

Cartier gazed at herself in the mirror wearing a strapless black Balmain bodycon dress with an aqua colored matte lipstick. With a liquid liner she did a cat's eye, styled her bob toward the back, and that was it. She looked absolutely stunning. Her Givenchy heels gave her petite frame the height needed to exude confidence and sexuality.

She thought about seeing if Apple would go with her to this day party, but this was a Brooklyn party although it was being held in Manhattan. Most likely Brooklyn folks would be in the house, and Cartier felt that Apple would bring trouble.

She strutted out of her building and glided toward her Bugatti. Inside the car, she did one final check of her makeup in the visor, smiled at herself, and uttered, "You go, bitch."

She started the car and sped off. She was ready to make an entrance. She drove toward the highway with her music blaring as she sang along with Gucci Mane, Kodak Black, and Bruno Mars to "Wake up in the Sky." For some reason, Cartier was in a very good mood.

"What the fuck is a day party?" Head had to ask Chemo.

"Just come through, bruh. You'll like it."

"Still, what is it? You know I don't like surprises."

"I know. The only difference is the time it starts," Chemo explained. "It's for old heads like us so we can still get our shine on and be home at a decent hour. If you're thirty and above, then you go to day parties."

"And what time does it start?" Head had asked him.

"It starts around five in the afternoon."

Head chuckled. "Five? And people really show up? Don't have me out here looking thirsty."

"Shiiit, Barkim and me been making a killing off these parties. Niggas can't get enough of them."

"A'ight, I'll be there," said Head.

"You know I got you," Chemo had replied with finality.

Day parties. Head still laughed at the concept. Back in his day, parties didn't start until eleven or midnight. Times were changing. But the idea of it intrigued him, and he wanted to see what all the fuss was about. Plus, the timing meant that it wouldn't take much lying for him to go to the party without Pebbles.

The early hours of these new parties were something that Head figured he could get used to. Even though he seemed against it with Chemo, it was a good concept for anyone in his age range. Thirty and above could go to work, go to the party, and make it home in time to get up the next day. When he was running the streets in his twenties, the Q Club, S&S, The Rink, and Tunnel in Lower Manhattan was where all the hustlers popped bottles and showed off their wealth and where the thorough niggas came with their A-game. You came through in your street clothes with phat pockets. Nowadays, everyone was getting suited up, their hairlines shaped up, mustaches and beards trimmed, and paying their bills with black cards. Dealers now had shell corporations that laundered their money, drove company cars, and the women weren't just becoming baby mamas. They were holding court on equal terms with men.

It wasn't the eighties and nineties anymore; this was the millennium where snitches and bitch-ass niggas were growing popular in the streets, and where fake hustlers and fake niggas were boasting about their fraudulent street credibility and were more popular on social media than in the streets. It all seemed like a lie to Head. He felt that the streets needed some definite correction in this new era—someone had to do something to bring realness and strength back. He saw that things were growing out of control, and it was the reason he needed to network and create a new family and organization—one that couldn't be corrupted.

Head's smooth dark-chocolate skin glowed against his tailored dark blue Tom Ford suit and his gold and diamond cufflinks. His red bottoms brought him up-to-date and kept him on trend. He was fashion forward and he knew that he could fit in any environment.

He glanced at the time and it was 3:55pm. He wanted to leave before Pebbles came home. She was out and about either getting her hair done or taking care of business.

Head marched out of the building looking and feeling like he was worth a million and more. He got into Pebbles' Audi, which Ray had looking brand new again. The bullet holes were gone and the paint job was pristine, and for that, Head gave him a little extra on the side.

Five minutes on the road, Head's phone started ringing. He glanced at the caller ID, and it was Pebbles calling him. He knew she was home and wanted to know where he was at. At first, Head was going to ignore her call, but he decided against it. He answered with, "Yeah, what up?"

"Where are you? I just got home," she said.

"I'm out."

Pebbles could hear the wind blowing through the phone, indicating that he was driving somewhere. "Oh? Going where?"

"I gotta go handle some business," he said.

"Oh. Business. Okay," she replied with meekness, pretending to believe him.

"Yeah. I won't be too long, a'ight?"

"Okay. When you get home, just tap me on my shoulder," she said.

Head smiled. He knew that was her cute way of saying she wanted to fuck tonight when he got home. Pebbles was definitely tugging at his heart.

Pebbles pretended to be docile, proper, and business-minded. She rarely raised her voice to Head, and she pretended as if she would fall for anything he told her, including the lies. Every few days he was supposedly handling business in Michigan, but Pebbles believed that to be a lie. Still, she said nothing each time he disappeared. She knew about the ghetto bitch Cartier, and she knew her type. Pebbles wanted to become the opposite of her. She also knew about the day party in the city. Everyone was talking about it, and she was disappointed that he didn't invite her to go. But the last thing a nigga wanted was a bitch who wanted to argue all the time. That was her strategy—to stay humble and to stay pleasing her man. That was how she would get him and keep him.

Parking was tight in the city, so Head opted to park in a nearby garage, which cost him a small fortune. Before walking away, he checked his image in the car window and liked what he saw. He walked toward Escape, and surprisingly there was a line of people waiting on the sidewalk to get in the club in broad daylight. Head proceeded forward, knowing he wasn't going to wait on any line.

There were two bouncers dressed in all black at the door. One had a list, and the second was doing the security searches. Head bypassed everyone on line and went straight to the entrance, where the two men gawked at him like he was crazy.

"Yo. What you need?" one of the bouncers asked.

"I'm on that list," said Head.

"You sure about that?"

"Yeah, I'm sure, nigga," Head replied in a stern tone.

Head locked eyes with the two men. He didn't want any problems, but if they decided to get stupid with him, then he was going to create problems. The seriousness showed in his eyes. Chemo had invited him to this event, and he wasn't about to be embarrassed in front of all these people.

"Yo, he good. Let him through," Head heard Chemo say.

Chemo smiled at Head, and the two greeted each other with dap and a brotherly hug.

"I'm glad you came out," said Chemo.

"Yeah, I wanted to see what this shit was about."

"You're gonna like it. It's different—lots of ladies and lots of fun. This is the new era we're in, brother. You gotta love it."

Head followed Chemo into the club. The moment he entered Escape, everything about it looked natural except the time. The music was blaring, the place was jam-packed, and the bar was swamped with customers trying to get their drinks. The lighting was dim and the VIP area was lit.

As Chemo continued to escort Head through the club, he saw a sea of faces from his past and briefly wondered which one had just tried to murder him. As he moved through the club greeting those he knew and receiving love and attention from many others, Head couldn't help but to scan the room for Cartier. They ran in the same circle, and he figured she would be at the party too. But after searching for her for nearly fifteen minutes, there was no sign of her. *Fuck!* he cursed to himself. She wasn't there.

Head had the best VIP table at the party reserved for him, thanks to Barkim and Chemo. They ordered four buckets of champagne, Voss water, Grey Goose, and Louis XIII cognac, and they were surrounded by beautiful ladies. There was conversation, laughter, and flirting, and Head was having the time of his life. He downed some champagne along with the Voss water, and dabbled with the XIII cognac, all while rubbing and massaging the thighs of a beautiful girl sitting on his lap.

"And what's your name?" he asked her.

"Cynthia." She smiled.

She was cute and sexy, and her bubble ass against Head's lap was creating some arousal. The day party was lit like it was New Year's Eve. The DJ was spinning hit record after hit record, the crowd was amped, and the place was so crowded that it looked like the party was going to spill out into the streets.

By the time Cartier finally arrived, Head was tipsy and on the fast track to becoming drunk. She moved like a panther through the crowd—confident, sexy, and self-assured. Head fixed his eyes on her from the VIP area. Cartier couldn't help but to stand out in the crowd. He watched her converse with Barkim and Chemo for a moment, and it didn't matter who was sitting on his lap; his attention immediately shifted to Cartier. Every step she took, Head watched like a field goal kick in the final seconds of the Super Bowl. He watched her approach the VIP area where he was seated, and the moment she stepped foot into the section, he was on her. He stood up and nearly threw a tipsy Cynthia to the floor.

The first words out of his mouth to her were, "Damn, you wearing the shit outta that dress."

Cartier shook her head dismissively. "Get lost."

Head stepped closer, trying to bridge the gap. He was inches from her but felt miles away. Cartier wasn't trying to connect. He intimately stared in her eyes and saw pain—or was it anger?

"I know you mad—"

She chuckled. "Mad? Mad was two weeks ago. Come again."

"I know I fucked up, but let me explain myself. Let's get out of here so we can talk." Head allowed his hand to brush up against her hip, hoping to spark something.

Cartier shrugged. "You did explain. You said everything you had to say in all them fuckin' letters, right? Tonight I'm here to party, not listen to a grown man whine about the past. Excuse me. I see a few niggas who might see a future wit' me in it. Thank you—next!"

She tried to push past him and he forcefully grabbed her arm. He loosened his grip when he saw the scowl on her face.

"I'm trying to be a lady, but you know I can act a fool."

"Please don't do that. You lookin' too sexy to be out here wildin'. I swear on my life, ma, I've been thinking about you every day."

Cartier looked at him stoically. His compliment didn't mean shit to her. "Me? Really? How your Insta-bitch feel about that?" she asked.

"She's not a bitch, Cartier."

"Oh, you taking up for her?"

"It's not even like that, and to keep it one-hundred, we not together. She's just mad cool," he said.

"So y'all fuck buddies," she countered.

"Listen, we started off wrong, and I apologize. Let's let bygones be bygones. If I can forgive you for breaking my fucking heart, then you can get past Pebbles."

She laughed. "And you're serious?"

"I missed you, Cartier. Let's go somewhere and talk, watch Netflix and chill for a few days," he suggested.

Cartier couldn't believe what he was saying. She instantly shut him down. Her only reply was, "Boy, bye!"

She walked off to find a section to sit without Head being up her ass with his pitiful apologies. Barkim and Chemo sent a few bottles her way, and she took delight in being the bitch she was while Head was looking like a lost fool. He couldn't even play it cool. Maybe it was the alcohol talking, but she didn't care. Tonight was her night to unwind and enjoy life, and she wanted to check in on Harlem to see how she was making out.

Harlem was making her rounds throughout the club looking gorgeous in a black corset and stilettos and her gorgeous white smile. It looked like she was getting the hang of things. Cartier smiled. Soon, Harlem came to greet her and she gave Cartier a big hug. There were lots of eyes on the two of them. Everyone started to wonder how they knew each other.

"How are you making out?" Cartier asked her.

"I'm doing fine; making my rounds and making my tips," Harlem replied. She flashed Cartier a small wad of cash.

Cartier smiled. "You a hustler. Go get that money."

Cartier gave her a handsome tip, sipped on her champagne, and allowed the top ballers to flirt with her. The attention was flattering, but not from Head. She glanced to her right and noticed that he was still watching her, and it was starting to become a bit creepy. When their eyes locked, she would frown at him like there was some kind of bug inside her mouth.

She only stayed at the party for an hour. She knew that you left them wanting more—and they all wanted more, especially Head. Passing Harlem during her exit, she said, "I'll see you at the apartment."

"Okay. Bye, Cartier."

Cartier left the building like the sexy boss bitch that she was. She came, she saw, and she muthafuckin' conquered.

Head stumbled to the parking garage where the Audi was parked. It was just after 11pm, and it was awkward to be leaving the club at that hour instead of arriving. Yet, he had a good time. The only low point was getting shaded by Cartier. The short time she was there, she had nothing to say to him, and that bothered him. He slid into the driver's seat, started the car, and headed home. During the drive he thought about Cartier as images of her sexy dress and her stylish haircut flashed through his brain. Thinking about her was making his dick hard.

Did I fuck up a good thing? he asked himself. Cartier was a natural born hustler, and from the way she handled herself tonight, he knew that Pebbles couldn't hold a candle to her. Cartier knew how to get money, while Pebbles was too busy spending it. Yet, he made his choice and he was about to go home and climb all over his decision. Cartier had him horny and he wanted to fuck.

The moment he walked through the front door Head started undressing himself. He went to the master bedroom and saw that there was no need to tap Pebbles on her shoulder. She was already awake, lying there watching TV in a T-shirt and panties. She turned and saw that her man had the hungriest look in his eyes.

Head peeled away the rest of his clothing and jumped onto the bed and came at her like an animal that hadn't eaten for days. He pounced on her like a sexual predator, spreading her legs and slamming his hard dick into her like there was a time limit. She immediately became submissive to her man and moaned as he fucked her vigorously. Something about him was different, but Pebbles couldn't put her finger on it. She couldn't focus on anything besides the frenzied fuck Head was dishing out, and the thought dissipated while she enjoyed the moment.

As Head banged her repeatedly, he was wishing he had his hard dick inside Cartier.

8

*O*nce again, the morning sun came seeping into Cartier's bedroom indicating to her that it was going to be another beautiful spring day. Cartier woke up around 10am and lifted herself out of the bed like she was a blossoming flower in a picturesque garden. She felt good. Last night had gone completely her way, and the way she left Head and the other ballers yearning for more of her attention was extremely gratifying. It played out just as she had expected.

She walked out her bedroom to see that Harlem's door was closed. She was asleep when Harlem came home. She wanted to see if the girl was up and ask her about her night. When she went to open the door, she found it locked. It was cool. She figured Harlem had a late night and wanted to sleep in. She deserved it.

Cartier went into the kitchen to start breakfast and to clean up. She was still on a natural high, feeling good and looking good. She thought about whether it would be rude to turn on some music and dance to it while she was cooking and cleaning, but she didn't want to wake up Harlem. But part of her said, *Fuck it!* It was her house and she wasn't about to tiptoe around it for anyone. Cooking and cleaning to music was like a family tradition. When she was young, Trina would always cut on the greats and blast them so loud that it felt like there was a concert happening inside their living room. Aretha Franklin, Diana Ross, Gladys Knight, Prince, and Michael Jackson would all croon throughout their apartment.

Cartier marched over to her high-end stereo system and she knew the perfect album to play. She streamed Beyoncé's *Lemonade* and she started to shake her head, sing along to tracks, and dance around her apartment like she was on an episode of *Soul Train.*

Niggas are something else, she said to herself. Cartier could relate to the entire album and she repeated some songs verbatim. Listening to a certain track made her think about Jason, her ex-husband, and it brought back feelings of how he had broken her heart in the same way more than once. But unlike Beyoncé, she wasn't so forgiving. Cartier thought about the time she had emptied her entire clip into that nigga and his fuckin' mistress. The memory was poignant, but it was a long time ago.

With her grits slow cooking in the kitchen, Cartier went into her bedroom and suddenly noticed something. When she had left for the day party yesterday she had four hundred dollars on her nightstand in twenties and fifties. Now there was less than two hundred. As if she wouldn't notice.

This little thieving-ass bitch! Cartier thought. If Harlem had stolen money from her when she could have simply asked, then what else had she taken? Cartier started to look around her bedroom, and it didn't take long for her to find that two of her handbags were missing, along with some shoes and wallets. Harlem hadn't been there more than a month and it was already going south.

Cartier stormed out of her bedroom and banged on Harlem's door so hard that it felt like she was going to take the door off the hinges.

"Harlem, open the fuckin' door!" Cartier hollered. "You better open this damn door right now!"

The door finally swung open, and Harlem gaped at Cartier with a sour look on her face. She was naked. What came as a shock to Cartier was when she looked past Harlem and noticed a naked man in the bed knocked out cold with his legs cocked open and his flaccid dick hanging to the side. It looked like Harlem had put that pussy on him something serious last night and laid him to rest. However, the funky room was messy and Harlem stood there looking defiant. She knew what Cartier's abrupt visit was about.

In that moment Cartier saw the girl who had the heart to prostitute her body instead of the innocent. She felt she had been manipulated. Cartier had to shelve the money discussion for now. She was fuming. She pushed past Harlem and marched into the room toward the sleeping man.

"Nigga, get the fuck up!" she screamed. She yanked the man by his arm, rudely stirring him awake, and dragged him to the floor where he fell with a thump.

"Get the fuck outta here!" Cartier shouted.

It was then that she got a clear look at his face. The young man was named Zaire and he quickly jumped up and was ready to react with his own hostility until he caught a good look at Cartier and recognized his surroundings.

"Yo, Cartier, my bad. You scared the shit outta me. I was 'bout to look for my ninas," he said.

Zaire knew Cartier and vice-versa. She didn't give a fuck, though. She didn't want him in her home.

"Get your shit, Zaire, and get the fuck outta here," she shouted.

Zaire didn't hesitate, knowing what was best for him. He hurriedly collected his things, barely got dressed, and rushed out the front door like the place was engulfed in fire. The moment he was out the door, Cartier pivoted and tore into Harlem.

"You bring that nigga here—into my damn home, you fuckin' bitch!" she screamed. "You know what the fuck he's about?"

Harlem had no idea. She stood there looking naive and stupid.

"I'll tell you what he's about," Cartier continued. "He's a grimy muthafucka that goes out there and does home invasions, and you fuckin' bring him here!"

"I didn't know. I'm sorry," Harlem replied despondently.

"Sorry? You'll just fuck anything, I see," Cartier retorted.

"It won't happen again."

"You got-damn right it won't fuckin' happen again. And by the way, where the fuck is my money and my shit?"

"I don't know what you talkin' about. I didn't take anything from you," Harlem replied.

The remark caused Cartier to stomp her way, looking like she was ready to throw Harlem out the window. She shouted, "Don't fuckin' lie to me, you stupid bitch!"

"I didn't take your shit," Harlem shouted back.

Cartier felt that the bitch was ungrateful and that she was trying to play her. She screamed back, "Who took it then?"

"I don't know! Maybe you spent it and don't remember. I ain't gotta steal shit from you, Cartier. I got a fuckin' job, and it seems like I'm the only one working in here," Harlem chided.

Oh shit! Cartier screamed to herself. The young girl was unquestionably feeling herself. She thought that she was so smart and grown.

"Bitch, you better watch your mouth in my home," Cartier warned.

But Harlem continued her defiant streak. She rolled her eyes like they were marbles rolling around inside of her head and rudely replied, "Bitch, go fuck yourself, cuz I don't need to take shit from you. So take that shit somewhere else!"

What the fuck!

Cartier didn't want to do it, but the young bitch had already said too much. Harlem didn't see the punch coming; it struck her just as fast as lightning would have—no warning, just blast and fire that damn near took Harlem out of her skin. She went stumbling backwards, and Cartier pounced on her like a cat on a mouse.

"You gonna fuckin' respect me!" Cartier yelled.

Harlem went down like she was Joe Frazier against Ali, and Cartier continued to beat fire out her ass. The fight was one-sided. Harlem had no chance in defending herself. While she was on the ground, Cartier dragged her across the floor like she was a rag doll and continued to punch her repeatedly.

"What, bitch? I told you, don't fuckin' disrespect me, especially in my fuckin' place," Cartier shouted. "You fuckin' trick!"

"Get off me!" Harlem screamed.

"You done, bitch?"

When Cartier finally let off her ass and gave her some breathing room, Harlem picked herself up from the floor with hurt and pain in her eyes. "You think you're so much better than me and Esmeralda? You're using me too! Just like her!"

Cartier didn't understand. She scowled and thought, *How dare this no-rent-paying, no-food-paying, no-paying-at-all little bitch gonna say some dumb shit like that?*

"You used me that night. You made me an accomplice to that attempted murder on your ex," she exclaimed.

Whoa! Cartier thought. *Did she really just take it there?* She felt that she had two choices with Harlem—kill the bitch or kick her out.

"You know what, you ungrateful bitch? Get the fuck out!" Cartier shouted. "I don't want you here anymore."

Cartier started stomping around the bedroom and grabbing anything that belonged to Harlem. She tossed all of it into the hallway like yesterday's trash. Next, she pulled Harlem out into the hallway and slammed the door behind her.

"I hate you!" Harlem screamed at the top of her lungs from the other side of the door.

Cartier exhaled. Being back in Brooklyn wasn't unfolding as she planned. And not only that, her damn grits were burning on the stove.

Cartier stood in the Cypress Hill Cemetery in Brooklyn visiting her best friend, Monya. She held a bouquet of white roses in her hand. It was a depressing moment for her. So much time had passed since her friend's death. She didn't say much. She just stared down at the headstone and wondered how things would have been different had they been born under different circumstances. The choices they had made, the things they had done, and the men they had fucked with had led to their downfalls.

She sighed heavily and said, "I'm sorry, Monya. I'm sorry this happened to you. It's not right that you're in the ground."

She crouched and placed the bouquet of white roses on her friend's grave. She then explained that Head was finally home from jail and already giving her problems.

"I think you would have liked him," said Cartier.

She chuckled and thought, *Monya, you always loved complicated relationships.*

Cartier continued with, "I've killed too many, Monya. I got too much blood on my hands. I've lost everything that I've ever loved—you, our crew, my moms, siblings, and what was the most precious thing to me, my baby girl. If I don't get out now then I know I'm next."

Cartier stood at her friend's grave for a long moment reflecting on her life and her mistakes. There were too many to count.

The sun sank low in the sky with the light gradually draining away. The warmth of the day had been replaced by a cool breeze. As Cartier's eyes were fixed on the headstone, she all of a sudden felt strange. A dark feeling hovered over her, and she didn't like it. The feeling was something that she couldn't shake off; it felt attached to her like the skin she was in. She looked around and carefully took in her surroundings, noticing a few others in the sparsely populated area, and she shuddered. She wondered why she was feeling so weird.

She continued her talk with Monya. "As long as I'm keeping it real, I did something that I don't really understand myself, which was opening up my door to a stranger. This chick, she's a little thief and not like us. We hustled for ours. She doesn't boost merchandise, which I could respect. She's the sneaky kind of thief that will dig in your wallet while you sleep."

Cartier paused for a moment to think about her actions. She concluded, "I think I looked out for her 'cause she reminded me of you."

Cartier smiled, looking down at the gravesite as if she actually heard Monya reply, *Bitch, ain't no-fuckin'-body like me.*

"You always thought you were so fuckin' cute." Cartier chuckled.

"Monya, do you remember the Harlem twins, Apple and Kola?" She shook her head rapidly. "Apple—she has this unquenchable thirst for the game. She's strong willed, but reckless. Sometimes I fear that I'll be visiting her buried six feet deep in the very near future or vice versa."

Cartier enjoyed her moment visiting her friend, but it was also painful, and she felt it was time to go. She crouched down and kissed her index and middle finger and pressed them against Monya's headstone, showing her love to the deceased.

When she got back to her car there was something on her windshield. It wasn't supposed to be there. She was in a cemetery, so who would be advertising something? Right away, Cartier opened her Hermes handbag and placed her hand on her pistol. The 9mm gave her some quick comfort. Her head swiveled like a rotating chair until she was certain there weren't any threats nearby.

She snatched the item from her windshield and flipped it over. It was white cardstock that displayed a skull, a dagger, and blood with the handwritten letter *O* in black ink.

O? What does it mean? Cartier asked herself. *And where did it come from?*

The card somewhat spooked her. Someone knew she was at the cemetery and she believed that she was being followed. First her home, and now the cemetery. It wasn't cute. However, she shrugged and tossed the damn thing over her shoulder. Someone was definitely playing head games with her. She got behind the wheel of her Bugatti and peeled out of the cemetery.

9

"O h shit," Head groaned with pleasure while he was sleeping. It felt like he was having a wet dream, but when he opened his eyes, he was waking up to the most amazing blowjob he'd had in a long time.

Pebbles had started deep-throating him. Her lips rapidly slid up and down his hard and long dick, her head moving like a bobblehead as she sucked and slurped. Head was in absolute bliss. The sensation of her full, sweet lips was making his toes curl and his eyes roll around in his head like he was possessed.

"What the fuck?" he muttered.

She curtly stopped her pleasurable act to reply, "Just relax, baby. I got you," and she went back to her business.

It took fifteen minutes for her lips to pull the cum from his dick. After Head nutted in her mouth, Pebbles rolled out of bed and left the bedroom naked to go make him some breakfast. Her cute face wore a satisfied smile that looked painted on.

Head had to collect himself for a moment. The blowjob had him stuck. He figured that she had gotten a new contract and wanted to treat him to something nice this morning. He wasn't complaining.

He remained in her bed, relishing the moment for a while, and then he got up and walked to the window butt naked and took a look outside.

He peered at the city block—a very busy Manhattan. Some time ago it was his city.

While Pebbles was in the kitchen cooking for him, Head decided to pick up his smart phone and check out her Instagram page. It was the quickest way to find out information nowadays. Once he was on her page, he saw Pebbles in countless posts taken in high-end stores—Chanel, YSL, Prada, Hermes—buying bags, shoes, scarves, belts, and outfits. She also had all types of hash tags—#spoiled #mymansbetterthanyours #wedoitbig. But what really got under his skin was that all those posts mentioned @Heads___Home. He went to the handle and there was his face with several pictures of them from when she came to visit him. Some were more recent and some were of him sleeping in her bed. He had warned her that he wasn't down with that kind of exposure, but Pebbles had created an account that made it seem he liked that dumb shit. He had over two hundred thousand followers.

"What the fuck!" he muttered to himself.

Pebbles was trying to make him a social media icon. But what bothered him too was seeing the new clothes, jewelry, and shoes in the pictures. He casually walked to her closet and looked through all her belongings. She had indeed bought everything with the twenty thousand he'd given her. The ignorant, materialistic woman had put her image before home.

"This fucking airhead," he said with disappointment.

To cool off, he decided to take a shower. While the water cascaded down on him, Head closed his eyes and he knew that it was time to put his plans into action. During his time in prison, he did a lot of reading, absorbing books that amplified his knowledge and spiritual awakening. He became enlightened to the world around him. His past was behind him, but his future was looming fast like a speeding train. As he lingered in the shower collecting his thoughts, he heard knocking at the door. It was Pebbles telling him that breakfast was ready.

"I'm not hungry," he casually replied.

His reply left her stunned. "Huh? You're not hungry? But I cooked you a good meal."

"I said I'm not hungry," he reiterated.

"Well, do you want me to join you?"

"Nah. I'm almost done," he said.

"You sure? I can come in there and soap you up from head to toe and continue what I started in the bedroom."

"I said I'm almost done."

"Okay. Fine."

Pebbles knew something had changed with Head all of a sudden. Why was he being so terse with her? She sighed. She figured it was either a bitch or business. Pebbles turned around and went back into the kitchen while Head continued to shower.

After spending about a half hour in the shower, Head exited the bathroom with a towel wrapped around his waist to see Pebbles standing naked in the hallway waiting for him to come out. She grinned his way but he didn't smile back.

"Henry, why the sudden attitude with me?"

He ignored her and went into the bedroom.

She followed behind him. "Did I do something wrong?"

He continued the silent treatment while he started to get dressed.

"I wake you up sucking your dick like a porn star and this is how you do me?"

He coolly glanced her way and continued to say nothing. Her nakedness wasn't enticing at the moment. The only thing he wanted to do was leave.

"Just tell me, what did I do wrong?"

He threw on his Timberland boots, stood up, grabbed a gym bag, coolly looked at her, and replied, "I'm out."

He walked to the front door. Pebbles was right behind him, looking desperate to hear him say something—some kind of explanation for the sudden attitude.

"Baby, just talk to me. Please," she begged.

She grabbed his forearm to prevent him from leaving so abruptly, but Head turned to look at her with a sharp stare that could cut through steel. Pebbles knew to remove her grip from him.

"Like I said, I'm out."

He walked through the door and Pebbles was left standing there naked looking like a lost puppy.

Outside, Head climbed into an Uber.

"Where to?" asked the driver.

"Valley Stream, Long Island," said Head.

"Okay."

Head sat back and gazed out the window. From Manhattan to Long Island was a long drive, but he didn't care. He needed to think. He needed to rebuild and stay focused.

An hour later, Head climbed out of the Uber at First National Bank in Valley Stream, Long Island. He peered at the building on the busy boulevard before heading inside to meet with the bank manager. After Head provided the information needed for security reasons, the manager escorted Head to an area filled with safety deposit boxes.

"I hope everything is to your satisfaction, Mr. Jackson," the bank manager said.

"It is."

"Well, I'll give you some privacy," the manager said and left the room.

With his key, Head opened one of the safety deposit boxes that he'd long ago set up via a dummy corporation. Inside was exactly $200,000. Head might not have buried his millions like Pablo Escobar, but he was diligent in hiding his cash in different locations.

He removed the money from the box and placed it into the small gym bag he brought with him. With the gym bag zipped and tossed over his shoulder, he left the bank two hundred thousand dollars richer. Subsequently, he got into a cab and told the driver to take him to Northern Boulevard in Queens.

The car dealership where all hustlers went for the hottest cars without any red tape was where Head wanted to be dropped off. The moment Head stepped foot onto the lot, he had a salesman approaching him with a wide grin and encouraging behavior.

"You look like a man who knows what he wants," said the salesman.

"It depends," Head responded.

"I'm Mark," he said, shaking Head's hand.

"Henry Jackson."

"So, Mr. Jackson, what brings you to our dealership? Are you looking for something in particular?"

"I need something nice."

"Well, look around you. We carry the best cars New York has ever seen. And as far as the paperwork, we can take care of that too."

"I know. That's the reason I came here."

"So I take it that you've done business with us before?"

"In the past."

Mark smiled. "Well, we're glad to have a repeat customer."

Head went looking around the car lot where exotic and luxury vehicles such as Ferraris, Bentleys, Maseratis, and Aston Martins were for sale for a hefty price.

"You look like a man that would do well in a McLaren," said Mark.

Head chuckled. "Seriously? Me in that?"

"It will definitely get the ladies' attention."

"I don't need a car like that to get the ladies' attention," he countered.

"I believe you. You do look like a ladies' man."

Head walked toward something that caught his eye. It was a black-on-black Range Rover. He knew he would blend better in a Range. He wasn't a rapper or a ball player, or even legit.

"I see you're an SUV kind of man. I should have predicted that," said Mark.

"I like this. What's the price on it?"

"It's ninety-five thousand. But for you, I'll let it go for ninety and it's truly a first-class travel experience. It comes fully loaded with top-of-the-line technology, touch-sensitive switches, along with beautiful leather interior—"

"I'll take it," Head interrupted his pitch. He didn't need to hear any more.

Mark helped him with the paperwork, and Head handed him the cash for the purchase. He then drove out of the dealership in his late-model custom black-on-black Range Rover. It was his type of ride—sitting up high and cruising around town like a boss.

After leaving the dealership, Head drove to the Courtyard Marriott in Queens where he booked a room for the week. He wanted a low-key hotel he could easily get to without traffic and hoopla until he was able to get his own apartment.

He breezed through the streets of Brooklyn a single man. And while cruising, Pebbles called him repeatedly but he refused to answer. She didn't leave him any of the messages he thought he would hear, like saying she needed money to pay her bills.

Back at the Courtyard Marriott that night, the only thing he could think about was Cartier.

10

*C*artier sat parked outside the Spanish restaurant in East Harlem on 116th Street. She hesitated to get out the car and go inside the place, which had a line of customers inside. But she wasn't there because she was hungry. She was there because she had been summoned by Caesar Mingo, who was the top man in New York City. It was the last place she wanted to be.

How the fuck did I get on his radar? she wondered. She had agreed to the meeting with Caesar, but it wasn't like she had a choice. When Caesar Mingo summons you to meet him somewhere, you had better show up on time and be ready to hear what he has to say.

Caesar didn't look like most cartel figures. He didn't wear suits, smoke cigars, nor was he born into the drug game. He was a handsome dark-chocolate man with shiny jet-black curly hair. He wasn't Mexican, Colombian, or Cuban. Caesar Mingo was actually a Dominican born in Mexico, and he was a former Major League Baseball player. He played for the Texas Rangers for three years before he was injured in a motorcycle accident. He was just a young man at the time, only twenty-one years old, and he was a hothead. Now, at 40, he'd long ago switched professions.

Caesar had been married to a Jewish lawyer named Lena for nearly two decades. They had to hire a live-in housekeeper to keep the house tidy.

Caesar and Lena had one child together, a chubby little boy named Oscar, and Lena hardly had any clients. She had hooked Caesar in high school because she knew he was going to play pro ball. However, Caesar was in love with a Puerto Rican girl named Clarita back then. Most of his peers were marrying outside their race to get the good endorsement deals, so he did what his mind told him to do, not his heart. Lena was overweight, lazy, and considered a slob, but no one dared to make fun of his wife. They figured he was with her for special reasons.

Caesar controlled 1/10th of narcotics on the east coast from his suburban farm in upstate New York. He was a powerhouse in the city and highly connected to the streets, to law enforcement, and in the political world. There was no telling how many cops and politicians he had on his payroll. But he lived a humble life—drove a minivan and Ford F-150. He was beloved in his community and he rarely came to the boroughs unless it was for something like today—for new business arrangements.

Caesar had done his homework and research on Cartier. She was low-level to him, however, he knew that she was capable of much more. He knew about her jail time for manslaughter, her run-in with the Gonzalez Cartel, and how she had taken out one of his top earners, Citi Byrne.

After spending some time in her Bugatti outside the restaurant, Cartier finally climbed out of the vehicle. Although she walked into the restaurant alone, her two new enforcers, brothers named Majestic and Scooter, were already seated among the customers. The brothers took orders well and were ready to protect her by any means necessary. They were killers, and they respected Cartier, whose name rang out on the streets of New York.

Cartier came to the meeting at the restaurant looking her best in an expensive silk dress, high heels, and clutching her designer handbag with her pistol concealed inside. As she took a seat near the entryway her eyes were darting everywhere, cautiously taking in her surroundings and examining faces. It was a typical atmosphere to a New York City restaurant—busy staff moving about fulfilling orders, chitchat filling the air, and patrons enjoying their meals. There was no sign of Caesar.

Five minutes after she arrived, Cartier was shocked to see him arriving driving a Chrysler minivan. She immediately knew it was him. He was alone except he had brought his three-year-old son with him. Cartier kept her eyes on Caesar from the time he parked the minivan, removed his son from the car seat in the back, and walked into the restaurant. He didn't look like an intimidating man, but anyone who really knew about his pedigree knew not to judge a book by its cover. He had on Crocs and an outfit that cost him no more than $30, and there were signs of a developing beer belly. His hairline was shaped up to perfection, his chocolate skin glowed like he got weekly facials, and it was clear that he had gotten a manicure. Caesar walked like a rock star, something only someone who had deep pockets could project.

Cartier stood to greet him. He gave her a stern look and said, "We'll talk in the back."

It was clear to her that he owned the place. She followed him through the restaurant to a private section in the back that was closed off from everything else. He closed the door behind them and they took a seat at a decorated table. She was nervous but she didn't show it. With his son seated on his lap, it was time to talk business. A waitress was assigned to take only their orders.

"Order whatever you like. It's on the house," Caesar told her.

"I'm not really that hungry," she replied.

"It's never good to talk business on an empty stomach. You come and you eat."

"Business?"

Caesar nodded.

She didn't want to argue with him. She smiled at the pretty waitress and said, "I'll have a turkey club and some fruit . . . and a bottled water."

"Asegúrate de que no estemos perturbados," Caesar spoke to the waitress in Spanish, telling her to make sure they weren't disturbed.

The waitress nodded and left the room. Once she was gone, Caesar stared at Cartier straight-faced and said, "I've heard great things about you, Cartier, and I bet you are curious as to why I called you to meet."

"I am."

"You're smart and motivated, and I see you as an asset to this organization—*valioso*," he said. "Those attributes are the sole reason I didn't have you killed when you took out Citi. Your actions left distribution wide open, and that's a position you're going to fill."

Cartier was aggravated. "I'm out the game—but you know this."

Caesar shrugged. "In, out—just semantics, little details we can't get hung up on. *Sí*?"

"Look, Caesar, I understand your position, but please get this. What happened with Citi was personal, and if that spilled into your business, then it is what it is. I can't rewrite history, but what I'm also not gonna do is be bullied into getting back into the game."

Caesar slowly nodded and replied with, "This isn't a negotiation."

"Everything is negotiable."

"As I said, with distribution now open, you will oversee Brooklyn and Queens and your coconspirator Apple will handle Manhattan and the Bronx. Yes?"

Cartier stood to leave.

"*Siéntate!*" His voice rose. "Why you make me angry?"

Cartier sat back down with a thud and rolled her eyes. "I can't do it."

Caesar chuckled. "So cute. You should see your face. Your eyes say they want to kill me dead. That kind of rage is what has kept you alive and will work well in my organization. Rival cartels infiltrated some of my Brooklyn and Queens territories when you killed Citi, and I will take them back. And I feel that you are the right person to help with expansion."

She was half-listening.

Caesar didn't have a problem speaking openly about drugs and expansion in front of his young son. The knock on the door interrupted their talk to some extent, but it was expected. It was the waitress entering the room with Cartier's order and a bottle of wine for them to enjoy.

"*Gracias*," Caesar told the waitress before she left the room.

Caesar went back to business. First he poured wine for him and her, took a taste, and said to Cartier, "I will start you off with ten kilos, but eventually, I want your numbers up to fifty kilos a month from me."

She was taken aback by the demand. "You're not listening. Give me one reason that would make me change my mind."

"The reason is obvious. Money. I could come at you with threats to have your fingernails removed with pliers and your body dipped in a vat of acid while you beg for the pain to stop. Or have Apple's daughter's skin peeled from her body with a cheese grater as you helplessly watch the young girl call out for mercy that won't be given. There are so many things a man in my position could say in hopes that we have a meeting of the minds. But, you see, I am different. I'm a very optimistic businessman, and I believe that you've never lived up to your potential. I want to help you with that."

"My potential? I've done very well for myself. I ran my cartel for years, accumulated some wealth, and now I'm retired and still young."

"That stolen money won't last long. You've already made unwise investments, beginning with that gaudy vehicle parked outside."

"It's a Bugatti."

"It's every drug dealer's mistake. If you died today no one would care. You have nothing, no one, and, most importantly, no legacy."

That remark hurt. Cartier thought about her murdered child, Christian, and her two sisters, Fendi and Prada, and then finally Trina. He was right. She had no one.

"And moving your ki's is supposed to give me all of that?"

"If you're smart then you take the money and do something good with it, create something so that long after you're gone your name will remain."

"But fifty kilos—I'm only one person."

"You are a hustler, I see . . . and I respect the work you've put in on these streets. Especially being a young black woman. And from my understanding, you've never been one to back down from opportunity or risks."

"No. But that's the kind of risk I'm trying to break myself away from."

"Why? I grow. You grow."

The problem was, she didn't want to continue to grow in the drug trade and take unneeded risks. When she was in charge of her organization, she was never that large.

"Fifty kilos a month is a lot for me to handle, Caesar," she said.

"The problem is, you are of little faith. Only in the darkness can you see the stars," he said.

Did he just quote the bible or something? she asked herself. He was different. And it seemed like he wasn't going to take "no" for an answer.

"Listen, I will do you this one favor. I will front you ten kilos on consignment. If you move them, good. If not, then you return them to me—no penalties," he stated. "And I will reevaluate letting you out of our business deal. But note that if you can't hold up your end, then Apple will have to take your place and be responsible for Brooklyn, Queens, Manhattan, and the Bronx. That would be a lot of pressure on the single mom."

She didn't like the terms, but she agreed.

"I guess I don't have a choice, right? Unless I'm ready to go to war again," she deduced.

"I knew you were smart. So, we do these terms, make some good money, and everything will work itself out. Right?"

"Yeah," Cartier replied halfheartedly. She stood up to leave.

"You don't eat?"

"Like I said before, I'm not that hungry."

"It's not good to waste food. Hundreds of people die every day because of starvation," said Caesar. "Take it with you to go."

It felt like more of a command than a suggestion.

She didn't want it in the first place, but she took it with her to go and couldn't exit the restaurant fast enough. Exiting covertly behind her was Majestic and Scooter.

"You good, Cartier?" Majestic asked her outside the restaurant.

"Yeah. I'm good."

"Do you need us for anything else?" Scooter asked.

"Nah. I'll be okay. Y'all can go. Thanks."

The two killers nodded and went their way. Cartier got into her car and lingered behind the wheel. She thought about moving fifty kilos a month. It was going to take a lot of manpower and skills and moving in the shadows. It was something she wasn't ready for, but she had to be ready for it. Caesar was a man you didn't disappoint.

She started her car and left. As she was driving, she thought about Caesar bringing his young son to that kind of meeting. She didn't understand why a man who was worth so much—a man who was head of the Mingo Cartel and who had enemies—would endanger his child. But unbeknownst to Cartier, Caesar had nearly five dozen men moving in and out of the restaurant and blending in. Some were even staff. They would have mowed down any threat in a nanosecond. Caesar Mingo was in good hands. He was always protected, even when you didn't see it.

Before Cartier crossed back over the Brooklyn Bridge, she called Apple to warn her. She had no idea how her friend was going to take being coerced, but Cartier feared there would be drama.

"Yo, you gonna live a long time," Apple said. "I was just talkin' 'bout you."

Cartier grinned. "I miss you, bitch."

"Then come through. I'm bored as fuck."

Cartier could hear voices and loud music in the background, horns and sirens, and a child hollering. Wherever Apple was, it was bustling with activity.

"Soon," she promised. "I'm calling to pull your coat to some bullshit, but before I go in, I need you to know that I'm not up for another South Beach."

"You worried 'bout Señor Mingo?"

"Worried is a bit strong, but yeah, that's why I'm calling. Did you meet with him?"

"His peoples called and we meetin' next week. But it's all good on my end. This phone ain't secure, so all I can say is that I'm leveling up. Whatever numbers that bitch Citi was doin', I'ma triple that. You know I'm the queen of New York and he got that good ish."

Cartier chuckled. Apple stayed in competitive mode. "Don't you mean the queen of Manhattan?"

"Nah, I don't."

"A'ight, whatever. So you good, though?"

"I'm chillin'. Lookin' forward to making this shmoney."

"A'ight, be careful, ho."

"Ya dead mama's a ho," Apple retorted.

Cartier chuckled. "Ya dead mama's a slut."

Cartier ended the call and headed home. At least one of them was excited for this new business endeavor.

The skies were cloudy and gray and rain was looming when Cartier walked out of her building. To her surprise, she saw Harlem sitting on the sidewalk leaning against her BMW with her head on her knees. She was clearly asleep. Cartier stared at the young girl and shook her head. It had been a week since she kicked her out, and it was obvious Harlem had nowhere else to go. She was homeless. Cartier sighed, almost feeling terrible. She had yanked Harlem from her pimp and then kicked her out on her ass.

"What I'm gonna do with this bitch?"

Cartier walked over and nudged Harlem to rouse her awake. Harlem's eyes popped open as if she was startled and they shot up to stare at Cartier towering over her. Harlem had no words. She was embarrassed. It showed on her face.

Cartier tossed her a set of keys and said, "Go upstairs, wash your ass, and get some sleep."

Harlem nodded. She was exhausted and sluggish. She rose to her feet and it struck Cartier that the girl looked like she wasn't eating at all. The look in her eyes toward Cartier showed gratefulness. "Thank you," she said.

She walked a couple of steps before Cartier grabbed her arm forcefully. Through clenched teeth, she said, "You steal from me again and next time I won't be so nice. Consider this your last warning."

Harlem nodded. She understood perfectly. She didn't want another ass-whooping.

It didn't take Cartier long to get back into the drug game. Caesar was right; the way she was spending money she would be broke soon, and she wasn't going back to her days of poverty. She was allergic to broke. She knew what it was like to try to live off tips, fuck niggas for a roof over her head, and work sixty hours a week for minimum wage. After South Beach it was her intention to settle down with Head and build something legit. But since he was being an asshole and it was clear that he couldn't forgive her for fucking with Hector, she realized that she had to move on from him. Although she hated to admit it, there was a thrill to moving coke. She felt powerful, respected, and feared—a great distraction from heartbreak.

11

The music was loud and the club was packed, but Harlem nimbly moved through the sea of people with ease, carrying sparkling bottles of champagne to the VIP sections of the club. Escape was the place to be. Whether it was the weekend or the weekdays, they always had a crowd.

Harlem loved her job. She was making great tips and making good friends. One particular friend she met was a regular guy in the club named Sincere and they had hit it off instantly. He was in law school and he was only twenty-six years old. He was tall, dark, and handsome, and he was nice. Harlem became smitten by him.

She had introduced Sincere to Cartier, and Cartier felt that he was a winner. But she also advised Harlem, saying to her, "Don't fuck him too fast—make him want you." Surprisingly, Harlem listened to Cartier's advice, and she and Sincere were taking things nice and slow.

Someone else who came into Harlem's life via the nightclub was Sana. She was a twenty-year-old biracial woman who had a black mother and white father—a father she had never met. She was a woman who could easily pass for white with her pale skin, thin nose, and short haircut dyed blond. And she only wore Ruby Woo lipstick from MAC. The two had an amicable relationship at work. Harlem considered Sana a friend.

"So you don't have anywhere to go?" Harlem asked her once she had dropped off the flaming champagne and headed back to the staff area of the bar.

"No. My mother's tripping, and she kicked me out. I was staying at the dorm rooms at my college, but they're so expensive that I couldn't afford to stay there anymore. So I've been couch surfing."

"That's fucked up."

Harlem could relate. She had been in the same situation not too long ago. She wanted to help out. Sana always kept to herself. She did her job at the club, got paid big tips, and would remain aloof from the other bottle service girls—mostly the black ones. Most of her friends were white girls.

"I know, but what can I do? I can't afford rent and tuition."

"Look, I might be able to help you out," said Harlem.

"You can?" Sana eyes lit up.

"I'm staying with a friend and she looked out for me, so maybe she'll look out for you."

Smiling, Sana replied, "If you can help me out with a place to stay, I would highly appreciate it and I would definitely owe you, Harlem."

"We good. I just wanna help. Come with me after work and I'll introduce you and we'll take it from there. Don't worry, girl, I got you."

Sana hugged Harlem. "Thank you."

"No problem."

After work, the girls traveled to Cartier's place via cab and got there in the early morning. It had been a long night at work and they were on their feet the whole time. Harlem wanted to strip away her clothing and flop against her bed face-first, and she wanted to sleep all day. But first she wanted to get Sana in good with Cartier.

They walked through the front door and immediately saw Cartier coming out of the kitchen with a cup of coffee. Cartier looked at Harlem and then her eyes cut to Sana, who she assumed was a white girl. "So you like pussy now, Harlem? You're bringing white bitches to my home to fuck?"

"No. It's not like that, Cartier. She's a friend of mine from work who needs a favor," Harlem explained.

"A favor? What kind of favor?"

"She's homeless."

"And?"

"And she doesn't have anywhere else to go, and I figured that since you helped me out—"

"That I'm gonna help out this white girl too," Cartier interjected.

Sana stood there quietly. She didn't know what to expect, but she allowed Harlem to talk for her. But she felt proud to hear Cartier call her a white girl. It was a compliment to her.

Harlem continued to talk, but Cartier had heard enough. She moved closer to the girls and stared at Sana with such intensity that it made her turn away nervously.

"Don't get shy. I like to look a bitch in the eyes when I talk to her. Look at me," Cartier said to Sana. "You need a place to stay, then I need to look you in the eyes when we talk."

Sana locked eyes with her.

"What's your name?"

"Sana."

She was pretty like Harlem.

"Well listen, Sana, this is my home and I make the rules here. Do you understand me?"

Sana nodded.

"Harlem will let you know, don't fuck with me, and if you break my rules or disrespect me, or if you have the audacity to steal from me, I will fuck you up. Do you understand me?"

Sana nodded.

"I'll let you stay for a moment, until you're able to get back on your feet. But don't ever take my kindness for weakness or you'll find out the hard way how much of a crazy bitch I can become. I can become your best friend or your worst nightmare."

"I won't disrespect your home," Sana humbly replied.

"Don't! That's all I ask from you."

With that said, Cartier walked away from the two of them. Harlem smiled at Sana and said, "I told you. I got you."

"Thanks, Harlem."

Right away, Sana got settled into her new place. She really liked the apartment; it was trendy and spacious—without a doubt something she could see having for herself.

Cartier received another anonymous threat, and this one was a white card with a skull, dagger, and blood with the handwritten letter *Y* in black ink. *Y?* The cards she was receiving from out of nowhere were starting to irritate her. She wanted to catch the person who was dropping them on her car, and she wanted to beat the shit out of them, torture them, and get to the bottom of things. But it seemed nearly impossible. The cards started to bother her and she decided to look for help in figuring them out, or catching whoever was responsible for them.

She met with Majestic and Scooter in confidence to fill them in on the strange messages. The three of them were in the living room at Cartier's place. It was late-night, meaning Harlem and Sana were working at the club, so they didn't have to worry about anybody eavesdropping.

Cartier said to her two shooters, "Someone's playing head games with me, and I need you two to be extra vigilant. I've been finding these note cards on my car, and it's starting to piss me off. I want the shit to stop!"

She handed the card with the *Y* to Majestic and he inspected it and handed it to Scooter.

"We on it, Cartier," Scooter replied, handing the card back to Cartier.

"We watchin' ya back n' I'll have some peoples keep an eye on ya place. Whoever is playin' fuckin' games wit' you, we'll find out n' take care of it," said Majestic with assurance.

Cartier liked the sound of that.

"And 'bout that other thing," Scooted started, "we were able to get a few mo' hustlers to cop ya product because of the quality of the coke, which is moving fast in Cypress Hills and Baisley Projects. Shit is doin' the highest numbers in those two areas."

"Yeah, a lot of these niggas are excited that ya back in the game. I got niggas hittin' me up n' they ready to link up wit' you," Majestic added.

Cartier already knew this. The streets were talking. Cartier Cartel was officially back in business, and a mountain of hustlers and shot-callers wanted to get onboard. They trusted Cartier, and her product spoke for itself. Niggas from OT were hitting her phone looking for distribution. Things were looking up. Still, Cartier knew that word of mouth through the streets could be a blessing and a curse at the same time.

12

The hot July sun was blazing outside, so Head decided to spend the afternoon in the comfort of his air conditioned hotel room. He was still at the Marriott, unable to come to terms with Pebbles and her social media shenanigans. Home less than sixty days and he had already managed to piss off the two women he felt something for. Head knew he still had strong feelings for Cartier, and he also knew that he cared about Pebbles. But he still had moves to make and a business to run. Things in Michigan were going easier than he had hoped thanks to the teachings and guidance he had received from Brother Kareem.

Kareem was a Hebrew Israelite and had been his cellmate the last four months of Head's bid. Kareem had just been hit with three life sentences for murder and drug conspiracy and a host of other charges that he never wanted to discuss. He was a man with a lot of regrets and nuggets of wisdom mixed with delusion he liked to spew. Kareem was in his late fifties and a career criminal. His salt-and-pepper hair peeked out from under his kufi cap and his Malcolm X horn-rimmed glasses sat perched on his broad nose. He was of average height for a man with a strong, muscular body. While serving life sentences, talking and teaching helped him pass the time, and persuading others to think like him gave him a sense of power in a powerless environment.

Head watched as all the younger inmates, usually men in their twenties, would crowd around Kareem in the yard or in the mess hall. It seemed Kareem's main focus was enlightening men on their birthright and how to go about manifesting the reality that all religions write about. To Head, it seemed Kareem was obsessed with polygamy and King Solomon in the Bible.

"The Quran, Torah, and Bible all say that we are not meant to have one wife," he preached. "The creator doesn't want us to adhere to man's law or societal norms. Y'all brothers got it twisted catering to these women—these Eves. Women were created to cater to the black man. The original man is us!"

He continued, "If God, Allah, Jehovah, or Yahweh—whatever you call your creator—didn't want this to be, then why when Eve was cursed did Yah say, 'And he shall dominate you.' Women aren't our equals, and if you believe that they are, then the most high will withdraw his protection from you as he did with Adam."

Kareem was quickly challenged by a young inmate named Tariq. "You keep talking that outdated Hebrew Israelite doctrine with your diluted messages, which are the white man's watered-down rhetoric. And what Adam are you talking about, because there was more than one Adam in the Bible? Adam is a tribe of people."

"The text says He made a group of Adams, which was man, and a group of Eves, which are woman, and then Yah created Eden for one Adam and one Eve."

"Where it say that? Show me the text that says that, Brother Kareem."

"I'm telling you what the text says."

"Show me!" Tariq yelled.

"Genesis says that in the first five days Yah made a group of Adams and a group of Eves and then on the sixth day it says Yah made another Adam and Eve and placed them in Eden."

Everyone could clearly see that the young dude was getting under Kareem's skin. Veins began bulging from his temples and his neck. Head had seen it all before, so he knew what was coming next.

Tariq rubbed is chin and said, "So the first group of Adams was the black man and the second adaptation of Adam was white? I'm confused, brother. I'm asking you to show me the tex—"

The punch to his jaw silenced Tariq, who quickly returned two body shots and an upper cut to Kareem's chin. The fight was quickly broken up by three CO's, and both Kareem and Tariq were dragged to the hole.

Head shook his head. "Stupid muthafuckas."

Two weeks later, Kareem was back in the cell with Head. Coincidentally, he had just gotten another letter from Cartier. He wanted to vent.

Now with his feelings open and raw, some of what Kareem had to say began to resonate. Head did treat Cartier as his equal. She busted her gun as he did his, sold drugs, and killed. Head thought that they had a mutual respect, but she disrespected him and fucked another man on his watch.

A lot of what Kareem had to say fell on deaf ears, though. Head wasn't buying into it. He would discard the radical parts of Kareem's religion and keep the nuggets that would further his mission on the outside. *The only way to truly find peace is to lord over women.* If there was one thing that Head had vowed, it was to never have his heart broken again.

So why can't I get Cartier out of my head? he wondered.

Head paced around his hotel room annoyed that he couldn't get that night Cartier came into the day party in that sexy dress out of his mind. It was weeks ago and yet he couldn't let it go. He missed everything about her. Seeing her there was like a breath of fresh air for him.

He thought about the first time he was intimate with Cartier and the way she made him feel. She was explosive, and he knew that together they could conquer whatever problems and obstacles came their way. Hell, they probably could have taken over the world if they wanted to. They were once a powerhouse couple.

Despite his reservations, he had to see her again, if only to get closure. Head knew of two people who could help him get in contact with Cartier. He was desperate to see her—talk to her—even if it was only for a moment. He picked up his cell phone and made the call to Chemo. The moment he answered, Head said, "I need a favor from you."

"What's that?" Chemo asked.

"I need you to get in contact with Cartier. I wanna see her, so set it up but don't let her know what's what."

"You don't got her contact?"

"Would I be asking?"

"A'ight, man. I'll do it," Chemo relented.

"Just call me when y'all meet and I'll show up."

"You gonna get me on that girl's bad side, and you already know how she is," Chemo slightly joked.

"Just do it."

Head ended the call. For some reason he was nervous, but he knew Chemo was going to come through for him.

The day was sunny with clear blue skies. The café on Jay Street in Downtown Brooklyn was quaint and bustling with customers. It was an afternoon to enjoy brunch, drinks, and conversation as pedestrians shuffled by and traffic from Fulton Street was starting to overflow onto the side streets. Despite the area's busyness, Cartier was enjoying her brunch with Chemo at an outside sidewalk table. They were having club sandwiches and talking about his club promotion business. Chemo had called earlier and asked her if she would be interested in investing in day parties.

"It sounds promising, but what do I know about party promoting?" Cartier asked.

"It's simple. We start by making an invitation list. For a large cocktail party, it's best to invite twenty percent more people than you can fit. I say that because typically seventy percent of invitees attend," Chemo explained.

"And you think it would be a good investment for me?"

"It would. Become a silent partner and see the returns that come in."

The proposal was intriguing. Cartier knew that she needed to invest in something lucrative and legit. In just a few weeks, Cartier's cartel was moving fifty kilos a month with Majestic and Scooter's help, and she needed to find ways to launder her money. Investing in day parties didn't seem like a bad idea. Still, she looked at Chemo and replied, "I'll think about it."

"Please do that. It's gonna be worth it," said Chemo.

While Cartier snacked on her grilled chicken salad and sipped her afternoon martini, from the corner of her eye she thought she was seeing things. But when she craned her head to the right and focused her vision on someone approaching, it was real. Head was coming their way like he had just happened to come through.

Cartier cut her eyes at Chemo. "You played me to come here for him?"

She leaped from her chair as Head grew closer. She was ready for another confrontation with him. She figured something was up when Chemo called and said he wanted to catch up and talk business. Her gut told her to be prepared for anything. It was the reason she came to the meeting looking stunning in a short summer skirt revealing her sexy legs, a sexy top, and high heels. Cartier knew the moment you fall back, a nigga crawls back. By the look Head gave her, she knew she had accomplished that mission. He couldn't take his eyes off of her.

"Can we talk, Cartier?" he asked humbly.

"About what? We ain't got shit to talk about, especially after how you disrespected me," she griped.

"I'm sorry. I was wrong. But just hear me out and give me a chance to speak my piece."

She stared at him. He sounded sincere, but she was on guard. While he stood there pleading his case to her, she noticed how handsome he still was. His outerwear was still street, but he sounded different. *Did prison change him?* He had always been a thug and masculine man, but there was something different about him.

"Look, I'll give you your chance to talk, but you better not bullshit me, Head. I'm not in the mood for any fuckin' games with you. You hurt me," she proclaimed.

"You hurt me too."

Cartier sucked her teeth. "Here we go."

"See? That's what I'm talking about. You think you're the only one with feelings."

"I know I'm not, but I've already apologized and it was so long ago. I made a mistake and chose Hector."

Hearing Hector's name made Head grit his teeth. "So you can understand my mistake in choosing Pebbles."

"Are you still with that bitch?" she asked blatantly.

"Nah. I got rid of her a while back. I'm staying at a hotel in Queens. I needed some time to myself. I needed to think. And all I could think about was you. I missed you, Cartier. I missed you a lot," he admitted.

His words weren't enough for her to fully trust him again. She still had her guard up, and she wasn't about to run to him just because he had dumped his bitch and was talking sweet things into her ear.

"Let me take you out," he suggested.

Cartier had to think about it for a minute. She then replied, "It better be someplace nice."

"You deserve nothing but the best," he said.

If the remark was supposed to make her grin, it didn't. She continued to stare at Head deadpan. She knew she had to guard her heart. It was going to take more than dinner and some smooth words to win her over. She had a lot to be angry about, and she wanted Head to get on his knees and grovel and kiss her black ass. But dinner was a start.

The Modern restaurant on 53ʳᵈ Street served French and New American fare with garden views at the Museum of Modern Art. For Cartier, it was classy and creative. She never expected Head would take her there for dinner. She wondered how he got reservations. The décor was extraordinary and the menu was tongue-twisting, but the food was delicious.

Having dinner at The Modern was part of the special day they'd had together. Head took Cartier shopping in the city and told her to get whatever she wanted on his dime. She took advantage of it and got herself some new shoes, a few pieces of jewelry, and some new handbags. She had a thing for pricey handbags.

She sat opposite him at the restaurant. Head was clad in a black button-down and some jeans, looking comfortable.

She took a swallow of wine while Head poured his heart out to her.

"For a man, when the woman he loves cheats, it affects him differently," he said. "I came down to South Beach to marry you and you turned me down—for him! I thought you loved me," he said. "That shit fucked me up. I ain't been the same since."

"Like you were an angel yourself, Head," Cartier came back with.

Head cringed at hearing her repeatedly say his street name but decided to not argue over it. He knew she would never call him Henry. "No. But I knew what I wanted, and that was you."

"I needed some time."

Head sighed and took a hefty drink of his water. The conversation was going left and he was growing frustrated. Part of him wanted her to keep begging for forgiveness—maybe kiss his ass a little more—but since she had caught him with Pebbles, Cartier was defensive. He didn't want to argue with her. He wanted to win her back.

"Look, let's not fight," he said.

"So let's not bring up the past. It's gone and forgotten," said Cartier.

"You're right. Let's just focus on our future. And speaking of the future, I'm hearing from the streets that you're back in the game full-blown."

Cartier knew what he meant. Of course the streets were talking. "It's my life, Head, and I need to do me."

"I'm disappointed to hear that. I thought you wanted out of the game. I thought you wanted something different. What you're doing out there is poisoning our people."

"Are you serious?"

"Yes." His stoic stare corroborated his answer.

"And this coming from the same man with drug distribution on his resume," she countered. "I mean, your story is all over the media—you're a legend out there and you wanna start judging me for what I'm doing?"

"Like you said, Cartier, we don't need to look at our past but our future. . . and our people are dying out there."

"You mean black people, right? If so, we aren't the only race who uses drugs. Have you read the news lately?"

"I have, and my eyes are open. You need to put your hustling on pause so I can school you, or preferably stop it altogether. I love you, Cartier, and I don't wanna see you in ruins."

"Nigga, if you came here to win me back, you sure got a funny way of showing it," she said, throwing back the last of the South African chardonnay in her glass and pouring another from the half-empty bottle on the table.

111

"I'm trying to enlighten you to something much greater than the streets," he stated. "If you have patience and let me work a few things out, soon I'll be able to give you everything you've ever wanted. I'll take care of you, ma. I promise. Just trust me."

Cartier stared at him with intensity. She was adamant that no one was going to tell her what to do. She didn't take orders from him or any nigga.

"Head, don't do that—don't try to tell me what I need to do, or what is best for me. I'm my own woman making my own decisions in what is my life."

"I'm not trying to control—"

"Yes, you are!"

Their conversation had spilled from their table, and other patrons couldn't help but overhear them. It was embarrassing. Their waiter had to come over and tell them to keep it down.

Head nodded. "We're sorry. We'll keep things down."

Once the man walked away, Head refocused his attention on Cartier. Now she had fire in her eyes as she glared at him. She downed the rest of her wine with an attitude.

He said to her with a heartfelt tone, "I want you to become a beautiful black queen for society to take note of—and for society to be jealous of, Cartier. You are that woman."

She chuckled.

"That's funny?" he asked her.

"No. But I find this person that you're morphing into amusing. Who are you trying to become? I mean, preaching to me about my shortcomings and my lifestyle, when the man sitting in front of me was once a notorious gangster and murderer. You don't have the right to come home from prison and try to reform me or change my life around, and especially not after I caught you with the next bitch that you went home with. It doesn't work that way," Cartier said with gusto.

She was being stubborn. Head wanted to control her as he did Pebbles, but her slick mouth and her stubbornness was starting to get under his skin. She had a strong will that wasn't breaking anytime soon. Cartier had always been smart and resourceful. Also, he would never admit it to her, but he was intimidated that she had gotten Caesar Mingo as her connect without his help.

Head continued with, "I just want to take care of you. Whatever you need, I want to provide."

"Nigga, as long as you knew me, have I ever wanted or needed a man to take care of me? That's not who I am. I'm not some needy bitch."

He knew she wasn't. The last and only person she relied upon to feed and take care of her was her mother Trina, who failed miserably.

"You know I didn't mean any disrespect," he said.

"I've been hustling on these streets since I was fifteen years old, and I'm not relinquishing my power to anyone," she said.

With that being said, Cartier pushed her chair back from the table, stood up, stared strongly at Head and said, "Now I need to go use the bathroom. Thanks for dinner."

Head could only watch her walk away with that bow-legged strut. He wasn't giving up on Cartier, though. He knew she would be tough, but he was up for the challenge.

13

Cartier leaving the restaurant had left a sense of urgency in Head. Navigating his Range Rover through the thick New York City traffic, he knew he had to capture her mind, body, and soul a different way. He almost forgot who he was dealing with. She wasn't weak in the mind like Pebbles. She could be just as manipulative as he was.

The city traffic stretched for blocks and it was frustrating. Head heaved a sigh of annoyance. Wherever he was going, he wasn't going to get there anytime soon. It seemed like the city was about to have a heart attack since every block was clogged with a traffic jam. Horns blew loudly and drivers cursed out their windows. New York City had too many people living in it, and it seemed like every last one of them was stuck in traffic with him.

Head huffed again and listened to the radio with his mind on Cartier. The only thing that broke his concentration was hearing his cell phone ring and seeing that it was Pebbles calling him. He was emphatic when he told Cartier that he wasn't with Pebbles. He reluctantly answered, knowing that she would keep on calling him if he didn't.

"What is it?" he answered indifferently.

"Where are you?"

"Why?" he replied with the same uncaring tone.

"Baby, I miss you, and I need your help."

"Help with what?"

"I'm about to get evicted. They put a letter on my door today, and I'm so scared. I can't lose my home."

"Why you calling me?"

"Because I need you!" she cried out. "And I don't have anybody else to call. Come on, baby, don't do me like this. I'm not throwing this in your face, but I held you down for three years."

"I'll be there in a few," he said.

"Thank you, baby."

He could feel Pebbles grinning through the phone.

"And listen, we need to talk," he added.

"Okay, baby. When you get here I'm gonna have something special waiting for you," she said merrily.

Head didn't respond to her comment. He wasn't too thrilled about her goodies after Cartier had left him aching for her undivided attention.

The midnight hour was approaching when Head arrived at Pebbles' place. When he knocked on her door, she answered wearing lingerie to impress him. But he wasn't impressed. He looked at Pebbles as a woman who couldn't keep her shit together.

"It took you long enough. I was starting to think that you didn't want this pussy," Pebbles said with a seductive smile on her face.

He pushed her to the side and marched into the apartment like he was on some kind of mission. Pebbles didn't know what to expect from him, and she was surprised that he would help her at all, but she was desperate and didn't have anyone else to call. After Head stormed out her apartment last month he began ghosting her. She had left numerous messages and he didn't return near one. Pebbles cried day and night because it was all so sudden and unprovoked. She knew he had run right back into the arms of Cartier, and Pebbles wanted revenge. But for now she was biding her time and playing her position. Her mother always said a nigga will always circle back around. And there he was.

"I know I fucked up with the social media posts, but could you please give me another chance? I don't want to lose you," she begged.

The first thing he did was go into his pocket and remove a wad of hundred-dollar bills. The knot looked like a small boulder in his hand and Pebbles' eyes lit up. He tossed it her way and she caught it like a home run catch.

"Thank you, Henry. Now let me return the favor because you always know how to take care of me," she said.

She moved closer to him, ready to drop to her knees and suck his dick. But Head resisted, uttering, "Nah. Chill."

She felt rejected but didn't want his slight to show on her face. If it was over between them, why would he be there bailing her out? He fixed his eyes on her like a parent ready to reprimand a child.

"What happened to the twenty large I gave you?"

"Baby, you know that money was spent on things I needed to expand my brand," she answered.

"You see, that's the problem, Pebbles—you putting things before your priorities. You have two kids that you rarely see 'cause you running the streets like you half your age! You're a mom, Pebbles. Did you forget that? Did you even send your moms any of that money?"

"How dare you!"

"Easily."

Pebbles stood there looking dumbfounded at Head. She had no idea why he was coming at her suddenly about her parenting skills.

"You're being cruel right now! I'm a great mom," she cried out.

"I'm saying these things because I want you to do better. You are a black woman caught up in this hype created by the white devil."

"Well, this is me. Take it or leave it."

"I already left it," he said matter-of-factly.

"Aaaaaah," she yelled out, hollering like a fool. "I hate you! I hate you! You used me, Head. You fuckin' used me!"

"Calm down," he began. "And stop being dramatic."

"I am not," she pouted.

"Pebbles, you need to change your ways. When you would come to see me all you did was talk about your kids, your responsibilities, and how you were building your empire. I've been home over two months and you ain't been with your kids yet. The woman you said you are is different from the woman you actually is."

"Look who's talking!"

"What you saying?"

"I'm saying you got weirdo tendencies too! I don't know who you consistently are either. You go to bed one nigga and wake up another, but I tolerate it because I learned that it takes a lifetime to really know someone."

Head slowly nodded and took in her words.

"Listen, I'm not your man and you're not my girl. I just got home and I need my freedom," he bluntly told her.

"But what about the promises you made to me when you was locked up? You promised that we would always be together and that you would take care of me and I would take care of you. We promised that we would always be there for each other. I sucked your dick, fucked you how you wanna be fucked, I invited you into my home, and you do me like this?"

He stared at her with no consideration for her feelings. "Those were words of a caged man, and you know how the game goes."

A river of tears flowed from Pebbles' eyes, and she fell to her knees. It looked like she was ready to have a panic attack in front of him.

Head went closer to her and crouched to her level. He took her chin into his hands and looked at her directly. "I love you and I will never leave you, Pebbles, but all this calling me twenty-four seven and wanting an explanation about my whereabouts—it needs to stop. You need to fall back from me."

It was going to be hard for her. She loved him more than anyone else. She didn't want to leave his side. She needed him. The sex was good, but he was her rock—her shoulder to lean on when things got hard. But she also wasn't stupid. Pebbles knew that their conversation meant that Cartier was most likely back in his life—that she had taken him back. She could see it in his eyes. His interest rested with another woman.

"Look," he continued, standing upright and staring down at her tear stained face, "I'm gonna start being out of town a lot more. I got something set up in Flint, Michigan and things are going good out there. I'm making some serious moves."

"Flint again?" she questioned.

"There you go with the questions. Didn't I just explain your position? Play your part."

"It's good to tell someone your secrets just in case something happens to you. You know the game."

"It's business, Pebbles—something you wouldn't understand."

After he said that, he went to the door. He didn't even look back at Pebbles as she continued to hug the floor in grief over his parting words. He coldly made his exit and closed the door behind him—like he was closing her out of his life.

14

artier opened her front door to see a smiling Head. "Can I get a key?"

"Nigga, please. You're lucky you even get to step foot into my home," Cartier replied.

Head laughed. He was happy to be there, and it showed in the way he seemed to glow. Cartier stepped to the side and Head walked into her apartment. For the past two weeks he'd been sleeping at Cartier's place. He had gradually come back into her life and was working on her heart. Cartier had decided to give Head a second chance. She believed that he and Pebbles were no longer together and that maybe the two of them could make it work again.

Their relationship had become amicable. They would talk and laugh; still, they hadn't had sex yet. Cartier didn't want to give him the pussy so easily. Head would have to earn it again, and she made that clear as day to him. He could come by and stay, and they could chill together, but she wasn't fucking him—not yet anyway. Head understood.

"So you're definitely done with Pebbles, right? I'm not your side bitch, Head," she had asked him.

"I don't fuck with her anymore. You see she don't call me anymore." He held up his cell phone like it would confirm his story.

"How I know who calls and who don't? I have to take your word—that's why I'm asking."

"Look, you don't have nothing to worry about. She was a mistake. Period."

Cartier decided to give him the benefit of the doubt.

Head felt like he was right at home with Cartier. The vibe with her was completely different than when he was with Pebbles. When the two of them were in the same room there was no telling what was going to happen. Their conversations were intelligent and mind-blowing—from politics, beliefs and religion, history, and the streets. There was a spark between them. There was history between them. And Cartier always challenged Head. She wasn't any pushover.

What Head respected most about Cartier after staying with her for two weeks was that she was on her grind. She had multiple irons in the fire, although he didn't agree with her drug distribution ring. She knew how to multi-task, and the respect she had on the streets turned Head on. She didn't need social media to represent her—to define her. She wasn't some shallow bitch looking for attention from complete strangers and pressing them for likes on her pages. She had no page.

"This is where I want to be, Cartier," he wholeheartedly expressed to her.

She didn't mind having him there either. They had their differences over the years, but Head had always been good company.

A few nights later Head was taking a shower and the bathroom door opened. Cartier pulled back the shower curtain to reveal her naked body and joined him. It was unexpected, but he welcomed her. The two became passionately entwined under the cascading water, and their sexual act went from the shower to the bedroom, where Head exploded inside of her like fireworks. It felt like love, and it had been a long time.

After their sexual tryst, the two lay snuggled in her bed having pillow talk. The 60" TV was playing the evening news. Something the anchor said caught Head's attention. Another young and unarmed teen was shot and killed by the police in Brownsville. The news angered him.

"The black community is raging out of control, especially with these police shootings," Cartier said.

Head looked at her and replied, "Black community? So you believe Brownsville, and every black neighborhood, is truly a black community?"

"Yes."

"Open your eyes, Cartier. There is no such thing as a black community, especially in America."

"What you mean?" she replied, intrigued by his remark.

"If it was accurately a black *community* then we would own things in the community. We would make our own laws and police our own people. We would run the schools, and we would have black businesses that stretched from block to block. So how can it be a black community when we don't own or control anything in that community?"

"So you learned all that in prison? You got your GED in black supremacy?" she joked with him.

"It's not a laughing matter out here, Cartier. This is serious."

"I never said that it wasn't. So what else they teach you inside there?" she asked.

"Don't mock me, Cartier."

"Who said I was mocking you?"

"I know you . . ."

"And?"

It didn't take long for them to get into a debate about society issues and politics. Head hated the white man. He felt that they were pushing global supremacy and they believed the black man was inferior. He believed that the white man was without a doubt the devil.

121

Cartier made the mistake of saying, "Not all white people are alike. And not all of them can be the devil."

"They got you brainwashed, Cartier," he barked.

"Nigga, you the one brainwashed with that foolishness you trying to preach to me," she countered. "Since when did you become a racist?"

"Black people cannot be racist," he returned.

"Says who?"

"Do you know the definition of a racist?" he responded. "A black man can be prejudiced, but he can't be a racist. Racism is systemic—it's institutional. Racism is prejudice plus power, and a black man can become prejudiced because of racism," he explained.

They continued to argue in bed over a variety of things, including a woman's right to choose.

"They should abolish abortion. These women flush babies down the drain like they flush the toilet. It's outta hand. Someone needs to speak up for these unborn kids."

"I know you ain't talking. How many bitches *you* ushered to the clinic? Y'all muthafuckas hardly spend any time raising these babies y'all wanna save. And don't get me started on the men who feel like they should get a medal for paying child support."

"That ain't all men." Some of the bass in his voice had disappeared.

Cartier continued with, "Those same politicians voting pro-life would send their mistresses to the abortion clinic if their careers, wealth, or home lives were threatened. Forty-five paid hush money, but what you think he would have done if she was pregnant? Abortion would be the first, last, and only option. It's always the perverts who vote conservative."

Head was silent.

"I thought so, nigga!"

"Come on, ma. Chill with the nigga talk."

"Negro, please!"

15

"Hey, do you have another cigarette?" Sana asked Cindy, a preppy white girl who shared some classes with her.

"Sure," Cindy replied.

Sana was hanging out on campus with her white girl crew, pretending to be all white and from one of the same upper-class neighborhoods they were from. Sana was embarrassed she had a black mother and a white father—a white man who had abandoned her and her mother a long time ago.

Sana's mother was tired of Sana desperately wanting to be identified as white, and she finally tossed her own daughter out on the streets. "Now go see if those white muthafuckas will help you out since you so badly want to become them," she had said to Sana.

And she did. She even cursed back at her mother. "Fuck you! A white mother would never do her daughter like this. That's why I hate you!"

Sana Laurent laughed and smiled in her white tennis skirt, powder white sneakers, and a classy white top, looking like she belonged to a privileged golf club. She puffed on her cigarette and enjoyed the company she kept. Cindy came from money, with both her parents being doctors. Tina grew up on the Upper West Side of Manhattan, and she had a nanny and a butler and a trust fund in her name. Margret's father was a hedge fund manager and every year he bought her a new fancy car to drive to school and show off in. Tiffany's mother was a topnotch attorney and her father owned several successful nightclubs in the Tri-State Area. These white girls had the money, the lifestyle, and the privilege that Sana had always dreamed about having. She envied them, but she wanted to learn from them and ride their coattails so she could become just like them.

"I heard the blacks are planning a march tomorrow for that black boy that got killed by that cop in Brooklyn," Tina mentioned.

"Another march—that's all those people do is march, protest, and complain about everything going on with their lives when they should blame themselves for what's wrong. They should be happy to be in this country and not in Africa being chased and eaten by lions," said Margret.

The girls laughed, including Sana.

Sana added her two cents. "It's sad. This country gives them all the opportunities to succeed, and yet, they choose to be lazy, violent, ignorant, angry, and want to blame all of their problems on white people."

"Yes. Preach, Sana, Amen! Amen! Hallelujah," Tina joked, mocking the black church.

"And don't get me started on the black woman, who wants to have multiple children but can't afford to take care of any of them. So they need government assistance and want to waste our tax dollars because they want to open their legs and get pregnant all the time by these thugs," Tiffany added.

"And I hate to say this, especially with so many of these black lazy girls getting pregnant and not being able to take care of their kids, but I agree with the GOP on a woman not having the right to choose. Hey, you made your bed now lie in it," said Sana. "Get a job and take care of your kids."

"I agree. Who's going to protect the unborn babies? And all these low-class black females and absent fathers get free health care and free abortions. But we and our families always work hard for our chance. They want to take advantage of the system, fuck like rabbits, get pregnant, and have no moral concerns when it comes to murdering their babies," Cindy said.

Sana and her white cronies continued to disparage the black race and the black woman like it was their job. Sana spoke openly about her conservative views and proudly supported Donald Trump and his Make America Great Again movement. She laughed with her white-privilege friends, lit up another cigarette, and said to herself, *This is home. This is where I was meant to be. They understand me.*

And then reality came knocking at her door.

"Hey Sana," Harlem called out to her.

Hearing that voice, Sana immediately pivoted and saw Harlem walking her way—the black Ethiopian girl with the darkest skin most people have ever seen and the ghetto name. Sana was about to panic. Her white friends gazed at Harlem in bewilderment with their mouths gaping. They all wanted to know if Sana knew this young, very black, and ghetto looking girl. Sana had a black friend—a REALLY BLACK FRIEND.

Before Harlem could get close, Sana said to her friends, "Her mother used to be my nanny, but I'll explain it to y'all later."

It made sense to the girls. *Of course*, it was normal to be kind to the help and their extended families from time to time.

Sana hurried away from the girls to keep Harlem from drawing closer. It was a nightmare that she was trying to avoid.

"What are you doing here, Harlem?" she asked.

"Did you forget? We're going to meet with Cartier today."

"Oh shit! I fuckin' forgot, girl. Shit, I be having so much shit to do and on my mind lately," she replied, flipping the switch.

"Who were those cornball lookin' white bitches?"

"Oh, they're just associates of mine from classes. I was using them for help with some of my schoolwork," Sana explained.

"They all look so fuckin' fake and corny. Them bitches probably think they're better than everyone else," Harlem said.

"I know, they are fake, and that's why I'm so glad you came and got me. I was 'bout to die over there hearing their bullshit," Sana replied.

The two laughed.

Harlem and Sana met with Cartier at a café in Downtown Brooklyn. Cartier was already seated at the sidewalk table enjoying an afternoon martini and some shrimp, while looking fabulous in her turquoise sundress. When the girls sat, she smiled at them and shifted into her big-sister mode.

"Where are y'all coming from?" Cartier asked them.

"Her school," Harlem answered.

"It's good that you're in school, Sana. That means something. It means you're going in the right direction. Definitely don't make the mistake Harlem and I made," Cartier advised the young girl.

"I'm trying."

"That's all we can do is try—to keep bettering ourselves," Cartier returned.

She wanted something different for these girls and she wanted Sana to convince Harlem to go back to school too. But when the subject would come up, Harlem didn't want any part of it.

"I'm a street girl, Cartier. It's what I know," Harlem had told her.

"It doesn't have to be all you know."

"I love it, though. I love the fast life, the partying, the men, the sex, and looking cute out here wit' these niggas sweating me," Harlem explained.

Once again, she reminded Cartier of Monya. It was scary. Harlem believed that she was the prettiest bitch that ever walked the earth. She had it going on, making great tips at the club and meeting new and important people. She didn't want to give that up for an education. Her education was the streets. It was survival.

Harlem believed she was a tough girl. Cartier gave her inspiration to become a no-nonsense bitch on the streets. But the reality was, she wasn't like Cartier. She wasn't that tough, and she could easily get her ass beaten to a pulp by mostly anyone. Harlem was more bark than bite.

16

"Are you serious? You tellin' me you think Prince was better than Michael Jackson?" Majestic exclaimed.

"He was. Prince had more hits, and his songs were much more meaningful," Scooter argued.

"Yo, you must be smoking crack if you believe Prince got more hits than Michael Jackson. *Thriller* alone sold more albums than all of Prince's albums combined. Michael is a fuckin' legend."

"And Prince isn't?"

The two continued to debate the topic while heading toward the Brooklyn trap house with fifteen kilos of cocaine in the trunk of their SUV. They had just picked up a shipment from the Mingo Cartel and were on their way to process it. So far, business with the Mingo Cartel was going well and there hadn't been any hiccups. Majestic and Scooter planned on keeping it that way.

It was a warm and quiet evening as their Durango arrived in Canarsie, a working–and middle-class residential and commercial neighborhood in the southeastern part of Brooklyn. They soon pulled into the driveway of a single-family home and cut the engine off. Scooter got on his cell phone to make a call to someone inside the trap house. When the man answered, he instructed them, "Yo, come out back and unload this shit."

Scooter and Majestic exited the vehicle with their pistols tucked snugly in their waistbands and their attention on a constant spin. The trap house and surrounding area was tightly secured with cameras strategically positioned and watching every movement, steel doors in the front and back that were so strong it would take the Hulk to bring them down, iron bars on the windows, and several armed goons inside.

Scooter opened the trunk and removed the black bag that carried the fifteen kilos. He closed it and went toward the rear entrance of the house. The back door opened for them and one of their workers, CC, appeared.

"Majestic, Scooter, what's up?" he greeted them with dap.

The two killers entered the house and everything appeared to be normal, but Majestic and Scooter had a sharp eye for spotting anomalies. The moment they stepped into the kitchen, they both sensed that something was wrong. The look on their workers' faces was the first thing that gave it away. They were trying to stay cool, but they were displaying some minor apprehension, as if they were under some kind of duress.

Majestic and Scooter simultaneously reached for their guns, but it was too late. All of a sudden they were swarmed and attacked by several masked gunmen that appeared to come out of nowhere. One of them struck Majestic with a pistol and shouted, "Get the fuck on ya knees!"

The masked men were armed with assault rifles and .50 cal Desert Eagles, weapons meant to cause severe damage to the human body.

"Don't die tonight, muthafuckas!" one of the gunmen shouted.

Majestic and Scooter stood there in silence, but their body language showed some rebelliousness. Majestic was bleeding from the back of his head from the whack, but he stood strong and defiant. It was going to take more than one blow to the head to bring him down and make him a bitch.

It was hard for them to submit to the goons' commands. They counted five of them. They couldn't see their faces, nor did they recognize any of their voices.

"Y'all muthafuckas think this shit is smart?" Majestic said through clenched teeth.

"Nigga, who told you to say any-fuckin'-thing?"

"Fuck you!" Majestic cursed.

Two gunmen rushed him and attacked while the other three continued to hold the others at gunpoint. The pistol whipping finally made Majestic drop to his knees. Everyone in the room was certain that the intruders were going to kill him. It looked like they weren't going to stop.

"Fuck you, nigga!" one of the gunmen cried out as he slammed the butt of his gun against Majestic's head.

When they were done, Majestic was sprawled against the floor badly beaten. Scooter scowled. He was helpless in defending his brother. The .50 cal aimed at his face was quite the deterrent. One bullet could easily take his entire face off.

After they were done manhandling and beating Majestic, they bound everyone inside with duct tape around their wrists and ankles and across their mouths. Then they snatched the bag with the fifteen kilos and rummaged through the house collecting a few thousand of dollars in cash. The five masked gunmen fled the trap house laughing and excited about their come-up.

Meanwhile, everyone left inside was shocked that they hadn't been murdered.

"If I could do it all over again, I would go to school and get an education," Cartier told Harlem.

"Like I keep telling you, Cartier, I don't think school is for me. I can get money out here without it—like I'm doin' right now," Harlem replied.

"Yeah, but this lifestyle can become transient and dangerous. I survived it not only by being smart, but being lucky too," said Cartier.

"Well, you have your way, and I have mine."

Cartier wasn't getting through to the girl, but she was going to keep trying. Their lunch at the café downtown had extended into two hours. As Cartier ordered herself another martini, her cell phone chimed and vibrated on the table, doing a small dance. It was Scooter calling her and she answered at once, knowing they were to pick up a shipment of fifteen kilos from the cartel.

The moment she answered the call, Scooter cried out, "We got hit!"

Cartier heard him say it, but she kept her cool in front of Harlem and Sana. She looked at the two girls, saying, "I need to take this. It's important," and she excused herself from the table and trotted somewhere private to talk.

"What the fuck you mean we got hit? What happened?" Cartier shouted into the phone. "In fact, don't say shit. I'll be there in fifteen minutes."

Cartier hurried back to the table.

"Yo, I'm out. I gotta go and handle some business." She tossed a few twenties onto the table to pay for everything and rushed to the trap house in Canarsie.

The scene inside the house was disturbing. Majestic's bruised face was coated with blood, but he refused to go to the hospital or get any medical treatment. The robbers had ransacked the place and taken money and drugs from her. The only good news was that everyone was still alive to tell their story.

"I'm fine," Majestic said. "I just wanna find these muthafuckas and kill 'em all."

"We gonna find 'em—real talk," Scooter assured him.

"What the fuck happened?" Cartier wanted to know.

"It was a setup," Scooter answered. "They were already waiting inside for me and Majestic."

"And how is that possible when this place is supposed to be locked down tighter than fuckin' Fort Knox?"

"I asked myself the same thing. We need to question every-fuckin'-body in here," said Scooter.

Cartier fumed. She had just gotten back in the game, and already she was taking a loss. She, Majestic, and Scooter were puzzled by the surprise attack. It didn't add up.

She looked at Majestic and asked him again, "You sure you don't need to go to the hospital?"

"I'm good, Cartier. I just want to handle this shit. They fuckin' come at me—at us—I'm gonna kill every last one of them," he growled.

"Good," she replied. "I want every worker we have interrogated. If this was an inside job, I'm gonna soon find out."

In total, four of her workers were lined up in the living room to be questioned about the robbery. Cartier felt that if they had nothing to do with the theft then they would be fine. But if they did, she was going to kill them right there on the spot. She approached every last one of them and grilled them. But each worker was adamant that they had nothing to do with the home invasion.

Majestic, however, was angry and wanted to torture them. His ego was bruised more than his face. He had convinced himself that one of his childhood friends was behind the jux. He planned on paying that friend a visit. Kendu had a serious gambling problem and he owed a lot of people a lot of money. Plus, Kendu was the only person besides them who knew the whereabouts of the trap house in Canarsie. Majestic deduced that Kendu had staked out the place, gotten some men together, and waited for the payload to arrive.

Once again, the dice didn't roll in his favor. Kendu cursed loudly and stomped his feet, throwing a mini temper tantrum at the craps table. He had lost ten thousand dollars. He was having a really bad night. He left the gambling spot a broke and upset man, but his night was about to become a lot worse.

The second Kendu exited the building, he saw Majestic's SUV parked across the street. Majestic was in the driver's seat staring at him. His look was menacing and it gave Kendu a deep chill. They were childhood friends, but Kendu was also aware of Majestic's deadly reputation on the streets. He wondered if he had done something wrong.

"Kendu, let me holla at you fo' a minute," Majestic called out to him.

"About what, Majestic?" he asked.

"About some business," Majestic replied.

Kendu had a bad feeling. There was no business with Majestic to talk about. He didn't want to approach the SUV. His instincts were on high alert, and they told him to flee—flee now.

"About what?" Kendu reiterated.

"Kendu, don't have me come out this truck," Majestic warned.

The two men stared at each other from across the street. Childhood friends or not, Kendu felt that he was in grave danger and he instantly took flight.

"Muthafucka!" Majestic cursed.

Out of nowhere a half-dozen men started to chase after Kendu. Kendu made a sharp left and cut down an alleyway with several goons right behind him. He scaled a short fence and continued to run. Majestic's men continued to give chase. From the alleyway, Kendu ran into the public street into open traffic and narrowly escaped being struck by a passing car. He started to sweat profusely. He glanced behind him and saw the thugs were still after him. He tried to run faster, but he stumbled on something on the ground and hit the pavement like a plane crash-landing.

He quickly tried to get up and continue to run, but it was too late. His fall gave the goons enough time to catch up to him and rough him up with their fists and pistols. A car pulled up and he was thrown into the trunk.

◇ ◇ ◇

"You rob me! Me?"

"C'mon, Majestic, I ain't had nothing to do with a robbery! I don't know what you're talking about!" Kendu shouted in fear for his life.

Kendu found himself in a concrete basement. He was badly beaten, and now he was a few feet away from two vicious pit bulls that were snarling and barking at him, their fangs ready to tear into his flesh. The only thing preventing them from attacking him were the large chains around their necks, which one of Majestic's men gripped tightly. But he would periodically give the dogs enough slack to inch toward Kendu.

"Majestic, please don't do this, man."

"Where's my shit?"

"I don't know!"

Majestic nodded to the man holding the dogs back, indicating to set them free. Immediately the dogs leaped onto Kendu and tore into his legs, their sharp fangs ripping apart skin and drawing blood. Kendu screamed out in agony while he tried to kick them off.

"Get 'em off me! Get 'em off me!"

Majestic nodded to the handler, and he pulled the dogs back.

"Where's my shit, Kendu?" Majestic asked again.

Whimpering and in pain, once again Kendu said, "I don't know, Majestic. I don't know what you're talking about. I didn't steal anything from you."

Majestic gave the order again, and the dogs brutally started to attack Kendu. This time it was longer. They went for several body parts and soon his face. His blood started to pool against the ground as his fingers

134

and toes were being ripped from him. His screams echoed through the basement as Majestic and his men gazed at the brutality with stoic faces. Once again, Majestic gave the order to stop the attack and the dogs were pulled back, their jaws soaked with their victim's blood. They barked loudly and lunged at Kendu to finish the job, but their owner kept them at bay for the moment.

"Look at you. You had enough? Just tell me what I need to know and this will end, Kendu."

"I was your friend. Aaaah, I don't know anything! Please. I don't know anything! Aaaah!" he cried out in anguish.

Maybe he was telling the truth, or maybe he wasn't. Either way, Majestic knew it was too late. He had come this far and Kendu was in too bad of shape. He nodded to the dog handler. "Let them finish what they started."

With that being said, the man released the growling dogs.

17

artier had to come out her pockets to pay for the stolen kilos. She felt embarrassed to do so, but the last thing she needed was any static with Caesar and the cartel. She had told Manolo, Caesar's right hand, about the theft and explained that she wanted to fall back from business with them until she could secure things on her end. She strongly felt that it was an inside job and she wanted to get her house back in order and find out who the source and culprits were.

She was shocked when Manolo said, "Caesar wants to see you again."

"Why?" she asked.

"I don't ask why. I only pass on the message. You go."

Cartier couldn't help but to be nervous about meeting with Caesar a second time. Her mind spun around with so many worries and concerns that she started to feel like a human fidget spinner. She tried to hold it together, but inside she felt like she was falling apart. She didn't want to worry herself, but Caesar sending for her so soon was unusual.

"When and where?" she asked Manolo.

He handed her a burner phone and said, "He'll call you soon with the location and time."

Cartier took the burner phone and Manolo walked away and climbed back into the passenger seat of an idling Tahoe, leaving Cartier pondering.

She made some changes to her business structure and changed up her stash houses and trap houses. She sent Majestic and Scooter on the hunt, and they were bloodthirsty dogs chasing scent after scent to bring back a bone for Cartier. She was transitioning back to her old self. The loss was a wakeup call, and Cartier knew she couldn't afford to take any more.

When Head heard about the robbery, he immediately went to see Cartier to lend his support. He asked if he could help her out in any way, but she declined. She wasn't looking for pity, and she didn't need anyone to hold her hand. She made it clear to Head that she was capable of holding shit down on her own like she had been doing and not to get in her way.

"I was just trying to help," he said.

"Do I look like I need your fuckin' help?" she barked at him.

"Hold up," he coolly began. "You not gonna keep talkin' to me any kind of fuckin' way. I'm a man. Not your bitch."

She exhaled. "I know. I just got a lot on my shoulders and wanna handle it on my own."

"You're stubborn, Cartier. You know that, right?" he said before leaving the apartment.

She knew. She had a lot on her plate—a lot of things to fix, and she didn't want anyone controlling her or telling her, "I told you so."

Cartier steered her Bugatti to the valet parking outside the Midtown lounge. The valet approached her car as she opened the door and climbed out looking red-carpet ready in her navy Alice + Olivia dress and silver red bottom heels. She was oozing confidence although she was nervous. She handed the valet her car keys and strutted toward the lounge.

It was a beautiful and warm night with a full moon glimmering in the sky. The Midtown traffic was thick, but surprisingly, the lounge was empty of customers. She was the only one there, besides a handful of staff. The moment she stepped inside, Cartier felt awkward as all eyes were on her. She wondered if she was in the right place.

The maitre d' approached her with a wide smile. "Cartier, right?" she asked.

"Yes."

"Caesar has been expecting you. Follow me," she said.

Cartier cautiously followed the slender and pretty blond woman through the lounge and into a back area, through a set of double doors, and into another room where there was a fireplace. Caesar was already seated with a bottle of wine and a bottle of champagne in a bucket of ice. This time he was dressed in a vintage Ritchie Valens La Bamba T-shirt, comfortable slacks, and Toms high-tops. When he saw Cartier enter the room, he immediately stood up from his chair to greet her.

"I'm glad you could make it," he said.

Like she had a choice.

He gestured for her to have a seat. "Come, sit and let's talk."

Cartier took a seat across from him near the fireplace. Caesar smiled. She didn't know what to expect from him. She was bewildered by everything—this meeting, the ambiance, their unexpected privacy.

"Here, we can speak openly," Caesar said.

Once again, they had their own private server—in fact, two servers, one male and one female.

"Whatever you want, have it. My chef is ready to prepare whatever you and I desire tonight," he said.

"So this is your place too?"

"Yes. One of many. As you can see, I like restaurants and lounges. I like to satisfy a person's desire, give them a welcoming place to relax, unwind, converse . . . give them something to enjoy," he said.

"It's a really nice place," she complimented.

"Thank you."

So far, things seemed copasetic, but she had no idea how the night was going to end. Cartier ordered the fettuccine with roasted chicken and lemon cream sauce, and Caesar had the spicy sausage penne with red pepper sauce. Along with their meals, wine, and champagne, they enjoyed fresh fruit on a skewer with mixed fruit mousse. Everything was top-of-the-line, including the service.

When Caesar popped open the champagne bottle, Cartier thought that he was going to try and seduce her. But he was all business.

"I heard about your loss the other day," he mentioned.

"It's a minor setback, Caesar. Believe me when I say it won't happen again, and I already paid Manolo what was owed," she replied. "Just as I've started to clean house. I'll find out who was behind the loss."

"I respect that you came to Manolo about it, and did not allow me to find out through the streets. Once more it tells me a lot about your character," he stated.

"I have nothing to hide from you."

He nodded. "And as you know, I don't like secrets."

"And I'm not trying to keep any from you," she said.

"How's the food?" he asked out of the blue.

"It's good—delicious."

"I'm glad you're enjoying everything."

She smiled and continued to nibble on her dessert. Throughout their intimate dinner, Caesar was mostly about business, but he also brought up some things about his personal life. Cartier found herself intrigued by him.

"You like baseball?" he asked her.

"Honestly, I never really cared for the game," she replied.

"At least you're honest. But I love the game, and in another life long ago, I played professional ball. It's still my passion to watch and teach it when I can. But you want to know why I love baseball so much? Because it's a game of patience and skills. It's not like football or basketball or soccer, where the game moves fast. It moves at a leisurely pace, allowing plenty of time for conversation and speculation about strategy. Unlike most sports, the defense controls the ball and it's not territorial in nature," he declared.

Caesar took a sip of champagne. He took his time to tell a story and Cartier was all ears.

"And unlike most sports, in baseball there is no clock. Each team has the same number of chances to score until the final out. So, each player has a chance to step up to the plate and perform. One man against nine players on the field, and that one man can either strike out or hit a home run."

She wanted to know where he was going with the baseball talk.

"Cartier, you're at the home plate clutching the bat in your hand, and you're staring at the pitcher, whose job it is to strike you out. But patience and strategy is how you win the game. You swing too fast or too late, you lose. And you have swung and missed the first pitch, creating your first strike," he said coolly.

She continued to listen as he used baseball to describe the drug game—or life itself. The drug lord, husband, father of one, and ex-baseball player was interesting. Caesar had many layers to him that Cartier wanted to comprehend.

"It is your job to know not only your own teammates, but the opposing teams too, especially the pitcher, because his only purpose is to strike you out. The game can't be played without him."

"I understand," she said.

Cartier's nervousness was gradually fading. Somehow Caesar made her feel a bit comfortable while they were alone. But there was more business to be discussed.

"So, do you have suspects in mind?" he asked.

"I'm thinning out the list now, and like I said before, I have two of my best men on the hunt," she replied.

"The question you should ask yourself is, who knew enough about your organization to hit you from the inside? And usually, it is someone that you trust the most who can hit you where it hurts, including the men you sent out on the hunt," Caesar advised.

She nodded and took note of the counsel he gave her.

"But, Cartier, I feel that your priorities are split and you need to become more focused. A mistake was made and it will be corrected."

"I understand. And I agree."

Although she agreed, she knew it was going to be hard to focus. She didn't want to get into bed with Caesar in the first place. She was threatened and coerced to do so. And she didn't know if he was trying to coach her or subtly warn her about the mistake.

Dinner with Caesar lasted over two hours.

"Did you enjoy?" Caesar asked her.

"I did. I loved the food and the conversation."

"I'm glad you did."

After dinner, a waiter came to their table carrying a soft leather duffel bag. He dropped it at Cartier's feet. She grew somewhat nervous again.

She looked at Caesar, who was expressionless. "What's this?"

"Open it."

Cartier reached for the duffel bag and slowly unzipped it. She figured it couldn't be a bomb, because Caesar sat only a few feet away from her. When she opened it fully, she was shocked by the contents. It was money—stacks of it. She looked at him with confusion written on her face.

"What's this for?" she asked.

"It was me who exposed you to too much product too soon. So consider this a one-time courtesy from my end—a refund. But moving forward, something like this should be prevented. No more mistakes, Cartier. Do you understand me?"

"I do."

Cartier excused herself from the table as their dinner concluded. Carrying the duffel bag, she left the lounge feeling like she had just left a date. Caesar was a complex man, and she didn't know of any cartel leaders who gave refunds. She was unsure about the entire ordeal, but once the valet pulled her car around, she snapped out of it. Like Caesar advised her, it was time to focus—no more mistakes.

18

The 757 came to a safe landing at Bishop International Airport in Flint, Michigan on a sunny Thursday afternoon. The plane started to taxi toward the terminal, and the passengers aboard were eager to make their exit from the plane. It had been a smooth flight for Head, and he had slept during most of it.

Head departed the plane with a small carryon duffel bag. He strolled behind the other passengers into the small terminal dressed for the weather in cargo shorts, sneakers, and a T-shirt. He looked more like a tourist than a notorious gangster and convicted felon. He carried a polite smile as he made his way through the terminal and toward the airport exit.

Head smiled vibrantly when he saw her standing in front of the idling black Yukon outside the terminal. Seeing Head, her smile matched his. Head took two steps her way, and Jacki came running toward him with excitement. She leaped into his arms and straddled him, saying, "It's good to have you back," and the two kissed passionately in public.

"We need to go," he told her.

She nodded. "You're right. There's a time and a place for everything."

Jacki collected herself and opened the passenger door for Head and he slid inside. She hurried around to the driver's side and got into the vehicle.

Once again she smiled at Head and said to him, "The others can't wait to see you either."

"I bet. It's good to be back."

Hearing that, Jacki smiled brighter and was enthusiastic. She was a young and pretty African-American twenty-three-year-old from a small town outside of Detroit.

"We've missed you," she said, still grinning.

"And I've missed y'all too," Head returned.

The black Yukon started the drive through the blue-collar city. Flint had become known for its water crisis, but it also had high crime rates and had repeatedly been ranked one of the most dangerous cities in the United States. Some neighborhoods seemed like ghost towns with vacant lots that stretched for blocks and blocks, and over the years residents had fled the area like there had been some nuclear fallout. Flint was the last place anyone would want to move to, but Head had made it his home away from New York.

Head gazed out the window in silence, taking in the scenery. He had a lot to do—a lot to accomplish.

Jacki steered the Yukon from the blue-collar city to a rural area on the outskirts of Flint where farmland and isolation stretched for miles. They soon arrived at a large home that sat on several acres of land. The Yukon traveled up the dirt road that led up into the property and came to a stop at a large cabin. Head lingered in the passenger seat for a moment, absorbing the view of the estate.

Jacki smiled. "We're here."

"Yes. We are," he said.

Head and Jacki got out of the car and approached the cabin. The interior of the home was a far cry from anyplace Head had stayed in New York. The rooms were huge, especially the master bedroom, which was nearly nine hundred square feet. There were two wood burning fireplaces, including one in the master bedroom, and vaulted ceilings and plush carpet throughout the six-bedroom home.

The moment he stepped inside, Head was greeted by several ladies over-the-moon excited about his arrival. Head was their Messiah—their savior. They were at his beck and call to serve and please him.

"It's good to have you back, Daddy," said Mandy.

"Yes. It is," Kandy agreed.

Head smiled at the girls and replied, "It's good to be home again."

Kandy and Mandy were pretty white nineteen-year-old twin sisters from Flint. Mandy was already seven weeks pregnant by Head. This would be her third child, as she already had a boy and a girl. Her twin sister Kandy didn't have any children yet, but she was hoping that Head would impregnate her soon so they could share something wonderful.

The twin sisters came from an abusive and broken home where alcohol consumption and meth use was a daily occurrence. Their father was a heavy drinker who didn't contribute anything to their lives besides misery and abuse. He was an angry man who beat them for simple things such as talking or laughing too loud. Their mother was a meth head who valued her drugs more than her twin daughters. When their household became a party crowded with family and friends, Kandy and Mandy suffered more from neglect.

As they grew, their immune systems suffered from lack of nutrition, and for years their skeletal bodies were only half alive from surviving on scraps from trash bins and the kindness of neighbors and food pantries. The twins' teeth were mostly rotten, and a yellow film covered their top and bottom rows.

By the time they turned twelve, an anonymous call to ACS prompted their removal from their deplorable conditions. Their sunken eyes and sickly appearance from years of malnourishment placed them at the bottom of the adoption lists, so they were in and out of foster care.

When Mandy and Kandy turned sixteen, they ran away together and took to the streets to steal and sell drugs. A few months earlier, right after their nineteenth birthday, they were introduced to Head, a handsome out-of-towner who spoke to the girls with respect. Head had a detailed plan—a vision of how he saw his future—and he explained that he wanted them to be a part of his legacy. He promised them a better life, a life that was a far cry from their previous one. He promised them the close-knit family unit they had never had.

Head's family worked as one unit toward one common goal. Head explained his Robin Hood dreams. He wanted to rebuild Flint, and then Detroit. Head wanted to gobble up all of the high risk, dilapidated, and condemned properties that he could afford. Most were city owned and were auctioned off for no more than the back taxes due.

Block by block, he would rebuild single-family homes, tenement buildings, and commercial real estate and rent to low income people of color. These modernized homes would accept Section 8, HUD, and other vouchers, but he wouldn't be a slumlord. There would be community centers that taught free computer coding classes, business and finance, advanced science, and practical job training. He wanted these black communities to be black owned, and once he began tearing down the old and building the new, there wouldn't be gentrification. He wasn't selling out. Head wanted his communities to reflect the 1920s Black Wall Street movement in Tulsa.

Kandy and Mandy were fully engrossed in his vision, hanging on his every word. It never occurred to either of them that they were white as they vowed to help him build his black world.

Also on the compound was a girl named Melissa. She was a twenty-year-old black woman with a young son, and she had her own hard-knock-life story. She too was from the hardcore streets of Flint and had been on her own since she was thirteen years old. At the age of fourteen, she started dabbling in drugs. First it was weed and alcohol, and then she graduated to the cocaine and pills. By the time Melissa turned eighteen, she had an arrest record a mile long, had been shot and stabbed, had overdosed twice, and was left for dead in an alley. She met Head at a sleazy bar where she tried to sell him a fake gold watch for ten dollars. She was in bad shape, going through self monitored withdrawals. Melissa was determined to stay clean, but it was hard and she needed money for food. Head gradually gained her trust and sold her his pipe dreams by driving her through the ghost-town neighborhoods. He convinced her that he would provide her a better life than the one she was living.

Last, but not least, there was Jacki, the young girl who had picked him up from the airport. At twenty-three, Jacki was the elder of the compound. She was from Detroit and moved to Flint with her boyfriend in her early teens. Jacki's main problem was that she was codependent. She needed a man in her life and would suffer anxiety attacks each time a relationship ended. Jacki believed she was born to be a man's wife, and that it was the only thing she was good at.

Head continuously preached to the girls that they were a family and that they were all contributors to the family. They all served a purpose.

"Our family is supposed to be strong and united, and our family must continue to grow," he continued to broadcast until he was sure that all minds thought alike.

It was an entire operation that no one knew about. Head was living a triple life in Michigan, and he had four young girls brainwashed with his beliefs. Among other things, Head learned how to be persuasive with his agenda from Brother Kareem.

"Would you like me to draw you a bath?" Mandy asked.

"That would be nice."

She smiled and headed to the master suite to draw her man—her black king—a warm bath.

Head didn't have to lift a finger. The girls were ready to wait on him hand and foot. Jacki was the best cook, and she wanted to make her man a savory meal, but Head said he wasn't hungry. He wanted to unwind, take a bath, and get some rest. It had been a long trip and a long day.

All four of the ladies wanted to join him in the tub. They missed him and wanted to please him. But he requested some alone time. He needed to think. And while the girlfriends were knocking on the bathroom door, his mind was on Cartier.

After his soothing bath, he went into the bedroom to get some sleep on the king size bed. Six hours later, Kandy was knocking on his bedroom door to alert him that a car was approaching the property from the road. Head removed himself from the bed, threw on a T-shirt and some jeans, and walked outside to see a black Dodge Charger arriving at the foot of his wraparound porch. Inside the Charger were two black men. His young girls joined him on the porch to see who it was.

"Do you know them?" Jacki asked.

Head didn't answer her. Instead, he approached the car. Two men climbed out and Head greeted them with dap and a brotherly hug.

"How was the trip?" Head asked them.

"Long," replied the driver, a man named Brother Taron. "But well worth it."

With that said, the two men walked around to the trunk of the car. Brother Taron removed a black leather duffel bag from it and handed it to Head. He unzipped it and smiled. Inside the bag was fifteen kilos of cocaine.

"Y'all brothers did nice," he praised them. "Were there any problems?"

"Nah, shit went smooth like ice."

With the acquisition of the fifteen kilos stolen from Cartier's trap house, things were looking promising for Head. One way or another, he was hell bent on squashing Cartier's independent streak, and ultimately she would have to rely on him. He could have easily murdered Majestic and Scooter, but he knew that as long as they were alive, then he could keep coming back for more product.

He wanted to break Cartier and remold her to see the future the way he saw it.

19

"And what are you making again?" Sana asked Harlem.

"It's an Ethiopian dish called *wat,*" Harlem answered.

"What?"

"Wat—W-A-T," Harlem corrected.

Sana wrinkled her nose. "Well, whatever it's called, it smells funny and it's stinking up the kitchen."

"Believe me, it is really good."

"I doubt it . . . just the smell of it is making my stomach turn."

"Don't knock it until you tried it," Harlem replied.

Sana leaned against the kitchen counter and crossed her arms. "And I don't wanna try it."

"It's a dish my mother taught me how to make," Harlem said.

Harlem had chopped up a red onion and simmered it in a pot. Once the onions had softened, she added some vegetable oil. Following that step, she added some berbere to make a spicy wat.

"I don't get it. You were born here, Harlem, and your parents abandoned you and went back to Ethiopia. So why are you cooking up some foreign shit? Keep things American. I mean, damn, your parents named you Harlem. You can't get any blacker than that," said Sana.

Harlem chuckled at the comment. "It's my culture."

"Your culture is here in this country."

"I may have been born here, but this country isn't my culture."

"So do you consider yourself an American or Ethiopian?"

"Both."

"Both? You need to be loyal to one nationality. And since your skin is so dark, you should just represent that African side of you. It definitely works."

Harlem looked at Sana, but she refused to reply to the ignorance. It wasn't the first time she had come across someone like Sana—someone judgmental and naïve, who added their two cents about her skin color and her Ethiopian culture. Unlike her parents, Harlem took pride in the Ethiopian ways and culture. She felt that it gave her an identity. She blamed her parents for not having an identity and being confused about who they were when arriving to this country—and who she was. But being with Cartier, she saw strength in her identity.

"I swear, if it ain't made in America, then it ain't right," Sana added.

Harlem rolled her eyes and sighed. Sana was something else. But she refused to argue with the girl because she was in a celebratory mood. The case the state had against her for prostitution was wrapped up with her pleading no contest. Her punishment was three days community service and a fine.

Sana stood in the kitchen wearing only a strapless bra and a pair of panties, showing off her bony ass. She considered herself an exhibitionist. She loved walking around the apartment nearly naked, and she didn't care who saw her, including Head, who was also staying there. She had been warned numerous times by Cartier to put some clothes on, especially when Head was there.

"When you're done with them pots and pans, you need to wash them out thoroughly, because I don't want to taste lingering effects from your weird food," Sana said, nodding in the direction of the sink.

"You're missing out."

Sana smirked. "I doubt it. I'll take some eggs or a steak any day."

Harlem continued cooking her traditional meal and refused to let Sana get under her skin. Not today.

"Damn, what the fuck you cooking in here?" Head asked as he walked in the kitchen.

Harlem sighed. She didn't feel like explaining her dish again—especially not to Head. He walked into the kitchen shirtless and wearing basketball shorts and he screwed his face at the smell of things.

"Shit smells like something's dying in here," he added.

"That's what I told her," Sana said.

"Don't eat it then," Harlem replied.

"Believe me, you don't have to worry about that with me," Head countered.

He then gazed at Sana in her bra and panties, showing off her tiny tits. He frowned at her. *The chick thinks she's cute*, he said to himself. But he showed no interest in Sana. In fact, he would fuss with Cartier about keeping a white woman at her place. One night, he requested that she be kicked out, ranting that white women were the devil and the downfall of a black man.

Cartier had countered with, "She's half-black."

Head was admittedly shocked to hear this.

Cartier wasn't about to take orders from Head. As far as she was concerned, Sana was doing big things. She went to a great college and held down a job. It would be cruel to kick her out when she was leveling up. It was her place, and she would let whoever she wanted stay there.

Head had just returned after being gone for ten days, and he gave Cartier a full business report on the progress he was making with his legit endeavors. She didn't drill him too much about his whereabouts and long absence, but she did require answers to any and all of her questions. He provided her with plane tickets and travel information to prove to her that he wasn't staying at Pebbles' place.

Along with his beefing with Sana, Head and Harlem weren't the best of friends either. The two were always arguing. He hated when Harlem took to the kitchen to cook her foreign African foods. For some strange reason, he disliked her culture. Harlem found it ironic, since he went around preaching black pride, black politics, black businesses, building strong black families and structure, and Black Lives Matter.

Harlem went to her bedroom to talk to her parents through WhatsApp. She was rebuilding her relationship with her parents, particularly with her mother, and she frequently talked to them through the app. Though she had never been to Ethiopia, she yearned to see it and experience everything her parents talked about.

"How are things there?" Harlem asked her mother, Eden.

"Things are good. Really good," Eden replied.

"That's good news," Harlem replied, taking a seat on her bed.

"But I need a favor from you, Harlem," Eden began.

"What kind of favor?"

"Since you are doing so well over there, can you send us some money again? It is truly needed," said Eden.

Harlem looked around her bedroom, grateful for all the nice things she had. "That's not a problem. I can do that."

Eden smiled. "We appreciate it so much, Harlem. You are a blessing to your parents."

"Look out for it tomorrow afternoon."

"How much will you send?"

"Work and tips have been good at the club, so maybe three hundred dollars," said Harlem.

"That is fine. Thank you."

"Goodbye, Mom," Harlem said, walking back into the kitchen.

"Goodbye."

After getting her food, Harlem went back to her bedroom to enjoy her meal in peace. She needed a timeout from everyone.

❖ ❖ ❖

Sana sat on the living room couch in her panties and bra, heavily engrossed in her crossword puzzle. She was obsessed with doing puzzles and playing word games in the newspapers or on her cell phone. She almost needed an intervention. Working the puzzles kept her thinking and focused, and she loved the challenge.

Head walked into the living room and gazed at her in her underwear.

She looked his way and asked, "Why don't you like white people? What did they ever do to you?"

He scowled. "Are you seriously asking me that question—what have white people done to me?"

"Yes."

"Let me say this to you, little girl. As a black man in this country, to be relatively conscious is to be in a rage almost all the time," he said, his body tensing up.

She looked back down at her puzzle and said, "You don't have to be in a rage. You just need to relax, that's all."

"Relax. Of course for you, it's that simple."

She looked up and smiled. "It can be."

"I have a question for you."

"Ask."

"With your light or white skin, what race do you consider yourself? What ethnicity do you consider your primary? Is it white?"

Sana didn't answer the question right away. Head stared at her with intensity until she finally answered, "I'm mixed."

"Mixed, huh?"

Of course, Sana was lying. She wanted to say white, but she felt that she was behind enemy lines and she didn't want to upset Head. There was this ferocity inside of him toward white folks that she felt threatened by.

"When you were mixed back in the day—a mulatto—you were still considered black and lynched by mobs of whites. Having a drop of black blood in your veins, in your DNA, meant you were a nigger."

Sana sat there quietly for a moment. It looked like she was taking in his words. She then smiled. "You really need to relax. When was the last time Cartier gave you some?"

"That's not your business."

"I know, but maybe if you were getting some pussy then you wouldn't be walking around here with your chest all out and preaching this black supremacy," she countered.

Head was taken aback by her boldness.

She continued to smile at him in her underwear. Her smile was vexing Head. It was becoming a strange encounter between the two of them.

"What's going on in here?" Cartier asked, walking into the living room and tying her robe together.

She observed Head and Sana staring at each other, and seeing Sana lounging on her couch in her panties and bra made her upset. She immediately barked at Sana, "Girl, what the fuck did I tell you about walking around here half naked, especially when he is here?"

"I'm sorry, Cartier."

"Don't be sorry, go and put some fuckin' clothes on."

Sana sprung from the couch and hurried into the bedroom. Cartier and Harlem were becoming tiresome with always telling her to put some clothes on when Head was there.

Cartier was three seconds away from putting her hands on the young white-looking bitch to get her point across. She didn't know what Sana was up to, but she wanted it to stop.

Cartier turned to look at Head and asked him, "What were y'all in here talking about?"

"Her privileged white skin," Head replied.

"Are you attracted to her, Head?" she asked him.

"Are you seriously asking me that question?"

Cartier stepped closer to him and locked eyes with him. "Yes!"

"I don't associate myself with the devil, Cartier. Her people—they're our oppressors and they have been for hundreds of years. Her people have done things to the black race that are unimaginable. I would never betray my race by sleeping with white women. Do you understand me?"

She didn't respond. She continued to stare at him. His eyes and voice were showing and speaking hate for white people, but in Cartier's mind, the nigga was still a man—and pussy was still pussy, no matter what race it was.

Cartier waved him off and went into Sana's bedroom to have a talk with her. She was lying on her bed still working on her crossword puzzle.

Sana looked at Cartier and said, "I'm sorry, Cartier. I was in there minding my business and doing my puzzle and he started talking to me."

Sana didn't know that Cartier had overheard some of their conversation. Lately, Sana had been walking around the place thinking that she was better than everyone else. Yet, Cartier was the one paying the bills. When they would go out in public together, Cartier noticed how Sana took to white people quicker than she did black people. Her speech and demeanor would change up around them, as if she desperately wanted to fit in with the white race and forget about the black DNA inside of her.

Cartier figured out that she was pretending to be completely white around a certain class of people and she wanted to talk to her about it—or better yet, call her out on her bullshit.

"Do you hate black people, Sana?" Cartier asked her bluntly.

"No, I don't. Why are you asking me that?" Sana replied timidly.

"Because I've been watching you lately, and it seems like you'd rather be white than black," said Cartier.

"But I am black," she said clearly inside the room.

"Are you sure about that? Because when you're out there"—Cartier pointed to the window—"you don't announce that like you just did in here."

"I just have a lot going on, Cartier."

"We all do. But don't be ashamed to be black too."

"I'm not," she lied.

"Listen, you have the best of both worlds and you should embrace both races equally. You don't have to choose one race over the other, because you're both," Cartier explained.

"I understand."

With that said, Cartier walked out and went into her own room. She opened her top drawer and removed the white card from it. She took a seat at the foot of her bed and stared at it. This one had the same skull, dagger, and blood with the handwritten letter R in black ink. The cards were starting to bother her. She had put Majestic and Scooter on a mission to find the culprits behind them, but after the ambush on her trap house, their attention was diverted.

Cartier couldn't front. She was worried. Whatever this was with the cards, she didn't want it spilling over into Harlem and Sana's lives, possibly putting them in danger. Cartier felt like she was the big sister inside the home, and they were filling the voids left by her two deceased sisters, Fendi and Prada. She missed her little sisters very much, and having Harlem and Sana around reminded her of them.

While Cartier was in her bedroom alone, brooding and at the same time reminiscing about her little sisters, Harlem decided to go for a walk outside for some fresh air and to work off her meal. She opened the front door to see Head standing in the hallway alone. He was on his phone and didn't notice her behind him. She then heard him say into the phone, "I miss you too, Pebbles. I'll see you tomorrow."

Harlem was shocked to hear that. She knew Cartier was going to go into a heated rage once she found out.

20

*H*ead was away again, leaving Cartier without her man. She hated his trips out of town, which he kept saying were about business. She believed that he was a busy man—but how busy?

Harlem and Sana were working at the club, and the apartment was quiet. Relaxing in her bedroom, she poured herself a glass of white wine, spread out across her large bed nearly naked, and loaded up Netflix. The night belonged to her, and she planned on taking full advantage of it. She didn't want to worry about the streets, business, Head, or any threatening cards. It was too stressful. Just as the intro to the movie finished, her cell phone started to ring next to her. Glancing at the caller ID, Cartier saw it was Caesar calling her at the late hour. She answered the call with, "Hey Caesar," like they were best friends.

"How is your night?" he asked her.

"It's going fine."

"That's good to hear," he said.

With Head gone so much, Cartier found herself on the phone with Caesar more and more. He called her regularly. He called her when his wife was home, when she wasn't home, and he even called her when he was taking his son on play dates. Soon she found herself confiding in him, telling Caesar things that she probably shouldn't, like how it felt to lose her daughter in Miami. She told him about doing years of jail time for a murder she didn't commit. She talked about Monya, Jason, her mother and her sisters, and she confessed how empty she felt inside from losing all of her childhood friends and how she was secretly suffering from abandonment issues.

Caesar was a great listener.

She soon found herself expecting Caesar's phone calls. She didn't know where things were going with them, but she liked the attention he gave her.

Her friendship with Caesar came at a time when Head wasn't around. He was always out of town, always traveling somewhere rebuilding his empire. *Business* became his favorite word to her. His hateful rhetoric toward the government and white people started to become scary—so scary that she believed he was a borderline terrorist and the C.I.A. and NSA were going to tap her phones and raid her home.

Cartier truly loved Head, but she started to grow concerned about the change in him, and she was becoming weary of his long absences from her.

Harlem dawdled by Cartier's bedroom door for a short moment, thinking on how she was going to tell Cartier the grim news. She couldn't keep silent any longer. Cartier needed to know the truth.

Finally, she knocked on the master bedroom door and hollered, "It's me, Cartier. We need to talk."

The door opened and Cartier stood in front of Harlem in a blue silk robe. It looked like she had just gotten out of the tub.

"What's up, Harlem? What do you need to talk about?"

The look on Harlem's face matched the words she was about to speak. "It's something you might not want to hear."

"Just say it. I don't like it when people try to sugarcoat shit."

"It's Head. I overheard him talking to Pebbles the other day when he was in the hallway. He didn't see me. I think he's still messing with her."

"And you sure it was Pebbles he was talking to?"

"I heard him say her name."

The deadpan look on Cartier's face was worrisome. Harlem was sure that she was going to fly into a rage and flip out. She remembered the night Cartier shot at him outside his great aunt's place. This time she believed Cartier was going to kill him. She had warned him to leave Pebbles alone if they were going to be together—but Head wanted to have his cake and eat it too.

"You okay?" Harlem asked her.

"I'm fine."

"I'm here if you need me, Cartier. You know I have your back," said Harlem.

"I know. I just need some time alone to think," she said.

Cartier closed her door and retreated back into her room while Harlem stood there bewildered by her calm demeanor. It wasn't the Cartier she knew.

"Okay, that was weird," Harlem muttered to herself and walked away.

She had done her part by letting the cat out of the bag. Now it was Cartier's move.

When Head arrived home the next day, Harlem swore World War III was going to erupt. Head came home smiling like he struck gold somewhere. He hugged and kissed Cartier with passion, and Harlem was stunned when Cartier didn't resist him—or that she didn't smack him so hard that his teeth would hit the floor. Instead, she smiled back and said the words to him, "I missed you."

"I missed you too," he said.

"How was your trip?"

"It was great. I got a lot done."

"That's good to hear."

Harlem stood in the background watching Cartier's bizarre behavior with Head, and it felt like a glitch in the Matrix. The only thing Harlem could do was play the background and wonder if Cartier was okay.

That night, after dinner and drinks, Head made up some excuse to Cartier why he had to leave the apartment.

"I gotta check on something. I'll only be gone for an hour or two," he said.

"Fine," she replied with nonchalance.

Head gathered his things and left the apartment. The moment the door closed behind him, Cartier grabbed her jacket and shoes and told Harlem, "C'mon, let's go."

"Where to?" Harlem asked.

"To see where this muthafucka is going tonight."

"You're going to follow him?" Sana asked.

"Yes. Something isn't right," said Cartier.

This was the Cartier that Harlem had been waiting for. The look in Cartier's eyes said it all. If she saw some bullshit tonight then she was going to raise hell. Harlem was right behind her, ready to have her back in case anything went down.

Sana didn't want them to leave. She voiced her reason with, "Don't go, because you're gonna get what you go looking for."

They refused to listen. Cartier and Harlem took the stairs down to the lobby. By the time Cartier pulled out of the garage in her car, Head was pulling out of his parking spot on the street. She proceeded to follow him.

Fifteen minutes later, Cartier brought her car to a stop in a well-off area of Manhattan. She observed Head climb out of his Range Rover and approach a building she wasn't familiar with. Her instincts screamed at her who he was going to see. Harlem had already brought it to her attention, now she was about to confirm it herself.

She and Harlem exited the vehicle and subtly followed Head into the building. Inside, they observed Head knocking on a door and when it opened, Cartier saw the bitch smiling at Head. She threw her arms around him for an intimate hug and deep kiss. Cartier observed the infidelity with her own eyes.

This cheating muthafucka! she screamed to herself. Seeing Head hugging and kissing on Pebbles wasn't the worst part for her. She was able to get a good look at Pebbles, and she nearly threw up when she noticed her protruding belly. Pebbles looked a few months pregnant, and there was no doubt that it was by Head. It was a crushing thing to see. The rage swimming inside of her was overwhelming, and it was something she could no longer control.

Before Head could step foot into the apartment, Cartier came charging at them from what appeared to be out of nowhere with Harlem following right behind her. She did a beeline for the both of them. Seeing Cartier coming for them, Pebbles' eyes widened in fear.

"You sonofabitch!" Cartier shouted. "You got this fuckin' bitch pregnant!"

Head was caught off guard. "What the fuck you doing here? You followed me?"

"You nasty bitch-ass nigga!" Cartier screamed and slapped the shit out of Head. "You out here fucking raw, gambling wit' my life!"

"Cartier, you need to chill!" he shouted.

"No. Fuck you!" she screamed. She wanted to punch him in the face—and punch him hard—so hard that she wanted to disfigure him.

Cartier refused to cry in front of Pebbles. It took all her strength to hold back her tears, but she did. She had to. It felt like everything was crumbling inside of her. She loved Head and she wanted to make their relationship work. She gave him a second chance and he threw it down the drain.

"You so fuckin' stupid! You keep going back to this bitch like she got boomerang pussy!" Cartier continued to rant and scream.

Pebbles stood in the doorway like a deer caught in headlights. She didn't know what to expect from Cartier. She was scared that she was going to be attacked next—whether she was pregnant or not. Pebbles was in her second trimester and didn't want to take anything for granted. She covered her belly with her arms protectively. But Cartier didn't go after her. Instead, she cut her eyes at Pebbles and glared at her with such intensity, it almost hurt.

"We're in love, Cartier, and our baby proves that. You're going to have to realize that it's over between y'all," Pebbles said.

"Over?" Cartier had to clap back. She cut her eyes back to Head and said, "You need to choose right now, nigga. Me or her."

Harlem was shocked that she gave him a choice. Head was too.

"What?" he uttered.

"I'm not going back and forth with no bitch, Head. You either stay here and play house with this dumb bitch or make things right at home."

Harlem and Pebbles were both dumbfounded by what was said. Of course, Pebbles thought he was going to stay with her. She was carrying his child, so why wouldn't he choose her?

"I'm not gonna say it again, Head," Cartier reminded him.

Head transitioned from a pillar of black unity and strength to a yes-nigga right there in the hallway. He shot Pebbles a look that spoke his answer before his lips did.

"I'm out. I'm leaving with Cartier," he said.

Pebbles' mouth gaped. "You're what?" she cried out.

Head didn't give her the decency or respect to give her an explanation, nor did he tell her goodbye. He pivoted, gave Pebbles his back, and marched away from her like she was a complete stranger and not the woman carrying his child.

"Are you serious?! I'm carrying your baby and you gonna walk away from me like that!" she shouted. "Fuck you, Henry! Fuck you fo' real!"

He continued to ignore her. Cartier, however, decided to take advantage of the embarrassing situation. She didn't have to lay a finger on Pebbles to hurt her. She stood there with Harlem beside her and smirked. It was a boss look that said, *He's mine, bitch, and I'm better than you.*

Pebbles tried to keep her tears in, but they were bubbling inside of her like a shaken soda. She wanted to attack Cartier with her smirking ass, but she knew that she didn't stand a chance—especially with her being pregnant and Harlem standing right there.

"No real nigga chooses beer over champagne." Cartier turned around and left.

"Damn, you did that bitch dirty," Harlem whispered to Cartier.

Pebbles stood at her door ashamed and humiliated. She had watched the man she loved walk away—maybe for good this time. She retreated into her home and slammed the door.

Pebbles was drowning in heartbreak and sorrow. It felt like she was having a heart attack. She couldn't breathe. Inside her place, she collapsed on her knees, subsequently folding into the fetal position in agony on the floor. She was hysterical. She cried and cried.

The more she pictured Head walking away, the harder she cried and the deeper her pain grew. His baby was developing inside of her. She believed that they were finally going to be a family. She gave him everything—she became the side bitch and gave Head the space he desired—and she gave him her heart. The way he stepped on it, like it wasn't shit, it felt like he tore into her chest and ripped it out.

After an hour of grieving and a whirlwind of emotions from anger, sadness, and uncertainty about her future, Pebbles finally gathered enough strength to pick herself up from the floor and make a phone call. She went from crying on the floor to being folded on the couch. The phone rang several times before someone finally answered.

"Hello."

"Ma, I need to talk to you," Pebbles cried out.

"Pebbles, what happened? Is everything okay? Is the baby okay?"

"The baby is fine. It's Henry. He just left me. He just walked away like I wasn't shit to him."

"What do you mean?"

Pebbles went on to explain the situation to her mother, leaving nothing out, including Cartier's smirk toward her. She sobbed while talking, and it took her mother to calm her down.

"Baby, just relax. Everything is going to be okay," her mother said.

"How?"

"He'll be back, baby girl. They always come back. The moment he becomes tired of Cartier's shit, he'll come running back into your arms. He's just in that stupid zone for a moment. They all fall into that stupid zone, Pebbles. But you're carrying his baby and that's special to a man. So calm down and get your shit right. Because when he do come running back to you, it's gonna be your choice to take him back or not. Baby, you know I've dealt with my fair share of pain and heartbreak from men for many years—always being the other woman. And one thing I know for sure is, I might have been the other woman, but I was always taken care of. So give him his space, but you continue to work on you while he's gone," she told her daughter.

After her talk with her mother, Pebbles dried the last of her tears and took a deep breath. She believed her mother was right.

He'll be back.

21

*I*f it wasn't one thing, then it was another. Cartier locked herself inside the bedroom for the entire day. She didn't want to be seen. She didn't want to be bothered. She had found another card in the driver's seat of her Bugatti—meaning someone had broken into her expensive car to place it there. This card had a menacing skull and trickling blood with the handwritten letter *A* written in black ink. She was being stalked by some unknown entity, and they weren't letting up.

In addition to the mysterious cards, Pebbles' pregnancy weighed heavily on her mind. Although she had the upper hand when she made Head leave with her, the bitch was still carrying his baby. The thought of it made Cartier incredibly depressed. He was fucking the bitch raw and put his seed in her.

Cartier didn't want to show her depression around Harlem and Sana. She didn't want to look weak in front of them. When she and Harlem were confronting Head and Pebbles, it took everything inside of Cartier not to break down emotionally, so she substituted that feeling of heartbreak with anger.

Meanwhile, Pebbles would call her phone to argue, and although Cartier had threatened the girl within an inch of her life, Pebbles remained angry and hostile toward Cartier. It wasn't over between the two of them.

Pebbles felt foolish for letting Head go so easily. She wanted Cartier to kick him out. Pebbles tried to get under her skin with statements like, "He put his baby inside of me, bitch. He wasn't thinking about you when he was coming in this pussy every night. I got his baby, not you."

"Say that shit to my face!" Cartier threatened.

Pebbles' calls created more animosity between the fractured couple. Cartier was furious that Head's baby mama had her cell phone number, yet she kept answering.

Head shrugged off his part in the whole fiasco. "You like this drama, Cartier. I told you to block her."

However, Pebbles' constant calls had upset Cartier. She wanted to kick Head out of her place and out of her life for good, but she didn't want him to go running back to Pebbles. She wanted to win. Her ego was in the clouds and it wasn't coming back down anytime soon.

Although Head chose Cartier, she refused to have sex with him. She walked around him with a stink-ass attitude, cursing him out and denying him of his needs and he didn't understand why. He had left Pebbles for her, so why was she so mad?

For days they argued back and forth—and Cartier even threatened to make his life miserable if he went running back to that bitch again. He didn't. Instead, Head jumped on a plane and flew to Michigan.

Michigan. Whatever trust she had had in Head had been eviscerated by the Pebbles situation. Now she wanted to know what the fuck he had going on in a different state.

The day was young and sunny, and Cartier was trying not to think about the Head and Pebbles predicament. The wine she was drinking while lounging on the couch was helping her to loosen up. It felt like she was on a rollercoaster ride with this relationship. The ups and downs were making her nauseous and dizzy. It was stressful, and stress was what she didn't need.

Her cell phone rang and buzzed nearby. She picked it up and saw it was Caesar calling her. She felt ambivalent about answering, but decided it wouldn't be wise to ignore him.

"Hello."

"It's a beautiful day and I have two tickets to see the Yankees play the Red Sox this afternoon. I'm inviting you," said Caesar.

"You want me to go to a baseball game?"

"Have you ever been to a ball game?"

"No."

"Well, there's a first time for everything," he said.

She sighed. *Why not?* "Okay. I'll go."

"I knew you would say yes. I'll be at your place in an hour."

"An hour?"

"Is that a problem?"

"No. An hour is good. How should I dress?" she asked.

"Just comfortable," he said.

An hour later, Cartier walked out of her building in Adidas fitted sweatpants, a thick sweatshirt, and a baseball cap. Caesar arrived alone driving a burgundy F-150. He climbed out the vehicle looking unassuming wearing blue jeans, a Thomas the Train T-shirt under a light fall jacket, and black sneakers. He smiled at Cartier and hugged her like they were good friends. No one would ever guess that he was a ruthless drug kingpin with the body count of a small war. Hundreds of men had been murdered by his command, and nearly four dozen had been murdered by his hands.

"You look very nice," he said.

She smiled. "Thank you."

"Shall we get this day started?"

"Yes. I'm excited."

"As one should be when attending a Yankees game," he said.

On the way to the stadium, Cartier became aware of the security detail subtly following him. At first, she thought they were enemies of his and it was going to be a hit. But Caesar's calm demeanor showed he was a cautious man.

As if he had read her mind, he said, "I pay good money for good men to watch over me in secrecy."

She had no idea how many men were watching his back, but it looked like they could rival the Secret Service with their clandestine protocol and their technology.

Cartier and Caesar sat nestled with the horde of fans inside the packed Yankees Stadium. It was a day of hot dogs, beers, giant fan waves, and cheering for the home team. It was the bottom of the 8th inning, and the Yankees were down by one run with a man on second base. Caesar explained some of the rules and regulations and who the major players were. His knowledge of the game and its players—past and present—was impressive. To everyone else, the two of them looked like a nice couple enjoying a baseball game. It's how Caesar wanted it to be perceived.

At the bottom of the ninth, the Yankees were at bat with one out when Aaron Judge stepped up to the home plate clutching a Louisville Slugger. He did a few practice swings at the plate and then assumed his batting stance with his eyes sharply on the pitcher. All eyes were on the batter and the pitcher, waiting for something exciting to happen. The pitcher threw the first pitch and Aaron swung and missed. The next two pitches were balls, making the count 1 and 2, and the one after that was a strike. One more and he was out. The pitcher threw a curveball at the plate. It came with a strong downward spin and was veering to the side. Aaron swung with all his might and *crack*—the baseball took off like a rocket and flew over third base and into the crowd.

Home run!

The stadium erupted as everyone rose to their feet and cheered as Aaron rounded the bases and stomped his cleats onto home plate. His teammates were there to greet him in celebration.

After the game, Caesar and Cartier sat on a bench in a nearby park having hotdogs and sodas. Cartier felt like a teenager again. The mood was upbeat and she was enjoying the company.

"So, did you enjoy the game?" Caesar asked.

"I did," she said between sips of her Coke.

Their conversation flowed easily, but Caesar knew something was bothering her. He was in the business of reading people and looking for signs of distress and peculiarity. He was skilled at picking up on body language and micro-expressions.

"I know something is bothering you, Cartier. I can see it in your eyes. What is it? You can talk to me," he said.

"It's my relationship with Head. He fucked up and got his mistress pregnant."

"That's a lot to deal with."

"It is."

Cartier seemed confused about their relationship, and he asked her a simple question. "Do you love him?"

"That's difficult to answer," she replied.

Caesar didn't understand her response to the question. He shook his head and said to her, "Love is the easiest thing to figure out, but people make it complicated."

She looked at him with curiosity.

Caesar went on to say to her, "I don't love my wife. I never did. Nor do I hate her. There are other emotions that are just as finite. I appreciate that she carried my son, and I'm infatuated with her intelligence—I admire her

Juris Doctorate degree. But it was never love between us. There are things I dislike about her, like how messy she is. I'm also annoyed that she's not a more attentive mother. And I'm aggravated that she's lazy. But although I don't hate her, if I had to, I wouldn't hesitate to kill her. And even though I'm not in love with her, I would also stop her from being killed."

Love, broken down and simplified by Caesar.

Cartier started to assess her feelings for Head. She appreciated that they had history, and she liked how both their names held weight in New York City. Them coming together as a couple kept her name ringing out more. And with women always judging when you don't have a man, she like being boo'd up.

Cartier had to admit to herself that she didn't really know Head like she thought she did. Maybe it wasn't that he had changed, but that he was being more of the same person he had always been. Only now did she see it. She still couldn't bring herself to say she didn't love Head out loud, but her talk with Caesar definitely had her thinking.

She liked hanging around with Caesar. He was intelligent and caring. She loved that he was a good listener. He came at a moment when she needed someone to talk to about her problems.

Spending time with Caesar made the day go by fast. Before they knew it, they had spent over three hours in the park talking. When it was time to go she didn't want to leave. It was odd because once again he didn't come on to her. At the end of their supposed date, Caesar brought up business. He mentioned the robbery.

"It's an inside job, Cartier," he said.

"I know it is. And I've already handled the problem," she lied.

"That's good to hear. I respect that."

Cartier was tempted to tell him about her other problem, about the notes that were being delivered to her anonymously, but she decided against it. She didn't want him to think that she came with a ton of problems.

22

*L*ove doesn't break your heart, people do.

It was a statement Cartier once heard from someone, and it was the truth. With Head away, she continued on with her business with Caesar. She wanted to keep herself busy.

The people in her household were changing. She noticed that Harlem had been moping around the place ever since the incident with Pebbles.

"It's not right, what he did to you. He doesn't deserve you, and you know it, so why keep allowing him back into your life?" Harlem asked.

"Because things aren't that simple," Cartier replied.

"He got someone else pregnant."

"And I already handled that. And besides, I hurt him before. No disrespect, Harlem, but this is my business, not yours."

Harlem pivoted and walked away.

Cartier suspected Harlem was upset and emotional for her own personal reasons. She had recently broken up with Sincere. She explained to Cartier that he was too immature for her. Also, she was pregnant. Lately, Harlem had been tired, throwing up nearly every morning, and missing days from work. Cartier had noticed her breasts had become swollen, and the signs indicated to her that the young girl was pregnant. She took Harlem to the local clinic and the doctors confirmed her suspicion.

"You need to tell Sincere," Cartier had told Harlem. "It's his baby, right?"

"Yes. It's his. But I'm not telling him shit."

"He has the right to know."

"Fuck him!" Harlem had cursed.

They argued about how to handle her situation. Harlem was being stubborn, and with Head back in town, things became even tenser between them. Harlem was always telling Cartier how she felt he was an asshole and Cartier was too good for him.

Head stepped out of the tub and toweled off. For a split second, he stared at himself in the bathroom mirror. He was in his forties, but his physique looked like a man's in his twenties. He kept himself in tip-top shape. Head felt that there was a war brewing between races and he had to prepare himself not just mentally, but physically too.

He stepped into the bedroom, where Cartier was lounging on the king size bed and watching TV in a purple T-shirt with her smooth, shapely legs showing. Head fixed his eyes on her and smiled. What he wanted was some pussy, but Cartier continued to deny him. He felt he'd been punished enough. In addition, Head felt that the tension between Cartier and Harlem was interfering with them patching things up.

"I think it's time for Harlem to leave here, maybe get her own place. She's been here long enough, Cartier, and besides, you're not her keeper," Head mentioned out the blue.

Cartier looked at him and replied, "Why? First Sana, and now Harlem?"

"Fuck Sana. Sana could stay."

"So Harlem gotta go? Again, why?"

"What you mean, why? The two of you ain't seeing eye-to-eye right now, and she's pregnant. You really want a crying baby around here?"

"How cold are you, asking me to kick out a pregnant woman?"

"So now you wanna make this place into a woman's shelter?" Head countered.

"She's a friend."

"You barely know her."

Cartier frowned. "If it wasn't for you, I wouldn't have met her in Central Booking in the first place. But since you wanted to be with that bitch and got me locked up, this is the result of it. I met Harlem and she fuckin' stays. This is my place, not yours."

Cartier removed herself from the bed and went into the bathroom, slamming the door behind her. She had enough on her mind. The last thing she wanted to do was argue with Head. He was back, but things weren't simple or loving between them—not yet anyway. She needed some time.

Even though Harlem had been bitchy and moody lately, Cartier wanted to help. Harlem planned on keeping the baby, and Cartier wanted to stand by her and cheer her up. They both were going through difficult situations. Cartier had received another white card with a black menacing skull with hollow eyes, a sharp dagger, and blood with the handwritten letter *U* in black ink. They weren't going to stop.

To get their minds off of their problems, Cartier decided to take Harlem shopping. With the weather changing and Harlem's belly growing, it was time to get ready for the fall season, and it was time to go shopping for the baby.

The two ladies entered the maternity clothing store on 125th Street and started browsing through the place. There was a wide selection of cute outfits for her to rock and loads of adorable baby clothes. Harlem fell in love with everything. She wanted the best for her baby, but she wanted to look good herself too. Her body was changing and she didn't want to walk around the city looking like a pregnant, fat slob in ill-fitting clothing.

Today, it was about Harlem. Cartier told her to pick out whatever she wanted. It was on her dime. It was Cartier's way to cheer her up. Sana had wanted to go with them, but Harlem vetoed it. She wanted to be alone with Cartier—like old times before Sana and Head came into the picture.

Harlem tried on multiple outfits and each one complimented her growing figure.

"You like it?" she asked Cartier, twirling around in the burgundy sweater dress she was trying on.

"It's nice. I can see you rocking that joint with your belly out to here," Cartier replied while she improvised a pregnant belly.

"It is nice. I'll take it too."

Harlem continued to try on outfits and picked up a few things for her unborn child.

"So, have you told him yet?" Cartier asked.

Harlem sighed. She didn't want to get into it with Cartier about telling Sincere about the baby.

"No."

"It's not right, Harlem. He needs to know."

"Cartier, please. Let's not get into this. I don't wanna talk about him right now," Harlem replied with a slight attitude.

"I'm just gonna say this . . . at some point, he will need to know."

"So what about you and Head? You forgave him like that? He did get the next bitch pregnant," Harlem fired back.

Cartier vaguely frowned at the remark. "Check your attitude, Harlem, and I'm giving you this one warning."

Harlem knew she had fucked up by saying that. It wasn't wise to bite the hand that was feeding you.

23

Head climbed out of his Range Rover in the Diamond District in Midtown Manhattan bundled up in a mink jacket. The wind forcefully pushed him forward as he walked the half-block distance to the store. The area was full of life that early afternoon. He entered a well-known jewelry shop called Jacob's Diamonds. He had a familiar relationship with the owner, and the moment he was inside, Jacob himself smiled at Head and welcomed him to his business.

"Long time no see, my friend. I heard you were home," said Jacob.

"It has been. Been home since the spring. But what's good?" Head replied, giving the man dap and a brotherly hug.

"Busy like always, selling luxury and wealth. What you here for? Because I have some nice pieces for you. The best. I know your style of jewelry, my friend."

"I'm looking for a ring," Head said.

Immediately, Jacob thought he was looking for diamond pinky rings or big boy rings that stood out. He started to remove the display case of gaudy looking rings to show Head, but Head right away corrected him.

"Nah, not that kind of ring. I'm looking for an engagement ring."

Jacob was taken aback. "Engagement ring. Congratulations. Who's the lucky girl?"

"Someone I've known a while. I need to make things right with her."

Jacob smiled. "In that case, I got the perfect rings for you to look at. Come with me."

Inside a private back room where Jacob only took his elite clientele, he placed a leather display case onto the table and opened it for Head to see. Inside was a series of expensive engagement rings.

"Nice," Head uttered.

"Yes, my friend. You've been a good customer to me for a long time, so I'll show you the best," said Jacob.

Head carefully looked at and inspected each ring. Each was flawless and brilliantly cut.

"Take your time, pick out what you like. I'll give you a good price."

Head soon found the perfect ring to propose with. He picked up a unique, rose gold ring with a flawless 4.52 carat round diamond.

"You have good taste."

"How much?" Head asked.

"It sells for one and a quarter, but for you, I'll let it go for one hundred thousand."

Head nodded. "I'll take it. Wrap it up for me."

With the ring securely in his pocket, Head sat inside his car for a few moments. Thoughts of his last proposal to her infiltrated his mind until he pushed them away. He always knew that he wanted to marry Cartier, now all she had to do was say yes.

24

The Blue Hill restaurant on Washington Place, which was in a townhouse-set location, was first-rate and elegant. Cartier and Head sat among the customers enjoying a wonderful meal together. It was late in the evening. The two were talking, but the conversation between them wasn't flowing like it did when she was with Caesar. It was Head's idea to take her out to dinner at a nice restaurant.

Cartier pushed away her plate of balsamic-marinated chicken and took a sip of wine.

"You're not going to finish your dinner?" Head asked.

"I'm not really that hungry."

"You want dessert?"

"No, Head. I'm fine."

"So, what's on your mind?"

"A lot of things."

"You know you can talk to me about anything, Cartier. I wanna be here for you."

She stared at him. She didn't know what to believe when it came to him. Since he had come home, he seemed to be all over the place. He had lied to her. He had betrayed her. It felt like he was using her. But still, she had feelings for him.

Head narrowed his eyes keenly on Cartier. He then reached for her hand across the table and gently started to caress it. It looked like he was fixing to say something important.

"I love you, Cartier."

She remained silent, wondering where he was going with this. She didn't have to wait long. Head placed a velvet ring box on the table and smiled warmly at her. Staring into her eyes, he opened it to reveal the large diamond engagement ring.

"Cartier Timmons, will you marry me?"

Cartier sat there in a silent mixture of surprise and confusion. She wondered what had triggered the proposal. But he was serious and she didn't want him to feel rejected again, like he had in South Beach. No matter how turbulent and crazy their relationship was, Head always knew how to come back into her life. But there were issues that they needed to work on.

"There's a long road to falling back in love with you, Head, and a ring isn't going to do it for me," she said.

"I know."

"I need trust," Cartier added.

"And that, I promise to give you from now on." He pulled out his cell phone and handed it to her.

"What are you doing?" she asked him.

"My pass code is 98-89-90, and from now on, no more secrets."

Cartier was shocked.

He continued with, "I love you too much to lose you. I want us to work out, babe. Together, we're the perfect power couple. We can run not only this city, but maybe this country. And I want you by my side, Cartier. I want us to have the type of love that will rival anything out there. They won't be able to fuck with us, because I got your back and I know you got mine."

Why couldn't she completely cut him loose? Why did she allow him back into her life? His words were deep and they lingered like sweat on her skin. The way Head stared at her, passionately and powerfully, it made her weak inside.

"Say yes," he added.

She managed to smile and say, "Yes. Yes, I'll marry you."

Head went over to Cartier and they passionately kissed with nearly all eyes on them. Cartier felt this was his way of making up for getting Pebbles pregnant. The mistress got the baby, but she got the engagement ring. She felt that it was another win for her.

She was getting married!

However, the joyfulness she felt was once again short-lived. When they walked to her car that night, she could see it from a distance. There was another gift left for her on her windshield—another white card with the same menacing black skull, a threatening dagger, and blood with another handwritten letter *D* in dark black ink. Cartier quickly snatched the card and shoved it into her purse.

"What's that?"

"A party promo." She didn't want to ruin their evening.

Cartier looked around to see if there was anyone watching her from afar, but she saw nothing strange.

Enough was enough.

"Congratulations on the engagement," Caesar said to her. "So, you said 'yes' to him. I guess it's love, right?"

Cartier held the phone out and looked at it like it was an alien being. How did he already know about the engagement? It happened yesterday, and she hadn't told anyone yet. She figured that Head must have run his mouth off to someone.

"Thank you, Caesar," she said.

"If you need anything, Cartier, let me know."

"I'm fine right now, but thanks, Caesar. I appreciate it."

Cartier was pleased to hear that Caesar didn't have an issue with her pending marriage to Head. She hoped her engagement didn't interfere with their business relationship—or their personal relationship. She liked talking to him.

At first, Cartier and Head were going to do a really big celebrity-caliber wedding at an exclusive location. Cartier wanted bitches to envy her. She wanted every bitch that was infatuated with Head to step the fuck off! But Head didn't want the extravagance. He convinced Cartier that they should have a private ceremony because he felt that all that attention on them would only attract the wrong people. They still had enemies out there. He sounded mature and explained that it was only about them—and no one else.

"Fuck impressing friends, yours and mine," he had said.

Cartier agreed.

A week later, they went to the Justice of the Peace to get married the day before Thanksgiving. They stood in front of the judge not as two notorious murderers or drug kingpins, but as a loving black couple who wanted a life together. As Head professed his love to Cartier, he never took his eyes off of her. He held her hands lovingly and made it clear that he wanted to spend the rest of his life with her.

Cartier, too, declared her love wholeheartedly to Head. She took a deep breath and uttered the words, "I do."

The two kissed, and it felt like it was meant to be.

Thanksgiving Day wasn't what Cartier had hoped. Sana woke up that morning and announced that she was now a vegan, and Harlem refused to eat dinner with them and just cried her eyes out in her room. Cartier thought she finally understood the root of Harlem's depression. With her being pregnant and not having a relationship with the baby's father, Cartier was sure that Harlem was missing her own family. Head and Cartier were leaving in the morning for their honeymoon, but she made a decision that when she got back she would somehow find a way to contact Harlem's parents and pay for them to fly out and see their daughter. Cartier wanted it to be a surprise.

The next morning Cartier and Head flew to the Bahamas. They stayed at Sandals Emerald Bay, which offered a luxurious and secluded setting on Great Exuma Island. Cartier was trapped in paradise and she loved every day of it. She and Head made love every night at the resort. It seemed like the pussy was extra wet and tighter during their honeymoon, and Head came continuously every night inside of her. He couldn't ask for anything better. He had Cartier again, and he was ready to move on to the next stage of his plan.

25

Cartier lay cuddled against Head in the backseat of the cab on their way home from JFK airport. Their seven-day honeymoon in the Bahamas was invigorating. They both felt refreshed and alive, and now it was time to get back to business. They were married—they were unified into one force, and it was time for them to show it on the streets. It's what Head believed.

The cab arrived at Cartier's place and they climbed out into the late fall breeze. The weather was a direct contrast to where they had just come from—sunny and bright skies with temperatures in the 90's.

"We should have stayed in the Bahamas," Head joked.

Cartier chuckled and replied, "That would have been nice."

They collected their luggage from the trunk of the cab and headed into the building. They were all smiles and looking harmonious together. Walking into the apartment, Cartier knew something was off right away. It wasn't a threat, but things were quiet during the day and Sana was lounging on the couch doing her crossword puzzles in her underwear. When she saw the newlyweds walk into the apartment, she refused to greet them with "Congratulations" or "Welcome home." Instead, she frowned at them—mostly at Head, because she didn't trust him.

"Sana, put some clothes on," Cartier barked.

"I didn't know y'all were coming home today."

"Well, we're back, and I want you to start walking around my place decently. Head is my husband now, and I'm not gonna continue to play this fuckin' game with you," Cartier warned.

Sana sulked. She removed herself from the couch and started toward her bedroom. Before she could go into the room, Cartier asked her, "Where's Harlem?"

"Oh, she packed her things and moved out," replied Sana indifferently.

Cartier was surprised by the news. "She did what?"

"She left."

"When?"

"Soon after y'all left for the Bahamas," Sana said.

"Did she leave a message for me? A forwarding address?"

"No. She was pretty tight-lipped about everything."

Cartier reached for her cell phone and Sana said, "Don't. Her phone doesn't work and she quit the club."

Sana was clueless as to what was going on. Harlem had stopped speaking to her, and she became very private after her breakup with Sincere and the pregnancy. The two girls used to talk and share everything, but then Harlem shut down and started to act differently—depressed and isolating herself. Sana and Cartier were concerned about her behavior, but they couldn't get her to open up about what was bothering her.

Cartier was visibly shaken by the news. Head seemed pleased. He said to Cartier, "It's for the better."

She felt it wasn't. Over the past few months, Cartier had grown attached to Harlem. They had a connection, and she cared about the girl's well being. Cartier was looking forward to playing auntie to a niece or nephew. But then something changed with Harlem, and Cartier couldn't put her finger on it.

For several days, Cartier tried to find Harlem. She went to women's shelters in every borough, she called Esmeralda, and she spoke with several of Harlem's coworkers at the club, but to no avail. Harlem was nowhere to be found. It seemed like she had just disappeared.

◇ ◇ ◇

A week back from the Bahamas and the threats to Cartier continued. This time two white cards were placed in her mailbox. They bore the same menacing skull with creepy, hollow eyes that seemed to be glaring at her, a jagged dagger, and blood with the handwritten letter *E* in black ink. Two *E's*? Cartier didn't know what to think. She couldn't make it stop because she didn't know where or who they were coming from. Someone had been watching her for a long time now.

Majestic and Scooter were able to find out that the cardstock was sold in almost any supermarket or office supply store, but who was behind it was still a mystery. And unless Cartier hired someone to covertly watch her back around the clock, it seemed that the chances of catching this elusive person were slim.

She wanted to tell Head about the cards, but she decided against it. She figured he would try to control her. He would want her locked in the apartment twenty-four seven and would want to keep tabs on her. She refused to have an argument with Head about the cards. He had enough on his plate and she had enough on hers.

The following day, Cartier met with Majestic and Scooter in the basement of a meat market warehouse in Lower Manhattan. She barked at her two hit men for not finding the culprit or culprits behind the cardstocks. She tossed the recent cards at Majestic's chest and exclaimed, "When will it stop? I need to fuckin' know who is behind this shit!"

"I'm on it, Cartier," Majestic said.

"How *on it* are you? I'm still receiving these bullshit cards! And I'm starting to think that these cards showing up and the hit on my stash house is connected," she shouted.

"It might be," Scooter said.

She locked eyes on her killers. "I need this to stop now. I want whoever is sending me this shit to be found—dead or alive, I don't give a fuck. But I want results from both of y'all. Do y'all understand me?"

"Yeah. We got you," said Scooter. "Believe me, they gon' get got, Cartier. It's our mission to find whoever da fuck they are."

"Don't make promises you can't keep," she replied.

"Oh, you know we keep our promises," Majestic said.

Both men wore serious expressions. They were extremely loyal to Cartier, and if they had to take a bullet for anyone, then it would be her. Had they worked for anyone else when the product was taken from the stash house and they weren't murdered, they would have been murdered. But Cartier believed them. She somewhat trusted them and they wanted to keep their arrangement. If they needed to assault and interrogate every person in the city, then they would. Majestic and Scooter were more determined than ever to find out who was leaving the intimidating notes.

"Yo, Cartier," Majestic continued. "This is some psychological bullshit on some other level. Whoever is behind this is touched in the head, maybe deranged. I would feel better if we had a man on you until we find out who's behind this shit. Maybe two."

Cartier thought about the request. She could handle herself when she knew who she was at war with, but this was an unknown enemy. They had the advantage—the element of surprise.

Cartier nodded. "Who I got on payroll that you'd trust wit' your life?"

Majestic grinned. "Other than me and Scooter, I'm feelin' Lil Foe and Roddy."

Cartier bought a Tahoe and tinted out the windows to hide the vehicle's occupants. Lil Foe and Roddy were now reassigned to watch her back. Head loved this. His wife being driven around the boroughs protected was a statement to the hood.

While cruising through the city on a breezy fall afternoon, Cartier seemed preoccupied by something. The SUV came to a stop at a red light at a busy intersection on 7th Avenue. Something instantly brought Cartier out of her trance. She fixed her eyes on a young woman pushing a baby stroller. The child looked to be a year old, and she was a pretty little girl with a head full of black hair. Seeing the mother and the baby walking across the street made Cartier think about Christian. She missed her daughter greatly and she fell into deep sadness thinking about the tragic way her baby was snatched from her. Though it happened years ago and she had long ago gotten revenge, it still haunted Cartier like it happened yesterday.

"I want another baby," Cartier said to herself.

"Now is not a good time for you to get pregnant. Are you crazy? A baby?" Head griped.

"You're calling me crazy for wanting to have your baby?" Cartier retorted.

"It's not like that, Cartier. I'm just saying, these are difficult times right now. You got your thing going on strong, and what if we go to war and you're pregnant? It ain't gonna be a good look."

He was talking, trying to make sense, but Cartier wasn't listening. In fact, she became more incensed.

"You don't want me to have a baby because that bitch Pebbles is already carrying your baby?!"

The situation brought back ugly memories of her and Jason. She painfully remembered being locked up while she was carrying Christian and believing that she was the only one pregnant by Jason. Shockingly, her best friend Monya beat her to it. It was an ugly reminder to Cartier that niggas ain't shit. Now, years later, she found herself in a somewhat similar situation.

"How you gonna have a baby when you're running one of the largest drug distributions in the city?" he asked, wanting to change her mind.

"I know how to separate my personal life and my business."

"Yeah, and speaking on business, now that we're married, I need to know things about your business just in case something happens."

"If something happens?" Cartier responded with a raised eyebrow. "You mean to me? What's gonna happen? I have men who know what to do, Head."

"I'm your husband and you don't trust me?"

"Let's not mingle our businesses. Okay? I'm not asking you about Michigan."

Head had told her that he was opening up a string of car washes with a partner that he had done time with and it was going to be huge. Head explained the cost of opening a business was cheaper out there and since the water crisis, easier. It wasn't a lie. Eventually he was going to own a string of car washes, all part of his black-owned business portfolio.

"That's different, Cartier. I'm legit and you know this. You still wanna play Scarface out there on them streets," he argued.

He wondered if she had any safety deposit boxes and where her new trap houses were. They were probative things that in a normal situation and marriage should be shared.

"Nigga, don't try to change the subject. This isn't about my thug life. It's about you not wanting me to get pregnant, even though your mistress is!" she yelled.

Head hated the word "mistress." He cringed each time she said it.

Cartier longed for this baby, but then something in her gut told her to chill out. And she did. She stormed out of the bedroom and left the apartment in a fit of rage, slamming the door behind her.

Sana watched her leave. She had heard them arguing in the bedroom, and she knew Head was not the type of man she wanted.

ead was out of town again—back in Flint. He would be gone for weeks each month, allegedly building his car wash business from the ground up. Cartier was increasingly thinking about a baby. It wasn't right for Pebbles to be carrying her husband's baby and not her.

She had called Head in Flint to bring it up again, but he was reluctant to speak about it. Whenever she would call, there was a lot of noise in the background and he would always say that he couldn't talk because he was working. But Cartier was adamant to talk, exclaiming into the phone, "Too fuckin' bad. We need to talk about this! Why can't you give me a baby? I'm your wife!"

Every other word recently was *wife* or *mistress*. Head had erupted with rage, screaming, "I told you, Cartier, leave the fuckin' issue alone! I don't wanna talk about no fuckin' baby right now! I'm busy. Don't fuckin' call me about this shit anymore!"

Cartier was shocked by how angry his reaction was. She didn't know why he was so opposed to building their family. Cartier felt like a fool. These are things you discuss before the marriage.

Sana knocked on Cartier's bedroom door and asked from the hallway, "Cartier, are you okay in there?"

"I'm fine," Cartier replied.

"Do you need anything? If you do, I got you. If you want to talk, we can do that too."

Sana opened the door and walked into the bedroom. She could tell that Cartier had a lot on her mind. She was sitting on the bed with an open bottle of wine and listening to old Toni Braxton songs. Sana joined her on the bed and took a drink of wine from the bottle. With Harlem gone, Sana and Cartier had become even closer.

"You okay, Cartier?"

"I'm just sitting here enjoying some time to myself and thinking, that's all, Sana," Cartier responded.

Sana smiled. "Well, you don't have to be by yourself. I can be your company."

Cartier smiled too.

"Are you thinking about Head?" Sana asked.

Cartier took the wine bottle back from Sana and took a gulp before replying, "I'm thinking about a lot of things."

They were quiet for a moment, feeling Toni's pain as she sang another sad love song.

Sana broke their silence when she asked, "Do you ever ask yourself what your purpose is?"

"Purpose? What you trying to say?" Cartier immediately became defensive.

"It's a discussion we had last week in class. My professor broached the subject in a philosophical and spiritual way and asked if any of us had an innate feeling that we were meant to do more with our lives. And if so, did we have a specific purpose that we were moving toward?"

Cartier didn't know how to answer. She didn't want to sound stupid, so she answered the question with a question.

"What about you?"

Sana replied, "I've been thinking for days on this, and I think I was placed on earth to eventually help the elderly. In what capacity, I don't know yet. But I know that I'll be a voice and will make a difference."

Now Cartier understood. What was her purpose? How could she make a difference and, most importantly, did she want to?

"Let me think on it and get back to you."

Sana grinned and nodded. She stood to leave when Cartier said, "And thank you."

"For what?"

"Making me think about something other than my troubles. If only for a moment."

After pouring herself three more glasses of wine, Cartier decided who she should call—who she could talk to. She dialed his number and Caesar answered.

She took a deep breath and exhaled. "Can we talk?"

"Of course, Cartier. I'm here for you," he replied.

The next day, Cartier found herself parking her Bugatti outside of a towering high-rise in Lower Manhattan. She got out of her car and stared up at the structure. It reminded her of her place in Miami. It was the best money could buy. This location was one of many for Caesar. He had homes, properties, and penthouse suites throughout the country. His net worth was rumored to be in the hundreds of millions—maybe even billions, but no one knew exactly. However, it was clear that he was exceptionally rich and powerful.

It was the first day of winter, so she bundled up in an expensive mink. Under it she wore a cream Chloé wool V-neck dress and ankle boots that showed off her shapely legs and cleavage. Cartier entered the ornate lobby, where she was greeted by the doorman. She informed him who she was there to see, and he called up to the penthouse suite to confirm her arrival.

After hanging up, he said to her, "He's expecting you."

She smiled and strutted through the lobby with her heels click-clacking loudly against the marble floor and pressed for the elevator. Once inside, she pushed for the top floor and sighed with nervousness. She didn't know what to expect tonight with Caesar. Things had been moving smoothly with them with only that one hiccup—that robbery. But arriving at his place, and being dressed the way she was dressed, she figured it might send him the wrong signals. She wanted his company tonight. She wanted to talk to Caesar and be able to express herself. Head had her fucked up, and she wanted to escape.

The elevator ascended straight to the penthouse suite without any stops. When the gold doors opened, she was instantly greeted by one of Caesar's men, Manolo. He nodded and told her to follow him.

Everything inside the penthouse suite was top-of-the-line and 3,000 square feet of absolute luxury. There were four bedrooms and a huge terrace with a private bar and barbecue overlooking the city. The place had a panoramic view of the metropolis, and there was a fireplace in the dining room along with a baby grand piano.

"I'm glad you came," she heard Caesar say behind her as she removed her mink and folded it over her arm.

She turned and saw him entering the grand room with a wide smile on his face. He was wearing a Disney shirt and jeans and he was barefoot, looking comfortable in his home.

"I'm glad to be here," Cartier responded.

"So, is everything okay with you? When we talked yesterday, you sounded quite upset."

She took another deep breath and locked eyes with him. Simply staring at Caesar made Cartier erupt into emotions. The tears started to fall from her eyes, and she dropped her coat on the floor. She was a strong bitch—respected and powerful, but for some reason she couldn't control her emotions. She was all over the place.

Caesar pulled her in close and allowed her to cry in his arms with her face against his chest. "It's okay. You can tell me anything," he said.

She didn't know where to start. He invited her to sit on the couch with him. He ordered his men and the staff to give them some privacy. Alone, Cartier finally opened up to him, telling Caesar all about her troubles with Head. He listened intently. He cared.

"You are a very beautiful woman, Cartier, and no man should have the authority to upset you like this," Caesar told her. "And if you need it to go away, it can go away."

"No. I love him, Caesar. Please."

"You love him, but does he love you the same?"

She didn't answer him. Instead, she sat there close to him in silence, maybe pondering the question inside her mind. Caesar kept his eyes fixed on her and started to gently stroke her hands. His touch slowly reached to her wrists and then he smoothly touched her thighs.

"I'm here for you, Cartier. You want a problem to go away, it can go away. You want it to stay, and then it will stay," he assured her.

She smiled. It happened quickly but subtly, nearly catching her off guard. Caesar leaned closer to her, pressing his lips against hers almost unwittingly and kissed her. She didn't resist. They kissed passionately as Caesar's hands roamed across her fine body and began to undress her bit by bit.

It didn't take long for the two of them to become sexually entangled in Caesar's giant bed, both of them naked and still hungrily kissing each other. Cartier was on her back, her legs spread for him. She wanted this, and he wanted it too. He had wanted Cartier since their first sit-down. With her pussy throbbing and wet, he penetrated her nice and slow. She moaned and wrapped her arms around him as his hard dick began to thrust in and out of her, and she straddled her legs around him as they fucked in the missionary position.

Several passionate positions and several orgasms later, Cartier found herself nestled against Caesar in his bed. Her face was against his chest and his hold around her was comforting. He wanted her to stay the night, and she decided to do so. She wasn't in any rush to go back home. She wanted to be comforted and continue their pillow talk. They talked and talked until she fell asleep in his arms.

The next morning, the bright sunrays shining through the large floor-to-ceiling windows kindly woke Cartier up. When she fully opened her eyes, she saw Caesar was already dressed. She figured that was her cue to get up and leave too. She removed herself from his large, comfortable bed and went searching for her scattered clothing.

"What are you doing?" he asked her.

"I'm about to leave. I assume you have a busy day today," she replied.

"No. You don't need to rush to leave. Lay back down and relax. I'll make us breakfast," he said.

Cartier was taken aback—*Breakfast?*

"What would you like to eat this morning?" he asked.

"It doesn't matter. I trust your judgment," she said.

"Good."

He left the bedroom, giving Cartier time to enjoy the comfort, coziness, and luxuriousness of the penthouse bedroom. She spent several minutes lying in bed and then decided to start her day. Last night was fun, but this morning she felt some guilt. She had just gotten married and had already cheated on her husband—and without protection.

Fuck!

Cartier showered and put on one of Caesar's T-shirts and joined him in the gourmet kitchen for breakfast. He placed a plate of omelets and potatoes in front of her. The aroma coming from the food was mouthwatering, and Cartier couldn't wait to dig in. Last night's sexual tryst gave her a healthy appetite. The first bite of the omelet nearly gave Cartier another orgasm. It was tasty and she already wanted seconds.

As she ate, Caesar sat across from her and sipped on his coffee. In a businesslike tone, he said, "Tomorrow, I will tell Lena that I want a divorce from her. And soon you can take the time to know my son."

She nearly choked on her eggs. "What?"

"If you want, you can run a faction of my business or you can become my housewife," he added.

Cartier stopped eating and dropped her fork. *Say what now?* She thought she had heard him wrong. He had to be joking.

"I want you fully committed into my life," said Caesar.

"I'm married."

"I am too," he replied.

The sex was good, but she wasn't about to divorce Head over last night. It was a fling. A one-night stand—nothing more, nothing less. *Wasn't it?*

"Does this mean that you love me?" she asked him.

"I love the way you make me feel. I love your feisty attitude, Cartier. I love how you're hard on the outside and soft and feminine inside. But to answer your question, I am not in love with you."

To Cartier, that wasn't enough. She had a man that loved her, she believed. "Well, I know Head and I have our differences, but I know he loves me and he tries," she stated.

Caesar laughed at her reply. "You crazy," he replied in his thick accent. "You believe your marriage is love?"

"It's something worth fighting for, and we do have love."

"Don't be naïve, Cartier. I know you're smarter than that."

She didn't appreciate how he was talking to her—like he was making fun of her marriage to Head. Caesar was a powerful and wealthy man, but Cartier wasn't about to be talked to like she was some off-brand bitch. It felt like she gave him some pussy and now he wanted to change up on her. Enough was enough.

She stood up abruptly from the table, slightly upset. Breakfast was suddenly over. "I'm done here, Caesar. I'm going home to my husband," she announced.

"I didn't mean to upset you."

It was too late for that. She strongly eyed Caesar and said to him, "And I would like to keep our business relationship business."

He nodded. "I agree."

But before she could leave the kitchen, Caesar had one concluding thing to say to her.

He stared at Cartier and said to her, "The only reason your husband is still alive is because of you. I could have easily had him killed and forced your hand to be with me."

Cartier stood there after hearing that chilling statement and she appeared to be undaunted by it. This time, instead of submitting to him because of his name and status, she intensely fixed her eyes on him and countered with, "No one forces me to do shit! Do you understand that?"

Caesar smiled at her reaction. He then said to her, "Now that's what I really like about you—your assertiveness and your slick mouth."

She spun around and walked out of the room. It was time to go.

27

Head huffed and puffed like he was going to blow someone's house down. He was about to come hard inside of Cartier. She was riding him like a bull rider, fighting to stay on the dick. Her pussy was dripping wet and contracting for Head. They were having their best sex ever—the time of their lives. It felt like the Bahamas all over again. It didn't matter where they fucked—the bedroom, the kitchen, living room, even in the shower; they were like two horny teenagers who couldn't keep their hands off of each other.

"I'm gonna come!" Head announced.

He grabbed her ass and looked up at her. Cartier was the best, and Head couldn't get enough of her. Since he had arrived back from Michigan, she had been extra horny and on Head like a bear after that sweet honey.

But it was guilt about her affair with Caesar. Cartier wanted to connect with her husband without arguing. She wanted to prove Caesar wrong.

"Come for me, baby," she cried out. "Fuck me! Fuck me!"

"Oh shit! Oh shit!" he cried out, feeling his sexual eruption brewing.

He reached up and cupped her tits as she vigorously moved her ass back and forth against him, her pussy swallowing his hard dick whole. She soon felt him come inside of her and she came too, as they took each other into the stratosphere.

Head had no idea what brought on Cartier's desire to fuck almost every day since he had been back in town, but he wasn't complaining. He took full advantage of her hormones raging out of control. Head wanted to spend some magical time with his wife before his next trip to Flint, and magical it was.

Sex made Head hungry. He got up and put on a robe and went to the kitchen. He made himself a healthy sandwich and downed a Pepsi. He felt good, like he was finally on the right track with Cartier mentally and physically. Eventually he wanted his wife to join him in Michigan and see all that he hoped to accomplish.

She would become his dominant queen among his sister wives. He knew his agenda was most likely years away because Cartier was so stubborn. It would take time for Head to fully indoctrinate her to his new beliefs, but he was hopeful that in the end it would all work out just as he had imagined.

One example to Head that he could manifest his polygamist dreams and live as King Solomon and build his Black Wall Street with Cartier was how she handled the Pebbles scandal. Brother Kareem told him that women were born to accept and forgive what society labeled as infidelity because that was a manmade law. He had preached that a man can't be unfaithful because men were never born to have one wife or one girlfriend. Although Cartier cursed, fought, and screamed about Pebbles, she ultimately accepted that she had been sharing Head with another woman. When she found out Pebbles was pregnant, Cartier put on the same show, but again, she accepted it. Head was sure that she would accept his sister wives. Maybe just not right away. There was still work he needed to do on her.

His next trip to Flint was in a week, but before he left again, he planned on making a pit stop. He had one home in order, and now it was time to get his second home in order.

Head knocked on her door several times before she decided to open it. Pebbles came into his view with a blank gaze. He couldn't tell if she was happy to see him or not. But she was. She reached out to hug him closely. They kissed each other and she pulled him into her apartment, ready to play house with her man—her baby's father.

Head crouched before her and kissed and caressed her protruding belly. He could feel his child moving around inside of her.

"Is it a boy or girl?" he asked.

"I don't know yet. I wanted you to be with me at the appointment to find out.

"Okay, set it up."

"I will," she assured him. "I missed you so much."

"I missed you too."

Pebbles smiled. Her mother was right. *They always come back.*

It didn't take long for Pebbles to be truly forgiving. They ordered Chinese food and then relaxed on the sofa. Pebbles was five months pregnant, and she was carrying large and low. She told Head about her food cravings and how she wanted to decorate the nursery. Again, it was something she wanted to do with him. He saw the boxes upon boxes of baby gifts that he assumed were things her friends had bought, or maybe she had bought them with the money he would send her each month.

Head amicably agreed to all of her demands as he massaged her swollen feet. His attentiveness helped Pebbles relax and think about their future. It was at that moment that she spotted his wedding band. A large lump formed in her throat that she swallowed away, along with the tears that wanted to fall. She wasn't going to do it. She wasn't going to fall apart in front of him again because she knew he would get up and walk out her front door.

"So," she managed to finally squeeze out, "baby shower or no baby shower?"

"I'm not really up for it. You know how I feel about people being in my business. And I'm sure your friends will be there snapping pictures and posting. But it's up to you. If you want one then I'll slide through for a minute." Head was getting cocky with his affair, knowing that Cartier would find out if he went to the shower.

Pebbles shook her head. "Then no baby shower. I don't need it. Well, we don't need it. Our baby will have everything with two loving parents."

"I want a boy," he volunteered.

The statement melted her heart. "You do?"

"Absolutely. I want someone to carry my name."

Head stayed with Pebbles for the week before boarding a plane and heading back out to Michigan. The elephant in the room was never mentioned.

28

SIX WEEKS LATER

The morning sickness had become continuous for Cartier. Since last week she found herself rushing into the bathroom, hovering her head over the toilet, and throwing up like she was bulimic. She stayed in the bathroom for well over a half-hour, throwing up or dry heaving. It didn't take a rocket scientist to figure out what was wrong with her. She assumed that she was pregnant, but she wouldn't be sure of it until she took a pregnancy test. Finishing her business in the toilet, she stood up and stared at herself in the mirror. *Pregnant,* she thought. It was what she had asked for.

She went into her bedroom and took a seat in a chair. She heaved a sigh. Once again, Head was in Flint handling his business. He'd been gone for a week now, and she missed him. He promised to be back home in time for Valentine's Day. Lately, their marriage had been going good—going strong. They were communicating and they were having great sex. She wanted to trust Head again, and so far, it was gradually working.

She hadn't seen Harlem in months, and though Cartier was worried about her, she couldn't dwell on the girl's absence. She had her own life to live, and if Harlem didn't want to come back or reach out, then that was her choice. She was a big girl and making her own choices, whether Cartier agreed with them or not. Cartier was hurt, though. After everything she had done for Harlem she felt she at least deserved an explanation.

Business with Caesar was still going strong. Since their sexual tryst, things had been strictly business between them. Cartier was making money hand over fist.

"I need something to drink," Cartier said to herself.

She went into the kitchen and poured herself a full glass of orange juice. She downed the juice quickly and poured herself another. It seemed like it was going to be a regular day for Cartier. The only thing she wanted to do was relax.

Seated at the kitchen table, Cartier decided to finally go through her mail. It had been sitting there for a few days now. She opened several pieces of mail that were irrelevant to her. But then she came across a letter that stood out. It was addressed to Mr. & Mrs. Henry 'Head' Jackson. She tore open the envelope and there was a letter inside. The writing wasn't even a full paragraph. It simply said: *Cartier, leave my man alone or die.*

First the cards, now a threatening letter. It had been months since she had received a cardstock. She fumed. *When is it all going to stop?* She read the sentence several times and wondered who could have written it. Cartier ran into her bedroom and pulled all the cardstocks from her dresser drawer and walked back to the kitchen to examine them. Was it the same person?

She grabbed her cell phone and started to dial Head's number. She was ready to call and confront him about the letter that was mailed to her—curse him out and ask him what the fuck was up. It had to be from a bitch he was fucking from Flint. But she thought against it and ended the call. Cartier came up with a better idea. She decided to fly to Flint in the morning to see for herself what was happening out there.

Lil Foe and Roddy were called upon to take the trip with her. She needed her hired shooters to have her back as a precaution. For all she knew, she was walking straight into some crazy woman's trap. Whoever she was, the note made it clear that she wanted Cartier's husband all to herself.

At the airport with just over an hour before boarding time, the three of them rushed to TSA for screening.

"Y'all take out your license and hold it with your boarding pass," she instructed. "And take off your sneakers and belts so we can just breeze through. I'm not missing this flight."

Both did as they were told. Cartier then called Majestic on a burner phone to make sure he had set up what she had asked. It was short notice, but he came through.

"Yo," he answered.

"Is it done?"

"Yeah, my little man will be waiting at an address that I'ma text you. Three ninas, five a piece."

Cartier hung up confident that she would be able to get her hands on the firearms needed before they rocked up to an unknown address. As they snaked through the line, she couldn't front. She was nervous. If she got there and it was an affair then she knew she would have to leave Head once and for all and not look back. But if it turned out that this mistress was really plotting to murder her, then Cartier wasn't certain that when she killed the bitch that she would have the strength to not have Head killed too.

They all placed their carryon duffel bags into the trays and stepped through the body scan one by one. Cartier went first and was cleared. As she grabbed her Prada and duffel, a small commotion began to stir from a group of TSA agents who were now huddling together. The line was paused, a few walkie-talkies were clicking on and off, and then several more TSA agents and airport security came running over. Cartier, Lil Foe, and Roddy exchanged bewildered looks. Most began to think the same thing: A bomb must have been discovered.

Within minutes Roddy was tackled to the ground and Lil Foe started swinging, trying to help his friend.

"Get the fuck off me!" Roddy screamed as they placed plastic flex cuffs on his wrists. He kept trying to wiggle free. Everyone gawked with their mouths open. What had the thugs done?

Cartier was wide-eyed and frozen. She watched as Lil Foe fought three TSA agents like a heavyweight prize fighter. His arms were swiftly swinging with powerful blows backing them all down. It was Cartier's inclination to jump in. She only hesitated to think about her unborn child.

Lil Foe caught eye contact with his boss and yelled, "Nah, Cartier. I got this!" and she chilled.

It seemed like the fist fight lasted forever before at least nine agents were able to restrain Lil Foe taking him to the ground. Ultimately, both men were dragged away.

Eventually everyone learned that Roddy had a gun in his carryon bag. Cartier knew it was unintentional, but damn. The passengers who were already cleared were allowed to go to their gates, and those who had not been cleared griped and screamed out in frustration because that section was shut down and they had to filter into other lines.

Cartier's flight was leaving in less than thirty minutes, and she didn't know what to do. She was amped from the commotion and decided that she needed closure. She had been up against worse, she thought.

The 757 touched down on the runway at Bishop International Airport early that afternoon. It wasn't how she had planned it, but Cartier arrived in Flint alone. She departed the plane with her carryon and went into the terminal. It was a brisk day in Flint, but she came dressed for the weather.

Outside the terminal she got into a cab and told the driver that she needed to make more than one stop.

"What's the first address?" he asked.

She gave him the address from Majestic. She still needed to go and purchase the burners.

The driver eyed his well-dressed female passenger. "Do you know where this is? It's not a good part of town."

"I won't be there long, but if you're worrying about getting paid, I can pay up front."

He didn't want her to pay up front because he planned on driving her in circles to run up her bill.

"First time in Michigan?"

"It is. But if you'll excuse me, I don't want to be rude, but I got calls to make and don't want to chitchat. I'm not in the mood."

"You're not being rude at all." The cabbie clicked on the meter and chuckled inside. He was only asking so he could determine how hard he could play her.

Cartier pulled out her cell and called Majestic, who answered on the first ring. Whispering, she told him what had happened and instructed that he find someone to bail Roddy and Lil Foe out. Majestic was uncomfortable with her going alone, but she convinced him this would be a quick trip.

She sat back and gazed out the window while the cab drove through the city. To Cartier, the place looked bleak—cold, unfriendly, and poor. *How can anyone live out here?* As the driver drove through the town, Cartier also wondered what would make Head start a business out here—in particular, a car wash. To her, it seemed like there was no money to be made in Flint, except maybe in drug dealing. Now that seemed profitable in such a town. She closed her eyes and fretted about what she was walking into.

Over an hour later, Cartier was awakened by the cab driver. All the stress and traveling had exhausted her. And she was starving. Right now she was craving Krispy Kreme glazed donuts and a slice of New York pizza.

She looked around and saw what looked like an apocalypse. Most of the buildings looked abandoned, but she could clearly see that they were occupied. She wished that she already had a burner on her instead of going to buy one.

"I'll only be a moment," she said.

He tapped the meter. "You see what you already owe. It's your dime."

Cartier eyed the nearly three-hundred-dollar tab. "It's not an issue."

When she tried to grab her duffel, which had the money for the guns inside, and her Prada bag, the alert cabbie thought he was about to get hustled.

"You can't take both. Why are you leaving with your luggage and purse if you're coming right back?"

"Didn't I offer to pay you up front?"

"I think I'll take you up on that."

Cartier rolled her eyes. She looked again at the dilapidated building and a wave of fear came over her. She didn't want to be left alone in the middle of nowhere in a state and town that she didn't know. She wanted to compromise. She peeled off six hundred from her stash and handed it to the driver and took out another fifteen hundred and stuffed it in her jacket pocket.

"That's what I owe and more. I'm going to leave my purse so that you won't be tempted to take off and leave me for another fare. I promise that I will give you a fifty percent tip if you wait for me, but I'm going to need your ID."

"My ID?"

She pointed toward his cab driver credentials. It was a no-brainer. Quickly he handed it to her and told her to take her time. He had already turned a sixty-dollar fare into three hundred and counting plus a hefty tip.

Cartier stepped out of the cab and the cold air woke her up. As she walked up the rickety porch steps and looked at the broken windows patched with cardboard and duct tape, she thought maybe she hadn't dressed appropriately for the occasion. She was wearing her most expensive mink coat, Rolex watch, engagement ring, and diamonds. Cartier wanted to look her best when she came face-to-face with Head's Michigan mistress, and she also thought she would have her two goons by her side.

You know when you have a feeling that your whole day is about to be fucked and you should just turn around and go back inside your house? Cartier had that feeling. Her intuition told her to get back inside the cab and make a beeline back to the airport. But her pride and stubbornness superseded all logic, and she forged on.

As she knocked her stomach was doing somersaults and she didn't know if it was her nerves or morning sickness. She heard heavy footsteps coming and she felt like a punk bitch. *Damn, maybe I should have left my jewels and the additional cash in my Prada.* She didn't know why she was having such reservations; Majestic had vouched for them. But instinctively she pulled off her ring and watch and stuffed them in her pockets.

A dirty looking dude with a dead eye opened the door smoking a blunt. He looked her up and down and then smiled wide. Instantly, she relaxed.

"You Cartier?"

She nodded.

"Come in. We gotchu."

Cartier was led inside the condemned building. It was just as cold indoors as it was out. She had to literally watch her step or she would fall through the floor. It was sparsely furnished—a chair here, a loveseat there.

Two huge rats came running past her feet, nearly aging her ten years. She wanted to yelp but bit her tongue.

Inside the living room were two other men smoking blunts as well. No one introduced themselves and they got right down to business.

"Where the others?" one asked.

Cartier didn't miss a beat. "Waiting for me outside."

"Outside?" he continued. "They too good to come in and meet us?"

"This isn't a family reunion. I came to do business. Let's get this over with."

He smirked and then flicked his finished blunt directly toward Cartier. He lifted up his shirt to reveal three guns tucked in his waistband. "You got the money?"

"Yeah, fifteen hundred, right?" Of course she no longer needed three guns, but she didn't want them to know that Lil Foe and Roddy weren't waiting for her outside. Cartier unzipped the duffel so she could quickly toss the guns inside and be gone.

"I said five!" the man unnecessarily yelled, his voice echoing through the almost empty home. "Five K a piece."

Cartier chuckled. "What I look like?"

The guy who opened the door came up behind her and placed a .45 to the back of her head and replied, "You look like a meal ticket. Now run ya shit, bitch, 'fore I park one in your dome!"

"Really? Y'all gonna do this shit to me!"

They were already on her, snatching off her mink coat and ripping the duffel from her hand. They patiently waited as they had her unscrew her diamond earrings from her ears. They tossed her items into a black trash bag in silence. Cartier had stopped talking, and they had no need to keep speaking. They spoke with their eyes, each exchanging hateful looks.

The trio backpedaled toward the back door with three guns trained on Cartier and then took off running through a back alleyway. Cartier had to hold back tears. There wasn't any reason for them to take flight. No one would be chasing them.

Humiliated, Cartier got back into the cab. It was evident that she no longer had her coat.

"What happened to you?"

"Just drive. Please!"

When they were far enough away she finally gave the cabbie the address that was on the letter that had been sent to her.

"How far is it from here?" she asked the driver.

"About two hours," he replied.

"Okay."

The cab traveled north toward the rural part of town. A couple hours later, they turned onto a dirt road and arrived at a huge estate. Cartier didn't know what to expect. There was land and trees and several vehicles were parked on the property. She wondered who owned the place. Where was Head? Why did she receive a letter from this place?

Cartier's options were slim. She had traveled so far and just wanted to see what was what. She couldn't turn around now, and she had no money left and owed a hefty bill.

"Listen, this is gonna sound like game, but that tip I told you about was stolen at our last stop along with your ID."

"Are you kidding me!"

"Calm down. I'm going to call a friend and have the money wired to me. If you wait here for me we can go together to a Western Union. I'll bless you with twenty-five hundred for your troubles and also my fare. But I'm going to need a huge favor. If I'm not out in ten minutes call the police. Do we have a deal?"

"Sure. Sounds good to me."

Cartier called Majestic before getting out of the cab and quickly told him what had happened. He was furious and began screaming about murder and revenge and she had to quiet his rage. She instructed him to wire her the money and get on the next flight out there. She was going to text him an address just in case. Majestic said he didn't like that just in case precaution and for her to wait on him, but she refused. She hung up and quickly texted Majestic the address from the envelope and removed herself from the backseat with her purse. Stepping onto strange grounds, Cartier felt naked and vulnerable without her gun. There was no telling what kind of threat awaited her inside the cabin or beyond. It was foolish to come alone, but she had made the choice and she wasn't about to turn back now.

With awareness, she approached the front door and knocked a few times. She felt a bit of apprehension, but she put on her game face to show whoever was on the other side of the door that she meant business. Head had to be somewhere on the property, and she wasn't leaving until she confronted him.

The front door opened and Cartier found herself face-to-face with a pretty, pregnant white girl.

"Hello," the young girl greeted politely. "Welcome. Are you new to our family?"

Cartier didn't know how to respond to the question. *Family?* she thought. *What family?*

"I'm Mandy. Come inside," the girl said.

Cartier slowly and cautiously entered the cabin. From her prompt observation, she saw that it was a homey place, and it was spotless. Standing in the main room, Cartier noticed three children running around the place, ages two through six. Clearly she could see they weren't Head's. From the window she saw the cab driver peel out, and she knew she should have done the same.

"You're pretty," one of the children complimented Cartier.

She smiled but kept her eyes sharp and open and she searched for that one anomaly. She had no idea what was going on. Moving farther into the place, there were three other women in different stages of pregnancy. One of them was Mandy's twin, Kandy, and then there was Melissa and Jacki. The women were all smiles and so far showed nothing but hospitality toward Cartier as they ushered her into their home, referring to her as their new sister.

"Our daddy, Malachi Muhammad, will be home soon to greet you," said Melissa.

Malachi Muhammad? Cartier wondered. *Who the hell is he?*

"Here, we're all one big family and we share everything," said Jacki warmly, an odd smile plastered across her face.

What kind of cult shit is this? Cartier asked herself.

Soon, they heard a vehicle arriving. The girls became excited, exclaiming, "He's back."

Finally, Cartier was about to meet this Malachi Muhammad.

The young girls became animated, as did the children. It felt like they were brainwashed by this one individual, and Cartier grew concerned. Had she made a mistake coming here? She had no idea who or what was about to come through that front door.

She stood there firmly and waited, feeling a tinge of apprehension. She attached her eyes to that front door. If needed, she would fight for her life and her baby's.

She heard someone coming up the steps and onto the porch, and then the front door opened and he entered the cabin—and he wasn't alone. Cartier's eyes grew wide with immediate shock. Her mouth gaped. This is Malachi Muhammad? It was Head, and standing next to him with her pregnant stomach was Harlem.

"Are you fuckin' kidding me?" Cartier shrieked. "What the fuck is going on here?!"

Head was shocked to see his wife. Harlem smirked at Cartier and rubbed her stomach. She couldn't wait to explain to Cartier that it was Head's baby that she was carrying and not Sincere's. The entire time, she and Head had been fucking right under Cartier's nose.

"Cartier, how did you find out about this place?" Head asked her.

She ignored his question and continued to glare at Harlem with her protruding stomach and wild smirk.

"Is Head the father?" she asked her.

"Yes. He is," Harlem replied smugly.

Cartier was devastated. It was all too much to take in at once. One thought that Cartier would react violently and tear Harlem apart, but shockingly, the opposite happened. She fainted.

artier opened her eyes and hoped it was all a nightmare. It had to be. There was no way Harlem was pregnant by Head. There was no way Harlem could have betrayed her like that, after everything she did for her. But lifting herself up and looking around, she wasn't in her bedroom and it wasn't all a nightmare. Everything was for real.

"You fainted," Mandy said to her.

She was trying to nurse Cartier, but Cartier rudely pushed her away. She didn't want anything to do with anybody inside the cuckoo's nest. She hurriedly removed herself from the bed and found herself dressed in a long white gown. They had the audacity to undress her and put her in some weird shit.

"Get the fuck away from me!" Cartier cursed at the young woman.

"We're only here to help you through this transition. There's no need to be afraid. Malachi has welcomed you into his home as one of our sister wives," Mandy replied.

"Please stop talking!"

Mandy was still trying to aid her, but Cartier was five seconds away from knocking the bitch out. She wanted to leave. She wanted to confront Head and Harlem. She had overcome the shock, and now she was mad.

"Where is he? Where the hell is my husband? And where is that fuckin' bitch? And why the fuck am I dressed in this fuckin' ridiculous gown?" Cartier screamed out.

"Please, there is no reason for you to be upset!"

"Don't tell me how to feel! Bitch, if you don't find my husband and that bitch in three seconds, I'm gonna fuck you up," Cartier threatened.

Mandy was taken aback by Cartier's hostility and aggressiveness. This was a peaceful family home.

"Sister, please, no violence. I only want to love on you until you feel the energy from Yah's restorative angels. He will fix you just as He's fixed us. You're broken."

"Bitch, don't be saying that dumb shit!"

"Cartier, please calm down," she heard Head say.

She craned her neck and saw Head standing in the doorway. He stared at her intently with his arms composedly folded in front of him, looking like management.

"What is this fuckin' place, Head?" she asked with attitude.

"It's home, Cartier."

His response went left field with her. *Home?* She wanted to charge at him and fuck him up, but she restrained herself. She wasn't in Kansas anymore, and she had no idea what the place was, yet.

"Although your arrival is unexpected, I'm glad you're here. It's time you know the truth," he said.

"Truth? The truth is that you're a lying nigga and I hate you. And where's that bitch Harlem? That lying, cunt bitch."

He stepped closer to her and said, "Cartier, lower your voice. I will not have that type of hostility and attitude in this place. If you give me a minute of your time, then I will explain things to you."

No matter the explanation he gave, Cartier felt that she wasn't going to accept it. She was tired of his lies, his cheating ways, and his deceitfulness.

"I'm a different man here, Cartier," he started.

"Are you fuckin' serious?"

He glared at her and uttered, "Let me finish."

She didn't have a choice. She was alone and hundreds of miles away from home.

"Society set about making rules—laws—that we as citizens have to follow or there will be consequences. I understand if there is no structure then the world could turn into lawless chaos, and we would begin to live like animals instead of humans. But a lot of the laws are outdated— these morality clauses need to be abolished. Nobody is going to tell me that it is for the greater good of the people that we can only love one person at a time," he stated. "Love transcends all understanding. Love makes you wanna do better, be better. When I'm here with my queens, I feel unstoppable. They make me feel like I can conquer anything I put my mind to. And as a unit, one unit, we're going to build things, create a legacy, and birth children that will pick up where we leave off."

He was losing her.

He continued with, "I love you, Cartier. I'm in love with you. And I know that what you can contribute to our family is priceless, but you gotta stop thinking basic. We're brainwashed as kids that we can only have one mom, one pops, and most times we see no pops. You know why? Because mommy done chased him out the house when she found him doing what he was naturally born to do, which is love more than one woman. It's no different than telling a bird to resist its urge to fly or commanding the lion to not roar."

Cartier was convinced that Head had officially lost his mind. He continued to preach to her about how he planned to build a black-owned empire on the backbone of his new family, but she stopped listening. Her only concern was leaving. But then something dawned on her. Was he behind the bizarre and threatening cards that were being sent to her?

"Have you been sending me threatening cards for months?"

"Cards? What? I have no idea what you're talking about."

"Don't play stupid with me, Head. For months, I've been receiving these cardstocks with skulls, daggers, and blood and a single letter written on them. Is it you?"

"Cartier, no. What are you talking about?"

She didn't believe him.

She wanted to get the fuck out of there, but Head took away her ID to get on the flight and he kept her locked in the windowless basement. He wanted to convince her to stay—to join their family, to become a sister wife. He wanted Cartier to believe that there was a better life in Flint—a life more rewarding than what was back in New York.

Cartier hollered and kicked walls and overturned furniture. She became a screaming banshee downstairs, shouting out, "Let me the fuck outta here!" She wanted desperately to escape. But the solid door was locked securely.

Cartier had tired herself out and decided to chill. She felt that any minute now Majestic and Scooter would come through bucking off shots until she was freed. The hate in her heart hoped that they killed everyone inside, including the kids.

Majestic and Scooter arrived in Flint a half-day later. They both hopped on the earliest flight out of JFK and landed in Michigan on a mission. Their boss was no longer answering her burner phone, and the last Majestic had heard she was going into an unknown address. This time Majestic had set up a sure thing. He got their cousin Loogie to drive up from Fort Wayne, Indiana and meet them at the airport.

Majestic and Scooter emerged from the airport looking ready for battle. Both had on jeans, Timbs, warm coats, and deathly glares. Loogie immediately spotted them and stepped out of his red Chrysler 300. The car was too bold for Majestic and Scooter's taste, especially with what they had planned, but they had no choice. Each man gave each other dap and then got into the vehicle just as airport security was walking toward them to insist they move along.

"Yo, thanks, cuz," Majestic said as he turned the heat up a few notches. "You brought those burners we need?"

Loogie nodded. "We straight." He turned toward Scooter, who was sitting in the back passenger's seat. "They inside the duffel under my seat."

Loogie peeled out, not yet knowing where they were going. Scooter leaned low and grabbed the heavy butter soft bag. He unzipped it and saw an arsenal of weaponry. There was a Tech Nine, an Uzi, two .45s, two nines, and a few revolvers.

"Damn, bruh, you think we got enough firepower?" Scooter joked.

"No such thing as enough," Loogie said arrogantly. "Y'all niggas seem like you at war. We don't know what we walkin' into."

Majestic nodded. "True." He reached into his pocket and pulled out a knot held together with a rubber band. "That's for lookin' out."

Loogie grabbed the money with his free hand without ever taking his eyes off the road. He stuffed it in his pocket, knowing from the weight of it that he was taken care of.

"Yo, so where's our first stop?"

Majestic gave him the address to Cartier's last known location. "First we go get our boss and then we hunt down that piece of shit, Andre, who violated her and disrespected me. I'ma make that nigga eat a bullet."

Forty minutes later they pulled up to Great Giant Supermarket.

"What the fuck is this?" Majestic asked as all three of them stared at the store in bewilderment. "You sure this is the address I gave you?"

"This is what you gave me."

Scooter asked, "Did you change the GPS to Michigan? Maybe it's still on your city."

"Nah, my shit is right," Loogie assured them. "Majestic, enter the address on your phone and see what's what."

Quickly Majestic typed the address in his smartphone and they were at the address that Cartier had given him.

"Something ain't right," Scooter said. "Where the fuck she at? She ain't in there, right?"

It was a rhetorical question. The men didn't know what to do. Majestic knew that Cartier said she was going inside someone's home. He surveyed the neighborhood, and there wasn't a house even close to where they were. He called her phone again and it went straight to voicemail.

"Fuck!" he yelled out. Where was she?

"Yo, I'ma go inside and ask some questions. Maybe there are two locations wit' the same address." Scooter needed to stretch his legs. "Y'all want anything?"

Both shook their heads.

Loogie asked what he already knew. "What's next?"

Majestic replied, "We find Dre."

30

For two weeks, Cartier had been locked inside the basement against her will. Every day she tried to strategize on how she was going to get out. Head always made sure to keep the door locked, and her pleas to be released fell on deaf ears. She had morning sickness and did everything in her power to hide it. If Head knew she was pregnant, there was no way he would let her go. She had no idea what Head and the others were going to do to her, but she had to keep hope that she would be released before she began showing. Cartier hoped this wouldn't become her final destination. She missed home. She knew people were worried about her, but she had no way of contacting them. She mostly wondered what happened to Majestic and Scooter. Had Head seen them coming and murdered them? Were they dead?

With only time on your hands to think, a lot of crazy thoughts pop up. Cartier was worried the most about Caesar. Her sudden disappearance would create a problem, and the last thing she needed was problems with a man like him. If she did manage to escape, then how was she going to explain her sudden absence to him? She feared there would be repercussions for her vanishing, and the cartel would believe she had been arrested and flipped.

The sister wives were very friendly to her and only entered the basement as a group and only when Head was home. Cartier peeped that because she would hear the door lock behind them and they had to knock to leave. They kept her fed, but only brought her food with a plastic spoon no matter what was being served. She knew Head was behind that. Cartier needed a weapon if she was going to survive this. A sharp knife would do. Day in and day out, she thought about bashing each of their faces in. But then what? She could beat the shit out of them all, but she would still be a hostage. And then she wrestled with putting her baby's life at risk.

Each girl talked to her as if she was a friend. They wanted Cartier to stay on her own free will. They wanted her to accept their family and accept Malachi Muhammad as her savior.

"He's a good man," said Jacki.

"He's a piece of shit," Cartier retorted.

"Nooooo," Kandy crooned. "He's a man of faith and love and togetherness."

"Malachi Muhammad is taking care of us. He pulled us away from our despair and gave us something to live for," said Mandy.

"We had nothing, and he's given us all of this," Melissa chimed in.

Cartier wanted to throw up. She felt like Amanda Berry. It was a nightmare. She tried to tell the girls that they were all brainwashed. What Head, or whatever they called him, was feeding them was a load of bullshit. It wasn't a family. It was a cult. But all the girls were happy with Head, and they would rather stay with him than go back to their alternatives.

The young white twins that were pregnant by Head particularly turned her stomach. After all the preaching about how the white woman was the devil and the black man's downfall, he had gotten two young white girls pregnant. Cartier couldn't believe his hypocrisy.

But that was just the beginning of Head's two-facedness. One day, Jacki came into her room and said, "I want to show you something."

Cartier thought about her options. Curse her out or play along. Knowing that the success margin of overpowering all four women, getting Head to unlock the basement, overpower him, overpower Harlem, and escape was a fairytale. She figured that the only way out was through making inroads with the women and pulling at their heartstrings. Cartier got up and took a short walk with Jacki as the other three stood off to the side with wide grins and prideful eyes.

There was a bookcase. Jacki pulled on it and it slowly opened as a hidden door. Inside the room was a full-blown drug factory. Cocaine, heroin, and pills were stacked, packaged, and ready for shipment. Cartier's mouth hit the floor. She had no idea. Who was Head? Who was the man she married? He had commonly preached to her about drugs poisoning their people, and how her drug dealing was work for the devil. He had scolded her about her actions in South Beach. He made it appear that he was a completely transformed man who regretted his past as a drug dealer. But this, everything she saw in the basement, it nearly rivaled her operation. He was moving drugs by the boatload. Was he serious?

"Impressive, huh?" Head asked her, showing up suddenly.

"How long has this been going on?" she asked him.

"Long enough to spread across several states and bring in millions."

She looked at him with utter disgust.

"Don't look at me like that, Cartier. In fact, you should admire and respect me. You and I together in business, can you imagine the territories we could take over? We can expand anywhere we want. We can work with or against Caesar. It's all up to you. If you get him to trust you then we can hit his shipments, infiltrate his operation from within, and then, baby, the sky's the limit."

Cartier was silent for a moment as her eyes drank in his operation.

Head then added sincerity to his voice and continued, "I know what you must be thinking, and before you say anything I just want to set the record straight. The only reason I didn't want you to get pregnant is because you are my foundation. Every organization needs a strong infrastructure, and I need your full attention. I know seeing all these women carrying my children must have you feelin' like you're not good enough, and I'm here to tell you that not only are you good enough, but you mean more to me than all of them put together."

"You're a fuckin' fraud!" she cursed. "My self-worth is never wrapped up in how a nigga feel or don't feel about me. And I know these bitches done super-sized your ego, but you ain't all that, baby. Your dick is just ok—no bells and whistles. Remember, I'm the same bitch who rejected you in South Beach when you came begging me to marry you. You know that the *only* reason we ended up together is because Hector was murdered, so stop actin' like you don't know who Cartier Timmons is."

Ouch. Her words hurt him deeply. Head cut his eyes toward his ladies and saw that she had their full attention. The story he had told them of Cartier and how she would kill for him was a slightly different narrative.

Head chuckled to hide his pain. "The big, bad, Cartier Timmons. Of course I know you. I know that you tried to kill me when I rejected you for another woman. I know that it wasn't only my enlightening conversation that made you go ape shit. I'd say the dick played its part."

The days of Cartier being shocked about anything were over. Of course, Harlem told him about their little caper. It was a good play, and if Cartier were in her shoes she would probably have done the same. Hood commandment number one was do your dirt all by your lonesome. And when you violate the code, you suffer the consequences.

"You might as well kill me right now, Head, because I will never become one of these brainwashed bitches you have running around here kissing your ass, thinking you're some kind of god," she strongly stated.

He chuckled creepily and countered with, "I wish it was that simple."

The following week, Cartier was still there.

She had watched the girls load up stash cars and go on drug runs. They all were completely under Head's control. Cartier tried a different approach. It seemed like Jacki was the alpha female out of the four and that Harlem must be the top bitch over Jacki. Harlem never came inside the basement because she knew what was good for her.

"Why do you do this for him?" Cartier directly asked Jacki. "Help me understand."

Jacki could only answer in a way that she understood. "I do this for me and it benefits us. I work better, live better, think better when I am paired with someone as one unit. I love catering to my man—cooking, cleaning, making love to him. It's what brings me joy. It's my purpose in life."

Purpose. There was that word again. "If that's true, then how could you share him with the others? It's not really a pairing, right?"

"Oh, but it is. Things are structured here and when Malachi Muhammad is with me, he's with me. His time, focus, and dedication is to me and only me. He makes me feel as if I am the only person he loves."

"But you're not, though. You may be the chick he loves on Tuesday, but then what? What about his Friday bitch?"

"You can't keep looking into someone else's backyard or you'll never be happy. If I worried about Wednesday through Monday, how does that serve me? It doesn't. All that matters is my perception of happiness. How he treats me."

"What about how he's treating me!" Cartier's voice rose an octave. "I don't want to be here. I want to go home to my family. As a woman you should understand that. As a religious woman you should empathize with allowing my family to suffer not knowing where I am."

Jacki nodded slowly, as if she was fully taking in her words. She replied, "But you don't have any family."

❖ ❖ ❖

Cartier tried to connect with Melissa next. She could see that she was a former addict; all the signs were there.

"How long do you think you can be around all those drugs before you relapse?"

Melissa's eyes widened. How did Cartier know her secret?

"I have it under control."

"Do you?"

Melissa frowned. "I said I did, so drop it. You're being cruel now, and that's not how we live. We live for love and unity, and once you join us then you'll see how Malachi Muhammad's teachings have given me the strength that I never knew I had."

"Does he know? About your drug problem?"

"I don't have a drug problem," Melissa corrected.

"But if he did know, isn't it cruel of him to have you tempted in this way each day for his own gain? His own greed?"

"I know what you're doing."

"And what is that?"

"I'm not letting you out."

"I'm trying to help us, not just me. You need to get out too. We both should leave together. You could come back to New York and I'll pay for your drug treatment at the best facility."

"You don't get it. I don't need drugs anymore. I used drugs to fill a void that I had, to numb my pain. Love was missing from my life, and I only saw the darkest parts of the human race. Malachi Muhammad has shown me compassion and self worth. I matter. What I do—what I contribute to this household matters. And his vision to buy properties and build communities brick-by-brick is more than you're offering. It's more than anyone has ever offered. We're going to make history, and you'll be sorry that you didn't get in on the ground floor."

This was harder than she thought. Cartier had met her match, and it was Head.

Majestic and Scooter had been safely back in New York for weeks. Still no Cartier. They left behind three dead bodies and had managed to retrieve her Rolex watch, which Andre had on his wrist when he was captured. Her other items were sold off. Back in Brooklyn, Majestic took over as the de facto boss until they could either confirm or deny her whereabouts. There was still a business to run.

Lil Foe and Roddy were back on the team, but both felt equally responsible for her disappearance. Majestic and Roddy felt the most guilt. They tried to remain optimistic that if Cartier did make it out of Michigan alive that she wouldn't hold them accountable for their missteps.

31

artier paced the basement. She was trying her best to maintain her sanity. She had been at the place a month, and she could only imagine what was happening to everything she had built. It had to be falling apart. She knew everyone was worried about her, maybe believing that she was dead. It was clear to her that Head wasn't going to let her go anytime soon—maybe not at all. Trying to penetrate the impenetrable wall of Malachi Muhammad was tough. Kandy and Mandy weren't down to help her out either. Everyone had their own unique reason for going along with her confinement. Still, she was determined to try and get back to her old life. She knew Head was growing frustrated with her every day she remained resistant to his cause, and it felt like things were about to come to a confrontational collision between them. Cartier felt Head would do something drastic to try and put her in check—to make her compliant like the others. But unlike the others he had brainwashed, she had something to lose.

Lying on her bed and contemplating her survival, the bedroom door opened unexpectedly.

Seeing Harlem come into the room was difficult. Cartier didn't know what to expect from her. In the past month she had gone to extensive lengths to avoid Cartier, but now they were face-to-face in the room. For a second, they glared at each other—the room thick with animosity. Cartier was ready to go ham and tear into Harlem. She was hard to look at. Seeing her pregnancy and knowing it was Head's baby stirred up a whirlwind of emotions inside Cartier.

After everything she did for the girl, she went behind her back and had sex with her man, her husband, and had gotten pregnant by him. She had been lying to Cartier the entire time. To Cartier, betrayal meant death.

"What the fuck do you want?" Cartier growled at her.

Harlem tossed something onto the bed, a small sack. She said to Cartier, "Just take it."

Cartier stared at the sack and was skeptical to open it and take a look inside. She didn't trust anything about the bitch.

"I should fuck you up, Harlem. I trusted you," Cartier continued to gripe.

"Look, I didn't come in here to fight with you. I came in here to help," she replied.

"Help me?"

"Open the sack, Cartier," Harlem continued.

Dubious, Cartier carefully reached for the sack and looked inside. She was in awe at what she saw. It was her ID, some cash, and a plane ticket. Her burner phone was missing. She looked at Harlem and asked, "Why?"

"Just go, and don't come back here," Harlem replied.

"You're letting me go, just like that?"

"Head isn't here. He won't be back for a few hours, so now is your time to finally leave, Cartier."

"And what about the sister wives?" she asked.

"They won't stop you."

"You know the moment I get back to Brooklyn, you and I are back to being enemies. This shit doesn't change anything."

"As I stand before you, Cartier—on my parents' lives—you and I are enemies now."

Harlem hated Cartier with a passion, and she could no longer take her being there a second longer. Her elaborate plan had backfired. Harlem was young and didn't fully understand matters of the heart. At her age and with her past, she thought love was black and white, and she was unable to understand the gray areas of it.

Harlem would have bet her life that when she told Head that it was Cartier who had shot at him at his great aunt's house, she had signed Cartier's death certificate. The day after she told him, Harlem mailed Cartier the letter with their address on it, knowing she would come. Harlem expected Head would seek revenge and finally see that Cartier didn't love him as she did. But instead of Head murdering Cartier, he set about making sure she was comfortable and tried to convince her to stay—to join them.

Cartier hurriedly got dressed and took flight out the house. She ran up the steps and bolted through the unlocked basement door. Her eyes scanned for the front door, and she ran as fast as her legs allowed.

Harlem gave her a set of car keys to leave in. Outside was a dark blue Ford Taurus. Cartier got behind the steering wheel and started the car. Her whole body was trembling from fear and adrenaline. She pressed her foot to the pedal and drove away fast. She refused to look back.

The flight to JFK airport rapidly ascended into the air with the landing gear retracting. Cartier was finally able to relax and exhale with the plane being in the air. It felt like she had escaped from Camp Crystal Lake with her husband being Jason Voorhees. Head had broken her heart into tiny pieces, glued it back together with lies, and shattered it again. Cartier was emotionally wrecked and didn't know if she could ever fully recover.

32

ana thought she saw a ghost when Cartier walked through the front door.

"Ohmygod, I thought you were dead!" Sana hollered. "I was worried sick about you."

She attempted to hug Cartier but got pushed away. Cartier was in no mood to have a joyous reunion. She was finally home and had a lot to deal with.

"Cartier, what happened to you? You've been gone a month. I called and called and tried to get in contact with you. I really thought you were dead," Sana repeated.

"It's a long story," replied Cartier.

Sana wanted to hear it, but she could tell that Cartier wasn't in the mood to tell it—not now.

"Did anyone come by here?" she asked Sana.

"Yes, a few people, including some scary looking men that were asking about you. I told them I had no idea where you were," Sana answered. "And Majestic and Scooter came by several times worried."

Cartier didn't need a description of the scary looking men. She already knew who Sana was talking about. For a moment, she didn't know which direction she was going. It felt like everything was happening too fast. She was stressed out. Her husband had six kids on the way, and she would become baby mama number seven in his sick, twisted new world. Cartier knew she was pregnant; she just hoped that it wasn't Head's. Now she hoped it was Caesar's baby, from that night they had unprotected sex and he came inside her.

Her first priority was to contact Caesar and explain her absence, and then she needed to contact Majestic and Scooter and let them know that she was still alive and see if they were able to hold down her business. While she was locked up in exile with nothing but time, she couldn't figure out why Majestic never came for her. She kept replaying the events and realized that when she hastily texted him in the cab, she had sent the incorrect address. Instead of texting the abbreviation for highway, she had texted the abbreviation for freeway.

Cartier spent the entire day on her phone trying to pull her life back together. One thing she made sure to do was contact a locksmith to change her locks on the apartment door ASAP. Head had a key, and she didn't want anything to do with him. When she contacted Caesar, he was upset.

"You rise back from the dead—it must be a miracle. Unfortunately for you, I don't believe in miracles," Caesar said.

"He kidnapped me, Caesar," she blurted out.

"Who kidnapped you?"

"My husband," she cried out.

Cartier was rambling. Not wanting to talk over the phone, he said to her, "We need to meet . . . soon."

"Just tell me when and where."

"I'll contact you with the time and location," said Caesar. "I'll be back in New York sometime next week. Don't leave town unexpectedly again."

Their call ended, and Cartier was extremely nervous and upset. She didn't know if her next meeting with Caesar would be her last meeting with anyone. She didn't want to panic, but now that she was at odds with her husband and somewhat on Caesar's bad side because of her sudden disappearance, it felt like she was living on borrowed time.

Since Cartier arrived home, she had been running around the place like a chicken with its head cut off. She made numerous phone calls and removed numerous guns from her bedroom closet to keep at reach. She went pulling everything out of the kitchen drawer and the mysterious cards were spilled onto the table.

"Cartier, please tell me what is going on?" Sana desperately wanted to know.

"I want Head and Harlem dead," she announced.

Sana was shocked by the crazy statement. "What happened? Did they have something to do with your disappearance?"

As Cartier was talking and crying out, the cards on the table caught Sana's interest, with her love for word puzzles. She went to the table and started to mess around with the cards. There were so many to try and decipher. After a couple of minutes, Sana uttered to herself mostly, "If there was an *O*, this would read, 'You're dead.'"

Cartier stopped what she was doing and stared at Sana. "What did you say?"

"I said if there was an *O*, then it would read, 'You're dead,'" Sana repeated.

Now Sana had Cartier's undivided attention. Sana had the letters spelled out on the table and had written the letter *O* on a blank piece of paper. Cartier was shocked. Her mouth dropped. *What type of head games is someone playing?*

"There was an *O* that I tossed away—I think when I was at the cemetery," Cartier admitted.

She would have never figured it out. She wondered who the fuck was behind this.

"Congratulations, you are definitely pregnant," the doctor told her.

Cartier wanted to be thrilled by the news. Previously she wanted to have a baby by Head, but now things done changed and she felt regret more than joy.

"How many weeks?" she asked him.

"Eleven weeks."

The time frame of her conceiving meant that the baby was a maybe baby—maybe it was Head's and maybe it was Caesar's. She placed her hand against her stomach and sighed. Her life was changing and she didn't know if it was going to be for the better or the worse.

"So far, everything looks healthy. We can schedule your first ultrasound to make sure," the doctor said.

His name was Allen Smith. He was thirty-five, handsome and he was polite with a bright smile. Dr. Smith had that personable touch that good doctors possess. He had a warm vibe, and Cartier trusted him to deliver her baby.

"Okay," she faintly replied.

"I know the father is going to be happy," Allen said. "Does he know?"

The mention of the baby's father unexpectedly made Cartier burst into tears. She was supposed to be happy and strong, but her emotions were all over the place. Though she was a hardcore bitch about her business, at the end of the day, she was still a woman with feelings. She wanted love and happiness, and she had none right now.

"I'm sorry, did I say something to upset you?" he asked her.

She continued to sob.

Allen approached closer and kindly placed his hand on her shoulder. He said, "Whatever is bothering you, I'm sure everything will work itself out. Just have faith."

"Everything is so fucked up," Cartier said between sobs and sniffles.

"If you're having this baby alone, there are plenty of women who are single mothers. But you seem strong enough to raise this baby on your own should that be the case," he stated.

He handed her some tissue to wipe the tears from her eyes. Allen had no idea who Cartier was. In his eyes, she was a single woman who was pregnant.

He took her hand and said, "My mother was a single mother and I turned out okay. I think."

The small joke made Cartier smile and chuckle a little.

"You see? There's that smile I've been waiting for," he said. "You'll be fine."

His words offered her some comfort. She appreciated his sharing and trying to make her feel better.

She left the OB-GYN in a lighter mood, but her problems weren't going to go away because some doctor made a few jokes. Cartier had issues that weren't common to the everyday pregnant woman. One of those issues was the death threat Sana had figured out. Cartier was convinced that Citi was behind the notes because although Kola described her as critically injured, her death was never confirmed. She and Apple both felt that Kola should have finished the bitch off.

Cartier thought about reaching out to Apple to tell her about her suspicion, but she decided against it. Cartier knew that Apple and her insatiable thirst for revenge would have her stressed more, and she didn't want to lose her baby like Kola lost hers. Besides, Citi was a punk bitch hiding behind some idle threats.

Cartier climbed into her car and sighed again. Eleven weeks pregnant—the biggest question was, who was the father of her baby?

33

A full moon hovered in the sky on the late, cold winter night. Cartier brought her Beamer to a stop on the dead-end block in a part of Brooklyn she didn't want to be in at the moment—Red Hook. She climbed out of her vehicle dressed warmly in her winter coat. Directly in front of her was a large parking lot once known as "Graving Dock One" located at the Vigor Shipyard. During its heyday, the dock was regarded as making Red Hook the center of the shipping industry in New York. But Cartier knew she wasn't there to receive a history lesson. Caesar had returned from his trip to Puerto Rico early and demanded they meet immediately. This was the place he requested to meet, and he wanted her to come alone.

Eyeing the two black SUV's parked near the warehouse, Cartier knew she was the last to join the party. Releasing a cavernous sigh, she cautiously approached the warehouse. She had no idea if she would come out alive.

It felt like she was in some kind of horror movie. The setting was extra creepy. Every step she took felt heavy. Her mind was racing with concerns, and she wondered if Caesar would kill a pregnant woman.

She knocked a few times on the steel door and it opened immediately with one of Caesar's thugs on the other side. The moment Cartier stepped into the sprawling warehouse, she heard screaming. It was a sharp and agonizing scream, and it echoed from deep within the building to where she stood.

"Wait here. He'll be with you shortly," said the armed goon.

The screaming continued, and Cartier could only imagine what was happening. It definitely was a man she heard screaming out in absolute agony. She waited there for ten minutes before the torturous screams came to a dramatic stop and Caesar emerged from the shadows in the warehouse with his hands and some of his clothes coated with blood. He seemed unfazed by the blood on him as he approached Cartier and slightly smiled.

"Cartier, it's good to see you back in town," he said.

She knew not to ask his business, although she wanted to know who was screaming in the next room.

"We need to talk," she said.

"Yes. We do."

Before she could say another word, she noticed two men behind Caesar carrying something in a large trash bag. It appeared to be a body inside; blood was dripping onto the floor, leaving a small trail. Caesar noticed her fixed gaze.

"Oh that," he said about the body being carried out. "Just a problem I needed to take care of. His answers to my questions were not to my liking, so I gave him some initiative to think rationally and clearly. But that is not your concern. From our last conversation, you said you were kidnapped and by your husband."

"I know it sounds far-fetched, Caesar."

"I've heard it all, Cartier, and I don't put anything past anyone," he replied. "And I've also spoken to your two men, Majestic and Scooter."

Cartier raised an eyebrow.

"And if you're wondering, they are still alive," he added. Caesar had stopped short of murdering her two men while she went missing because he believed she was avoiding him.

It was a relief to hear for Cartier, but she wasn't out of hot water yet.

"I'm going to need you to elaborate on this kidnapping situation."

It was cold in the warehouse, but Cartier felt hot like the temperature in the room had rocketed to 110 degrees. She unzipped her coat to show him her stomach. He was taken aback.

"You're pregnant."

"Yes, as you can see."

"Is the baby mine?" he asked.

"I don't know."

She didn't understand why she couldn't lie to him. It would have been easier. But Caesar was like a human lie detector, and besides, she was in enough shit with him already.

The announcement changed the vibe inside the room. He moved closer to Cartier and placed his hand against her stomach. He wanted to feel the life growing inside of her—the chances of it being his seed she was carrying. It was heartfelt. He wasn't getting any younger, and Cartier made him feel alive.

"Of course I demand a DNA test to see," he told her.

She nodded.

"I will know either way because I only make sons."

She chuckled. "Is that so?"

"It is so. And if the baby is mine, then this definitely changes things," he stated.

"How?" Cartier wanted to know.

"My wife Lena, she needs to go, and your husband too," he said unemotionally. "It can all be done the easy way."

"You wanna kill my husband?" she asked incredulously.

"He is a distraction, as is my wife. And if what you're telling me is true—that he kidnapped you for a month, then—"

"No!" she yelled.

"You still love him, after he kidnapped you?"

"It's not that . . . I just don't want him dead right now. What you do with your wife, that's your business, but Head is my personal business, and I can handle it."

Cartier didn't know what came over her. A few minutes ago she was worried about being murdered by Caesar, and now she was defying him for some reason. Though Head kidnapped her, lied to her, betrayed her, and mistreated her, it didn't sit right with her to have him killed—at least not right now. And it was evident that he felt that same way toward her. He could have easily retaliated against her once Harlem snitched about the alleged hit. But he didn't. And for some reason she thought about all those children he had fathered with his stable of needy women. They would all be born and never know who their father was. Cartier couldn't have that on her conscience. Besides, she didn't know whose baby was inside of her.

"You are a brave woman, Cartier. And I keep reminding you of it, but sometimes bravery does have its consequences."

She stared him directly in his eyes and responded, "I know."

"It's good that you know."

"Are we done here?" she asked, zipping her coat back up.

"I guess we are."

He smiled at Cartier and left the building. He would temporarily spare her husband's life. If he murdered Head against her wishes, then Cartier wouldn't give him her heart. He wanted her love—her undivided affection. He truly loved her, but he had to be a patient man. He didn't want to force her hand. He figured Cartier was a smart woman and she would wise up eventually and understand what was best for her—for her future.

But his patience with Lena was up. He would ask her for a divorce, and she would quickly agree.

34

artier's nerves felt like they were about to jump off a cliff. The air around her felt stifling. She wanted to breathe again and relax—even escape somewhere. Last night felt surreal, because it was an encounter with Caesar she thought she wouldn't survive.

The past few months of her life had been chaotic and melodramatic, but Cartier could only remember a few times when she experienced short-lived peace and tranquility. Thinking about her life—the whirlwind of drama and loss—could easily thrust her into depression. Her husband kidnapped her, got Harlem pregnant along with several other women, and he wanted her to join his cult. She was pregnant and wasn't sure whether the father was her trifling husband or a murderous drug kingpin. Everyone she ever loved was dead, including her mother and daughter. She couldn't help but to feel like she would be next. It was starting to feel like the grim reaper was sitting on her shoulders, mocking her. Speaking of her husband, he hadn't tried to contact her in any way since Harlem had let her go.

Her mood started to feel like the weather outside; cold and gloomy. Cartier took a good look at herself in the mirror. What she saw was something she suddenly wasn't proud of. *Where is my life going?* she asked herself. *What's my purpose?*

She was about to have another baby. Boy or girl, Head or Caesar's, her child was going to be loved unconditionally. She didn't want to make the same mistakes she made when she had Christian. The choices she made brought the demise of her family, and staring at her reflection in the bedroom mirror, the truth was staring right back at her. She was a murderer and a hustler, and so was the child's father, no matter who it turned out to be. And she didn't want her child to follow in their footsteps.

"What are you gonna do, Cartier?" she asked herself.

One of the things she respected about Caesar was how he had a mysterious "vanilla" life upstate for the sake of his child. It was a front, but it worked. She wanted the same thing. She wanted to start a new life—a new Cartier Cartel. She wanted to start a cartel of positive women. It would be a girl gang for something good. Everything needed to change in Cartier's life, starting with her men, her habits, and her outlook on life. She wanted that legacy Caesar had told her about the first time they met—a true purpose.

Cartier called Sana into the kitchen for a chitchat while she prepared to stuff her face with the bag of White Castle cheeseburgers and onion rings she had just bought. Cartier bought twenty burgers and six orders of onion rings and she didn't want to share, yet she knew she had to offer.

"You want some?"

Sana frowned. "Vegan, remember?"

Cartier smiled. "Right. You know, I'm surprised you just now hopped on the vegan bandwagon."

"What does that mean?"

Cartier murdered the tiny cheeseburger in two bites. "You have that look that says 'I'm vegan, do yoga, drink matcha tea, juice my veggies, align my chakras each morning, meditate, and hike.'"

"Are you making fun of me?" Sana didn't appreciate being called away from studying to be insulted.

"Stop being so sensitive," Cartier replied, and then stuffed an onion ring in her mouth, licking the tartar sauce from her fingers. Her mouth was chewing so quickly but she managed to carry on a conversation. "I'm just saying that I'm proud of you for bettering yourself without help from anyone. It's good to strive for the best version of ourselves."

"Thanks, Cartier. But whether I've said it or not, you've helped me more than anyone and never asked for anything in return. I appreciate you so much, and I know that I'm better because I met you."

Now Cartier was grinning. "So listen, I've been thinking a lot about that conversation we had about purpose—the one your teacher brought up. I said I would get back to you, and I'm still stumped."

"Well, what gives you the most joy?"

Cartier exhaled and then shrugged. Her answers were inappropriate. "It should be positive, right?"

Sana nodded.

"I like lookin' out for people—the underdog."

Sana quickly agreed. "That's true. The way you took in me and Har—the trifling one—shows that's what you love to do."

"But I can't look out for everyone."

"Maybe you could look into mentoring or public speaking. Maybe speak to disenfranchised high school students who are made to feel marginalized by society because of class, sex, or creed."

Cartier shook her head. "Nah, not for me. All those young students would learn from me is how to curse someone the fuck out."

They both grinned.

Sana had to admit that Cartier was rough around the edges. What could someone like her, who means well and has a good heart, do to have purpose and help her community?

"What about a group home? There are several in New York state. Maybe you could reach out and assist one in some capacity."

"A group home?"

"Yeah."

"Maybe…"

"As you can see, the place is really spacious and in a very good area," the female real estate agent informed Cartier.

Cartier and Sana were taking a quick tour of the place, a three-story Neo-Grec brownstone in Park Slope on a tree-lined street that needed some renovations. It was the fifteenth property she had shown to Cartier, and Cartier could tell that the realtor was ready to move on to her other potential buyers. However, Cartier wanted to make the right decision. This was important to her.

The real estate agent continued with, "It was built in eighteen ninety-nine and it's twenty-seven hundred square feet per floor."

"And what is the asking price again?" Cartier asked her.

"Two-point-five million," replied the agent.

It was a hefty price to pay, but Cartier needed the space and a Brooklyn location.

"The ground floor has a private entrance and is zoned as a rental. Down there you have three bedrooms and two bathrooms. The previous owners used it for their in-laws. You can open it back up to the main house or keep it as is. The upper two levels has a separate entrance and six bedrooms with four bathrooms. It's been on the market for less than a week, and it won't last long at this price. And as you can see, though it needs some work done, the foundation is still steady, and the original craftsmanship to all fireplaces and mantles is intact."

"I like it," Sana said.

The realtor smiled at her, hoping the young white girl helped her with the sale of the place.

"Two-point-five, and with renovations—what I'm looking at, something over three million?"

"It would be a wise investment."

It would.

"Fuck it, I'll take it," Cartier said.

"You won't regret it. I'll get the paperwork started."

Sana smiled. She couldn't wait to move in when the place was ready. Cartier and the realtor walked off to talk in more detail. Cartier didn't want to drop two million on a home and alert the feds, or worse—the IRS, so she decided to finance the home through a shell company that Caesar helped her set up. The estimated monthly mortgage was $11,500.

When Cartier and Sana stepped outside the brownstone, they hugged.

"I'm so proud of you," Sana sang.

Cartier didn't admit it, but she was eager to get out of her rental. Too many people knew the address, and she would rest easier if she rested her head at a new location.

After closing on the brownstone, Cartier's next move was to see an attorney. She and Sana strutted into a prestigious law firm in Lower Manhattan to meet with a woman named Megan McKinney. McKinney's specialty was in intellectual property. She was able to advise Cartier on issues relating to trademarks, service marks, and patents. Cartier had trademarked Cartier Cartel's Clubhouse, and she was working toward opening its doors to underprivileged youth. She wanted to do community outreach and help guide wayward teenagers with nowhere to go on education, job placement, mentoring, and internships. Cartier wanted to get grants from the government to help with legitimate cash flow to keep the place functioning.

What Cartier saw in Flint with Head opened her eyes, and it disgusted her how Head was misguiding those young women. She knew how it felt to be taken advantage of as a young girl. Back in her young days, a bitch named Shorty Dip took advantage of Cartier and her friends. She had Cartier and her crew shoplifting and taking all the risks while Shorty Dip reaped the benefits from it.

It was going to be difficult caring for her baby and running things too, so she put Majestic in charge of her distribution operations, and they would meet once a week. Business on the streets was good. Having a buffer between herself and the drug operation allowed her to focus more on her day-to-day planning of her group home and on giving birth to a healthy baby.

Astonishingly, Sana became more of a help and benefit to Cartier than anyone else. Sana was great at getting through to her generation, and with her knowledge about computers and numbers, they became a great team. Sana actually cared about Cartier, and she was grateful to help out any way she could.

Spring rolled around, and just as the frost dissipated, so did thoughts of Head, Harlem, Pebbles, drama, heartache, and heartbreak. Cartier kept herself busy and focused on what mattered—her pregnancy and CCC group home for girls. She hadn't heard from Head in months since escaping his compound, but then that streak was broken.

35

The pain was nearly unbearable for Pebbles, even though it was her third time giving birth. It felt like she was going to be in labor forever.

"Push! Keep pushing," the doctor encouraged. "Come on, just a few more pushes."

"Aaaah! Oh god!" Pebbles cried out.

The head was crowning, and Pebbles was pushing the best she could. She hollered in pain and wanted it to be over with. Surrounded by medical staff with the room feeling crowded, the one person she wished was there was Head. She yearned for him to be by her side at a wonderful moment like this—to hold her hand, comfort her, and tell her that everything was going to be all right. She knew he was in town, and she expected him to be there for his baby's birth.

She continued to push, feeling her baby would come at any minute. She thought Head was going to miss his daughter's birth. But surprisingly, he came marching through the doors and into the room ready to witness everything. Seeing Head there, Pebbles smiled and exhaled.

"Thank God," she uttered.

Head came to her bedside and took her hand into his and said to her, "C'mon, baby, you can do this. Push!"

And she did. She grunted, growled, cursed, and squeezed Head's hand like she wanted to break it into two pieces—but she pushed and pushed until their baby girl was in the doctor's arms, crying loudly. It already sounded like she had a healthy set of lungs.

After cleaning her off and physically inspecting the newborn girl, the doctor handed their prized daughter into Pebbles' arms and Pebbles beamed with joy. She was the most beautiful thing Pebbles had ever seen. Head smiled too. They had created a life together—a black life—and Head wanted to teach his daughter so many things.

"What are you going to name her?" one of the nurses asked.

Pebbles gazed at her baby girl and replied with, "Piper."

"It's a beautiful name," the nurse responded.

"It is." Pebbles smiled.

At that moment, Pebbles felt that she and Head were a family. It was an awesome feeling and she didn't want it to fade. Lying there skin-to-skin with her newborn daughter, she already felt connected, and having Head by her side in the room, she wished he would never leave.

"I love you."

He smiled and replied, "I love you too."

Those simple words made for a heavenly moment, and Pebbles felt that things were about to change. She thought Head would be around and treat her more like a wife than a mistress. Now that she had birthed his daughter, Pebbles believed that she had been promoted to a different position in his life.

Head spent a week with Pebbles and his daughter. When Pebbles and the baby were discharged, she came home to a beautiful new nursery. It was all paid for by Head. Only a few days old, and Piper already had everything a child could dream of, even though she didn't know it. Head even bought his baby girl a diamond ankle bracelet. He wanted her to have the best, and for her to be the best.

However, Pebbles' family moment and her bond with Head were short-lived.

"I gotta go," he announced to her one morning.

"So soon?"

"I need to take care of business. You know that," he said.

Head packed his things and left for Michigan a week after Piper was born. Pebbles never asked him any questions. She let him go on his merry way to whatever business in Michigan he had to take care of. She simply went with the flow. Head was paying all her bills, and once her body snapped back into shape, she planned on getting back to work.

The knock at her front door caught Pebbles off guard. She was trying to breastfeed Piper when it came. She knew it wasn't Head because he had his own key to her place. Pebbles placed her baby girl in the crib, covered herself, and went to see who it was. When she glanced through the peephole, she was completely taken aback by the visitor. In fact, she became worried. Cartier was standing in the hallway.

"What do you want, Cartier?" Pebbles asked from the other side of the door.

Pebbles knew Head had married Cartier, and she still allowed him to lie in her bed and continued to have sex with him.

"We need to talk," Cartier said.

"We have nothing to talk about. Get away from my door before I call the police."

"I came to talk, and you wanna call five-oh?"

"You're here for a reason and I know it's not to talk. Stop being mad because your man chose me."

Cartier shook her head. Pebbles was always talking slick through a phone line or thick door.

"First off, let me get this out the fuckin' way—I will always be that bitch who niggas will give a ring to and want to marry. Head's not my man; he's my husband."

"And, if it wasn't for the mistresses, then marriages wouldn't last as long as they do. And if it wasn't for the mistresses, y'all husbands would be completely miserable and bored, so you should be thanking me," Pebbles countered.

Cartier chuckled at her remark.

"Look, Pebbles, I didn't come here to fight or argue with you. I came here to talk—woman to woman," Cartier said.

"Again, talk about what?"

"It's about Head. I promise that no harm will come to you," said Cartier sincerely. "Look, I'm pregnant too, and it's Head's."

Pebbles huffed. It was a shock to hear. She wanted to believe Cartier, but the bad blood between them made her dubious. However, she couldn't run from Cartier forever. Maybe they did have something to talk about.

Cautiously, Pebbles opened her apartment door. Cartier stood there with a slightly protruding stomach. She entered and the first thing Pebbles said to her was, "I don't want any shit from you. My baby's sleeping in the next room."

Pebbles had her cell phone in hand and 911 on speed dial.

"I told you, I didn't come here to fight," said Cartier. "Look at me."

"So, you're pregnant?" Pebbles took a seat on the couch and motioned to the chair nearby for Cartier.

Cartier nodded and took a seat. "Nearly five months."

"Well, like it or not, our children are gonna be related," said Pebbles.

"I know." She hated it, but it was the truth. "I have something that I think you should know."

"What, Cartier?"

"Do you know about Head's other life?"

"Other life?"

"Yes. I found something out about him, Pebbles—something you should know too."

"Listen, whatever you know or found out about Head, just keep it to yourself," Pebbles replied in exasperation. "I don't wanna know. I don't care."

Cartier was shocked by her reply. She came to inform the bitch, but it was obvious that she wanted to keep herself in the dark.

"The only thing I care about right now, Cartier, is my daughter, her father, and how her father treats me when we're together. I don't want to know about anything else out there. Our issues are our issues, and I'm cool with the way things are. But I don't want any more surprises and bullshit in my life. Head's business out there is his business, not mine."

She said a mouthful, and Cartier couldn't believe Pebbles could be so simple-minded. She thought that maybe she and Pebbles could become allies instead of enemies, but now Cartier felt she had made a mistake coming to her and believing the girl had any common sense.

"I guess that's it then." Cartier stood to leave.

Pebbles nodded. "I guess so."

36

artier got out of the black Tahoe with the assistance of Lil Foe. He jumped out the driver's seat and opened the back passenger side door for his boss. With her drug operation expanding, she had Majestic hire additional men, which freed up Lil Foe to start back driving for her. It was really more for convenience than her security. Roddy was needed with distribution, and that's where he felt most comfortable.

"You want me to follow you up or you good?"

"I'm good, Foe."

"A'ight. Call me and I'll pick you up in the morning if you need me."

"Cool."

"You sure you don't need anything before I go? Snacks, soda, pickles?"

She laughed. "Nah, I'm good. Be safe."

She wobbled her way into her building and took the elevator to her floor. Her Brooklyn brownstone was still under renovation, and the cost was climbing to $600,000 for repairs. She wanted the place finished by June. She didn't want to spend a minute longer at her current place.

She stepped off the elevator and approached her door, but before she could walk inside, she heard Head say, "Cartier, we need to talk."

His voice sent chills down her spine. She spun around and saw Head coming toward her. She immediately frowned at his presence. She was armed with her .380 and wouldn't hesitate to use it on him if he came to act up.

"There's nothing to talk about, Head. I don't want you here!" she retorted.

Head would soon be the father of six babies with a possible seventh on the way. Cartier's protruding stomach was now noticeable, and Head glanced down at it and said to her, "Why didn't you tell me?"

"Tell you what?" she countered. "It's not yours!"

Head stared at her stomach, trying to guess how far along she was. "I don't believe you," he said.

"Too bad, nigga."

Head tried to follow her inside her apartment, but she quickly vetoed that. "Cartier, I just need to talk. To explain some things."

"Why haven't you signed the divorce papers my lawyer sent you?"

"That's why I'm here. Why are you doing this?"

"If I have to spend one more second talkin' about this bullshit, I'ma blow my own fuckin' head off. Not today, Malachi Muhammad. I'm done."

Cartier went inside her apartment and slammed the door shut in his face.

Head took a gulp from the tequila bottle clutched in his hand and knocked repeatedly on Pebbles' apartment door. It was 2am and he was clearly drunk and depressed. He leaned against her door, too inebriated to pull out his key, and continued to knock, creating a disturbance inside her building.

"Baby . . . open the door. Please. I-I wanna see ya," he slurred. "Open up, baby . . . open-open up."

The door swung open and Pebbles quickly pulled him inside. She wanted him to stop making a ruckus.

He staggered into her living room and smiled at her, stammering, "Where . . . where my baby girl at?"

"She's sleeping, Henry, and I don't need you waking her up," Pebbles said to him.

"Can-can I give her . . . a kiss goodnight?"

"You're drunk," she said.

No longer able to maintain his balance, he stumbled and fell onto her couch. The half-empty bottle finally fell from his hand. She sighed. It was going to be a long night. She helped him to his feet and into the second bedroom, where she helped him undress.

"I miss her," he cried out all of a sudden.

Those three words sent warm and fuzzy feelings into Pebbles' stomach. She thought he was talking about Piper.

"I miss her a lot, Pebbles," he reiterated.

"Just get some sleep," she said.

"I miss her!" he said, more forcefully this time.

"Shhhhhh. Didn't I say be quiet? You'll wake up Piper." It was hard to shut up a drunken man.

"Baby, she don't want me anymore. And I still love her."

Wait, what? "You miss who, baby?"

"I was foolish. I did all this shit to hurt her. I wanted her to hurt like I was hurting. I don't wanna lose her." Head began sobbing. His actions frightened her. He was animated and full of grief like someone had died. "I fuckin' went too far wit' this shit."

His body was heaving in and out like a man in great pain. If he were not crying over another woman, she would have been saddened that he was in such agony. It didn't matter that he was smashed, which was causing him to be hyper-sensitive. Pebbles stood over him frozen. What was going on? First Cartier came over wanting to spill secrets and now this?

She eventually sat down next to him and grabbed him in a warm embrace. Head rested his head on her breasts and began to calm down. Pebbles finally wanted answers.

In a soothing voice as she rubbed his temples she asked, "Are you upset over Cartier? Is that why you're crying?"

Head began to calm down. "What! No!" he denied.

"You don't love her, Henry?"

"I don't love that bitch! She asked me for a divorce! I'm divorcing her trifling ass! She be cheatin' and shit."

"She's has someone else? Is that why you're crying?" Pebbles voice was still measured and soothing.

"I fucked up, Pebbles. This all on mmm-me." His voice cracked as he tried to keep it together. "I got something to tell you, but if I do you gonna leave me too."

"I won't leave you, baby. Just tell me."

He screamed out, "You lying! You will too!"

"Shhhhhsh! Stop yelling!" she snapped, and then continued with, "What is it that I need to know?"

"Piper, my baby girl, she has siblings on the way I want her to meet."

"Oh, is that why you're upset?" Pebbles sighed in relief. "I already know that Cartier is pregnant and we're on better terms."

"Not Cartier! That's not my fucking baby! She's a cheater. She's a cheater and I hate her!"

Pebbles was confused. However, that small voice in her mind told her what was coming next. It was why Cartier came over.

"If you're not talking about her, then who is having your baby?"

Head sat straight up and looked her in her eyes. "Haven't you been listening? Piper has five siblings on the way."

Pebbles blinked rapidly. "Did you say five? How is that even possible? Are you telling me that someone—not Cartier—is having quintuplets?"

"I'm telling you that there are five great women that I want you and Piper to meet. Mandy is due any day now, so Piper will have a brother or sister very soon, Pebbles. I need you to get acquainted with these women. The same women that Cartier met, but she fucked everything up. She fucked everything up."

The conversation reverted back to Cartier, and Pebbles had to walk away. She left Head in the spare bedroom brooding and feeling sorry for himself until he finally passed out. Pebbles sat in her kitchen numb for hours, just staring straight in front of her. She tried to process what he had said, but there was no getting around that fact that there were five women having five babies by the man she loved. And if Cartier was pregnant by Head, then that made six. How was Pebbles ever going to explain to her daughter, who would be the oldest of seven, this ghetto soap opera?

The next day, when Head finally woke from his drunken stupor and came back to his senses, Pebbles had nothing to say to him. She gave him the silent treatment all morning.

"Everything okay?" he asked.

"Everything's fine," she replied dryly.

"Well, I need to go. Okay?"

"Fine."

Head kissed his newborn baby girl goodbye and left the apartment. Pebbles didn't want a hug or a kiss from him. Head found it strange, but he shrugged his shoulders and went on his way.

Soon after his departure, Pebbles was on the phone with a locksmith. She wanted to change her locks and finally be done with Head. She would allow him to see his daughter, but she would no longer be his mistress, his side bitch, or otherwise.

No more head games.

37

He's probably seeing her again, Harlem thought to herself. She didn't want to think about it, but the thought of Head with Cartier tore her up inside. She was completely in love with him and she didn't want to lose him—not to Cartier, Pebbles, or anyone. Harlem wanted to be the primary woman in Head's life. She and Mandy had given birth to his children, but she gave birth to his son, Henry Jackson, Jr. She was happy living in Flint, but she seethed when Head was away.

While he was gone, Harlem was holding down the fort. With Head away, the atmosphere on the compound suddenly shifted and changed. Though she was a sister wife and Head preached to them about unity and togetherness, Harlem treated the other girls like dirt when he wasn't around to see.

The girls were in the basement processing the drugs, cutting up the cocaine, and packaging the heroin and pills for distribution while Harlem was coordinating the drug runs. It was a business she felt proud to be in charge of. She had come a long way from being an escort for Esmeralda, and she wasn't going backwards. Though she owed Cartier a lot, she wanted to be in her shoes. Harlem wanted to become like Cartier—but a better version of her.

Harlem made sure the kids were studying and that the house was spotless. She made sure Mandy, Kandy, Melissa, and Jacki performed their daily duties. She did everything Head demanded of her, and she felt overlooked by him. She was a new mom and no longer wanted to share Head. She became more vocal when brokenhearted.

When Head returned to the compound, she could tell that he had a lot on his mind.

"You look stressed out, Daddy. Let me make things better for you," said Harlem, ready to please him in any fashion and help him unwind from his trip to New York.

"I'm fine," he replied, not wanting to be bothered.

"Well, everything's been taken care of. During your absence, I had everything moving smoothly."

He ignored her statement as he sat in his armchair and threw back a shot of vodka.

"She wants a divorce," he blurted out.

"Isn't that good news, Daddy?" Harlem said brightly.

Once again, he ignored her and continued to think about something. She hoped it wasn't about Cartier.

"I'm not giving her a divorce. She's my wife and she will always be my wife," he said.

"You should give her what she wants. We don't need her. You have me, Daddy. I'm here for you twenty-four seven. I can take care of all of your wants and needs. I can easily take her place and treat you so much better."

Head snorted. In his book, Harlem wasn't even runner-up. She was tied in third place with Jacki.

"I love you, Daddy. I do, and together, we can do whatever we want out there. It's your world, Daddy. It is. I believe in you," she said.

Head turned to look at her and coldly responded with, "Stop with that Daddy bullshit! You sound like a whore!"

"Yes, Malachi," she replied quickly.

"And stop tryin' so fuckin' hard. You ain't her. You never gonna be her!"

Head had this wild look in his eyes that began to frighten Harlem.

"I wish I could erase all y'all bitches—the kids too—and memories and all this fuckin' foolishness. Fuck it! I would do anything to get her back into my life. I took this shit too far! This fake-ass King Solomon bullshit!"

Head flung the vodka bottle across the room, and it crashed against the wall. Glass and liquid splattered everywhere.

His response shocked Harlem. It was hurtful. Still being subservient she asked, "Do you want me to clean that up?"

"I want you outta my fuckin' face, outta my fuckin' life. If I wake up tomorrow and never see you again, please know that I will give no fucks."

It was apparent to Harlem that she would never take Cartier's place and she would never have Head's heart the way Cartier did. They had history. Harlem quietly walked away, refusing to allow him to see her cry.

38

re you ready to know what you're having?" Dr. Smith asked her. Cartier wanted to have a gender reveal party, so she had asked Dr. Smith to not tell her at their previous ultrasound. She had changed her mind about the party, and now she wanted to know.

Cartier nodded. "I'm ready."

They both were looking at the monitor as he moved the probe along the ultrasound gel and then finally stopped.

"It's a boy."

"Are you sure?"

He laughed. "Oh, I'm sure."

"I'm having a son. My first son," she announced with joy.

"Congratulations! Well, everything reads well, and your blood work came back fine. You're going to have a healthy son," he said.

She grinned. Cartier needed the good news. Everything seemed to be falling into place.

"You seem happier since our last visit," he said.

"I have a reason to be happy."

"Do you feel like sharing the news?"

She did. "Before here, I went by a property that I'm renovating and it's almost complete. The Cartier Cartel's Clubhouse is a go. All my hard work is going to pay off."

"Another congratulations," he said. "And this project, what does it deal with?"

"It's a community outreach program for young teenage girls to help them get an education, job placement, and mentors and internships."

Dr. Smith couldn't hide it; he was impressed and proud of her. "You're doing a lot."

"I'm just trying to give back, that's all."

"You're doing more than others, that's for sure. But listen, if you need me to help out in any way I can, don't hesitate to let me know."

She didn't understand how her doctor could help out with her project. And seeing the slightly perplexed expression on her face, he explained himself more.

"Since this is my own practice, and until the girls can get healthcare, I can offer them free checkups and screenings. I can also talk to the pharmaceutical companies to give sample contraceptives and medicine. And I can drop by the place to teach the girls about their health and safe sex and give out brochures—whatever I can do to help out in the community."

Cartier was surprised by his generosity. She needed more contacts like Dr. Smith.

"I'm floored, Dr. Smith. You are a wonderful man, and I'm thankful for all your help."

"I've seen how bad it is out there. I have dozens of young girls come see me, and the condition most of them are in, it's heartbreaking."

"It is."

Dr. Smith told Cartier about a young girl who was eighteen years old. She had fallen on hard times. She was the perfect candidate for her project because at the moment she was staying with relatives, and her aunt was very abusive toward her.

Cartier asked for the girl's number and said, "I'll look into it and see if I can't help her out."

He smiled and replied, "We need more blessings like you in this community."

Cartier had gotten dressed and was standing to make her follow up appointment when Doctor Smith asked if he could speak with her in his office. She went in and sat down.

"I don't usually do this, but after I deliver your healthy baby, would you consider going out on a date with me?"

Her eyes widened from shock. He saw the look on her face and was completely embarrassed. "I mean, I know that's a few months off and only if you're not with someone, of course . . . and I could recommend another doctor—I mean, I know this is awkward, but I wanted you to know that I would like to get to know you. Please, say something." He was rambling.

Cartier finally smiled. "It's not awkward at all. Well, maybe a little with you seeing my goodies and all. Maybe this is sexual harassment."

Now his eyes widened.

"I'm joking," she chuckled. "Let's revisit this after you deliver my son, because if something happens to him during my delivery, you won't live long enough for our dinner date."

He waited a beat and then burst out laughing. "You're a funny one. Looking forward to our first dinner. Take care, Cartier."

"You, too, Dr. Sm—Allen."

It was another clandestine meeting with Majestic and Scooter in an undisclosed part of Brooklyn. Cartier arrived in the Tahoe under the cover of night, and she never got out of the vehicle. Her protruding stomach was making it more difficult to get around. She could feel her baby kicking, and it was a gentle nudge against her skin.

Majestic and Scooter arrived alone. Though they ran the day-to-day operations, Cartier was still the one calling the shots. Her men were holding things down in the streets, from cash transactions to murder if needed. They were also excited to become uncles. When word got back to them that she was having a boy, they were happier than she was.

"A nephew, that's what up," said Majestic.

"You know we gon' look out fo' da the little nigga, fo' real, Cartier," Scooter added.

They treated Cartier like family and fawned over her like she couldn't do anything wrong.

"But business been good and quiet on the streets—no problems since that stick-up last year," Majestic told her.

"What 'bout ya husband? Just give us the word and he can be dealt wit', Cartier. He violated you and almost put us in a bad position with Caesar," Scooter kept reminding her. They had been begging to murder Head since she had gotten back from Michigan.

"I'll handle him on my own time," Cartier replied.

"Indeed," Scooter said.

Their meeting was short. Cartier got the information she needed from them, along with a duffel bag full of cash to launder, and she went on her way. With Majestic and Scooter in charge, she was able to insulate herself from the drug trade and the streets. But the one thing she couldn't insulate herself from was Caesar. He had called her to meet again.

Despite being pregnant, Cartier entered the Brooklyn lounge that Caesar owned looking like she could walk the red carpet at a swanky Hollywood award show. Her sexy red spring dress covered her pregnancy with class and style. She arrived at the place with butterflies swimming around in her stomach. She didn't know if she was nervous because Caesar was unpredictable or because she was still attracted to him and might be carrying his baby. She was hesitant to show up, but at the last minute she changed her mind.

The lounge was full with customers, but the teeming atmosphere was of no concern to her. The moment she stepped inside, she was greeted by a young woman and was escorted to a private room for dinner.

Caesar was already seated at the table. Seeing Cartier walk into the area, he stood up from his chair and helped her take a seat at the table. Her body was constantly changing, and getting up and sitting back down was becoming slightly more difficult for her every day.

"You look exceptional tonight," he said.

"Thank you."

"Once again, I'm glad you came to join me for dinner. I know our last encounter was a bit awkward."

"It was."

"This is my way of making it up to you."

Everything was beautiful. The décor was overflowing with colorful flowers and balloons and flowing drapes. There was a bottle of Chateau Cheval Blanc on their table, which cost over $1,000 a bottle. Two servants were on standby, and the chef waited in the kitchen, ready to prepare whatever they desired.

Caesar grinned and said, "I heard that you're having a boy... *Noticias maravillosas.*"

He knew everything. It was scary.

"Yes."

"And have you thought about any names yet?"

"No. It's too soon."

"I'm sure you will come up with a nice name for him."

"I will."

Caesar snapped his fingers and the two servants hurried his way. He ordered a few appetizers, opened the bottle of wine, and was about to pour her a glass, but then reminded himself that she was pregnant.

"Not good for baby, right?"

She smiled and nodded.

With their meals in preparation by the chef, the two continued to converse. "I got great news for you," Caesar said.

"What is that?"

"My wife and I are getting a divorce," he said.

"I hope it isn't because of me."

"No. It was time."

"Well, I asked Head for a divorce, but he refused to sign the papers."

"Again, that's a problem I can easily solve."

"And like I told you before, I can handle my own problems, Caesar," she reminded him.

As they talked, Cartier couldn't deny how incredibly attracted she was to him. Was it her hormones or was it real? But it was his conversation that she really adored. It drew her in like a magnet, along with his power and status.

The dinner went great, but it was getting late and Cartier had a busy day tomorrow.

Caesar wanted her to spend the night with him, but she respectfully declined. It was just too messy right now.

he renovations on the brownstone were nearly complete. The money Cartier had invested into the property was worth it. It had nine bedrooms, three floors, and one of the floors was a walkout basement, which would belong to Cartier. The rest of the place was for the young girls to stay. It would become a sanctuary with the latest amenities for troubled teenagers. She wanted to give these girls the best that money could buy. For years she had been harming her community, and she felt it was time to do something constructive. Each floor had three bedrooms, and the house could take in eight girls comfortably. Sana would be on the first floor and would oversee a lot of the day-to-day operations.

Cartier did a walkthrough of the place and she was pleased with the work done so far by the contractors. Things were going great. The paperwork for the grants was almost complete, and she was just waiting for the walkthrough by the state. The home and the renovations had cost her a pretty penny, and almost all the money she had made from South Beach went into the property. The grants were definitely needed.

Linda, the young girl Dr. Smith had told her about, would be the first to live in the Cartier Cartel's Clubhouse. When Cartier brought her to the brownstone to show her the place, Linda thought she had died and gone to heaven. She fell in love with the place and couldn't stop smiling. Cartier felt like a mini Oprah Winfrey.

She pointed out a few changes she wanted to her contractor. "Can we knock that wall down to give it more room and light in here?" she asked the contractor.

"It's feasible, but it might interfere with the building inspection," he replied.

She wanted the best, therefore she was demanding. As she talked about construction, her cell phone rang in her hand. Glancing at the caller ID, she had no idea who was calling her. She answered anyway.

"Hello?" she answered.

"Good morning, is this Mrs. Jackson?" the person on the other end asked.

Mrs. Jackson. It was her husband's last name, so she knew the phone call had something to do with Head.

Reluctantly, she replied, "Yes, this is her."

"I'm sad to inform you, Mrs. Jackson, but your husband had a heart attack in his car and has passed away."

The news hit Cartier like a ton of bricks falling from a high building. Head was dead? And from a heart attack? Did she hear the lady right? How was that possible?

All of a sudden, what was happening in the brownstone didn't matter to her. The news of her husband's death sent her into a downward spiral of sadness. Though she and Head weren't on good terms, his sudden death was upsetting.

"Excuse me," she said to the contractor.

She hurried out of the building upset and dashed to her car. The only thing she could think about was Head dying from a heart attack. He was a healthy man and it didn't seem possible.

It was standing room only. The entire hood came out to show respect to a legend. Hundreds of people gathered inside the Brooklyn funeral home, and Head's funeral could rival a state senator with the turnout, the flowers, and the showiness. He was an important figure in the community, mostly for the wrong reasons, and everyone wanted to see if it was true. No one could believe a notorious gangster like Head could die from a heart attack, and not by gunfire or while in some pussy at a ripe old age. He was in his mid-forties and was still considered a young man.

The folks inside the funeral home empathized with his widow, Cartier, a street legend in her own right. She sat stoically in the front pew, dressed in all black. Next to her was his Aunt Gloria, who was in tears, grieving over her grandnephew. Flanking Cartier and Gloria in the front pew was Apple and Kola on one side and Sana and Linda on the other. Cartier, looking very pregnant, was poised and surprisingly docile when Mandy, Kandy, Jacki, Melissa, and Harlem showed up to the funeral with their children. Pebbles also arrived with Piper in tow.

Cartier cut her eyes at Harlem, but she kept her cool. The young girl was clad in all black, looking smug. It was ironic how the two of them went from friends to enemies, and all because of a man who was now dead.

Almost every known gangster, drug dealer, thug, and kingpin came to show their respects to the deceased. Barkim and Chemo were there too, and they were both shocked silent by the display of baby mamas and the buffoonery of it all. Head never shared details of his alternate life in Michigan with them.

Even a few of Head's enemies from back in the day showed their faces at his funeral, coming in peace. Cartier wondered what Head would be thinking right now if he saw some of the people that showed up to his home-going service. In fact, she chuckled at the thought, and those seated by her found her behavior odd.

The gossiping and whispering was nonstop. Folks were talking and criticizing her, hearing about the rumors of the young baby mamas and multiple kids Head had. Some folks even tried to subtly mock Cartier for marrying a womanizer like Head. But she showed no signs of weakness or fatigue.

However, Apple wasn't so calm. She sat in the pew near Cartier with a scowl on her face. She wanted to rip Head out of his casket and kill him again for playing her friend for a fool. And that's what Cartier looked like to the public—a fuckin' fool to become baby mama number seven under these circumstances. It was completely pitiful.

During the service and the eulogy, each woman and child all did their act to prove who loved him more. When the end of the service came, Kandy, Melissa, and especially Harlem all fell frantically on top of Head's casket, screaming and hollering and moaning—professing their undying love for him.

"Oh God, please bring him back to me! Oh God, I miss him. I need him, God. What am I gonna do without him?" Harlem cried out.

"I'm going to always love you, Daddy," Kandy cried out expressively.

Jacki cried out, "I can't live without you!" before she threw herself on the floor and wailed like a police siren.

God was cursed for being so cruel and all the theatrics one could see at a hood funeral were in full swing. Harlem had a new tattoo of Head's name on her shoulder. When Mandy and Kandy saw it, they went and got matching initial tattoos on their wrists, and Melissa put his date of death in roman numerals on her ring finger. Their kids were crying and showing out too, emulating the actions of their mothers. Meanwhile, Pebbles and Cartier sat stone-faced during the service, not shedding a single tear in public.

Watching the young baby mamas act up at Head's funeral when Cartier was the only female with his last name really opened Pebbles' eyes. She was one of them too—one of the dumb-ass baby mamas that Head used and controlled. She felt ashamed of herself.

After watching the pallbearers carry the casket outside and place it into the hearse, Pebbles went over to Cartier. She felt it was the right time to approach the wife—not to beef, but to talk—woman to woman.

"Cartier, can we talk for a minute?" she asked politely.

Cartier looked her way with a blank gaze. Pebbles stood in front of her holding her baby and looking meek.

"Sure," Cartier replied.

Pebbles went to her to not only offer her condolences, but also to apologize.

"He loved you deeply, Cartier," said Pebbles. "Before he died, I didn't want anything to do with him. I changed my locks and was finally done with Head. And right now, hand to God on my child's life, I'm a better woman and I really want us to become friends for our children. I wanted to apologize."

Cartier could see that Pebbles was serious. Her watery eyes didn't lie. She was ready to move on too. Cartier felt she was growing, and Head's death was the rite of passage into a better life for herself. There was still room for growth and change, and it started with forgiving Pebbles.

The two women hugged each other. And then something Pebbles said popped into Cartier's mind. *Did Pebbles say that she wanted to become friends?*

40

Inside the hotel suite in New York, Harlem was living large now that Head was dead. She ordered room service, ran herself a soothing, warm bubble bath, and took advantage of her new life. Now that Head was dead and gone, she had taken over his Michigan operation. She knew the business like the back of her hand, and she had access to all of his connections. The icing on the cake was that the silly Flint bitches were now all under her thumb and allowed her to call the shots. But there was one problem, and it was Kandy. She was becoming increasingly vocal about why Harlem was in charge, whereas Mandy, Jacki and Melissa needed someone to take charge.

Harlem was relaxing on the king size bed with Henry, Jr. and decided to make a video call to her mother in Africa to show off her new life.

Eden came through the cell phone with a large smile for her daughter and her Ethiopian accent.

"Daughter, how is things?" she spoke.

"Hey Mom, everything is perfect," Harlem greeted.

"How's my grandbaby?"

"He's fine. He's so good too. Hardly gives me any trouble at all."

"That's how you were as a baby. We had no issues with you. You were a good girl."

Harlem beamed from the compliment. "And it's done. It's finally done. Thank you."

"Great."

Harlem spoke freely on the encrypted line about how easy it was to murder Head after he continually professed his love for the ghetto Cartier. At first, Harlem was possessive over Cartier and she wanted her to leave Head alone. When Head began secretly flirting with Harlem and she knew he had money, her allegiance toward Cartier began to dissipate. She was far from dumb and naïve. When Harlem found the *D* on Cartier's car and saw the look of shock on her face, and then Cartier mentioned the *O* at the cemetery, Harlem knew that someone was trying to spook her. Harlem waited for more notes, but none came. Then one day she decided to pick up where the anonymous stalker had left off and she created her own message: You're Dead, resending the *D* that she had originally confiscated.

Harlem wanted Cartier to stay away from Head. When that didn't happen, she told Head that it was Cartier who had shot at him, and her mother told her to send the letter exposing their situation. She did what she was told, and Cartier came running to Flint looking for the culprit. Although it did get Cartier to finally see what Head was really up to and allowed her to let him go, it didn't push Head's hand to murder Cartier, nor did it stop Head from loving her. He obsessed over her and it seemed his sanity was fleeting. Almost every day Head threatened to kick them all out so he could go back to Brooklyn and leave them all with nothing.

Eden advised her daughter to kill him. She told her how to mix the white oleander poison in his drink, watch him die, and then take over everything he'd built.

"There is no need to go after Cartier," Eden had told her daughter. "She has nothing but a baby. Just focus on the money, Harlem."

Harlem wouldn't listen. Her ego couldn't erase Head's words about Cartier. It didn't matter that Cartier was the hand that fed her—that she was the one person who cared enough to get Harlem off the streets and put down ten thousand dollars to pay a debt for a stranger she had met in jail. Cartier treated her like a sister, but all those acts of kindness from Cartier had long ago been forgotten.

Killing Head and getting away with it had made Harlem feel powerful, the same power Cartier must have felt when she beat her ass and kicked her out on the street after giving her a taste of the good life. The way Harlem remembered the slight, she had to beg and grovel to get back inside the apartment. The only thing Harlem cared about now was eliminating what she felt was a threat. Cartier. Who knew what Cartier would be capable of once she gave birth? What if Cartier decided to seek revenge for Harlem fucking Head under her roof? What if she tried to take over his business? No, Cartier was a liability, and she needed to die.

With the Cartier Cartel's Clubhouse finally up and running, the eight girls who moved in were astonished that they had something so special. It was all for them, and they were thankful. Sana was thankful too. Because of Cartier, she did an entire 180 with her life and her way of thinking. Cartier was a needed blessing in her life, and she wanted to take full advantage of it, unlike Harlem, who became deceitful and cunning. She thought the bitch wasn't going to be heard from or seen again. So Sana was shocked to get a phone call from Harlem in the middle of the day, asking her to meet her at Mickey's in Lower Manhattan at 3pm.

"Not interested," Sana said. "What you did to Cartier was unforgivable and there is no excuse."

"Please, Sana. I have something really important to tell you. You need to know."

Harlem ended the call abruptly. What Harlem said piqued Sana's interest, and for a moment, she debated if she should meet with Harlem or not. She was loyal to Cartier, but Harlem's tone and relentlessness to meet made her wonder.

"Fuck it," Sana uttered. She decided that she would meet with Harlem and hear what she had to say.

From the cut, Harlem watched Sana leave the brownstone fifteen minutes after 2pm. It was predicted. She smiled. Her plan was coming to fruition. It was risky being back in Brooklyn and seeing Cartier again, but Harlem was determined to win.

Five minutes after Sana left, she marched toward the beautiful brownstone in Park Slope, entered the wrought iron gate, and knocked on Cartier's door on the ground floor. It was the same brownstone she had followed Cartier to after the funeral, when the limousine had dropped her off.

Harlem took a deep breath. She was ready for anything. The door opened and she stood face-to-face with Cartier, who was shocked that she was there—and with her baby boy in her arms. Harlem chanced that there wouldn't be a physical attack if she brought Henry, Jr. with her. She was right.

"What the fuck are you doing here, Harlem?" Cartier growled at her.

"Please, I need to talk to you, Cartier. I don't know what to do. I didn't know where to go," she pleaded.

"And you have the nerve to come here!"

"I'm sorry for what happened. I want to explain everything to you."

She didn't want to let the traitor into her home, but Harlem continued to tug at her heart, especially while holding her baby in her arms. Cartier once loved her, and now Harlem was trying to play the victim.

"Please, I just need to talk. I have so much to tell you," she continued to plead.

Relenting, Cartier allowed her into the home.

Inside, Cartier didn't want to beat around the bush and play host to her. She glared at Harlem and said, "Talk."

She was due any day now and was easily aggravated. She felt bloated and swollen, her feet hurt, and she was gassy. She didn't have the patience for Harlem's bullshit.

"I'm sorry, but it was Head. He used me and he manipulated me. I didn't mean to hurt you," Harlem said.

She continued to beg for forgiveness and tried to explain herself by putting all of the blame on Head. Now that he was dead, he wasn't there to defend himself. It got so real and emotional with Harlem that she started to leak tears from her eyes.

"I'm so sorry, Cartier. After everything you did for me, I didn't mean for any of this to go down like that," she explained with great remorse.

"Listen, let me make you some coffee, since I know how you Ethiopians love coffee, and we can continue talking," said Cartier.

"Thank you. I would definitely like that."

She followed Cartier into the kitchen. She continued to tug at Cartier's heart. As Cartier was about to make the coffee, Harlem said, "You know what? Instead of coffee, can you make me some tea?"

Befuddled by the request, Cartier responded, "Tea?"

"Yes. With honey and lemon," she added.

"Since when did you start drinking tea? Are you English now?"

"No, but since my pregnancy and having the baby, tea has been something that I crave," she explained.

It made sense. Cartier knew firsthand how pregnancy could change a woman's taste and appetite.

Cartier waddled back and forth in the kitchen making Harlem and herself some tea. Just as Cartier was ready to plop down, Harlem stood up with Henry's bottle in her hand and asked if Cartier could place the milk in the fridge. While Cartier was busy with the bottle, Harlem cleverly slipped some oleander into the teapot. Cartier then poured both of them a cup and joined Harlem at the table. Though she was bitter with the young girl, Cartier felt the need to reconcile with her. Maybe she was right, and Head got into her head and influenced her. Head did have the gift of gab and he knew how to use persuasion well. Harlem was a young and vulnerable girl and she didn't stand a chance against him.

Harlem pretended to take a sip of tea and they continued to talk. When Cartier took a few sips from the poisoned tea, Harlem smiled. It would only be a matter of time before Cartier was gone too.

Spending some time inside the brownstone, Harlem decided it was time to leave. She wanted to meet Sana at Mickey's, but not before she washed out her cup.

As she was leaving, Pebbles showed up and it left Harlem baffled. The two women were supposed to hate each other, but it was apparent that Pebbles was there on good terms. She hadn't anticipated Pebbles showing up there.

Fuck!

Pebbles twisted her entire plan. She wanted to go back inside to make sure Pebbles got a helping of the tea, but she would look foolish turning back around.

Pebbles displayed a smug look toward Harlem, like *Bye, bitch!*

Harlem stood outside trying not to panic, but she did. She prayed that Pebbles drank the tea too, hopefully knocking out two birds with one stone. But if she didn't, then she had a problem. Pebbles would become a witness to her being there at the brownstone.

Not sure what to do, Harlem called her mother via WhatsApp and explained the situation to her.

"Oh lawd, I told you, girl, to leave her 'lone. Now look what happened," Eden exclaimed.

"I couldn't. She needed to go too," Harlem snapped. She didn't want to hear doom and gloom from her mother—not right now.

"Don't hang around. Leave, Harlem—just leave there. If you stick around, it's only gon' look suspicious," Eden told her.

Harlem knew her mother was right. She decided to head to her meeting with Sana and hoped that she could use that as her alibi.

41

"Do you want some tea, Pebbles? I just made it," Cartier said.

"No, I'm fine. I don't plan on staying long," she said.

"So, what brings you by?"

"Like I told you at the funeral, I want us to work out and become friends for our children. I'm a new me, Cartier, and I feel good about myself," she stated.

Cartier smiled.

Pebbles was still looking for absolution. She congratulated Cartier on her clubhouse and praised her for what she was doing in the community. She wanted to help too.

"It's the right thing to do. I'm looking ahead, not backwards," she explained.

Pebbles withheld one key piece of information from Cartier, and it was like a noose tightening around her neck. When Head came home last year, she wanted to scare Cartier into leaving her man alone. She started leaving notes on Cartier's car that was going to spell out, Die Slow—subsequently telling her to leave her man alone without mentioning Head's name. Pebbles sent the *D* and *O* and then came to her senses, realizing what she was doing was childish, stupid, and beneath her.

It didn't feel right telling Cartier now, when she didn't go through with the scare tactic and with Head being dead. But it didn't feel right not telling her the truth either.

Cartier was annoyed and confused, but she wasn't angry. She was more grateful that Pebbles had solved part of a mystery. If she sent the *D* and *O*, Cartier assumed that it was most likely crazy-ass Head who picked up where Pebbles had left off in an effort to scare her into his protective arms.

Cartier told Pebbles that she didn't hold her accountable for Head's actions anymore and that they couldn't be best friends like that, but they could be cordial for the kids. Things were still fresh between them and it was going to take time.

Cartier stood up and stumbled. She caught her balance and leaned against the kitchen counter.

"Cartier, are you okay?" Pebbles asked.

"Yeah. I think so," she replied faintly.

"Are you sure?"

"I'll be fine. I just need some water."

Cartier tried to walk again, but again she stumbled and fell gravely ill. She paused for a moment, looked at Pebbles with concern, and passed out on the kitchen floor.

"Cartier!" Pebbles cried out, hurrying to her aid.

Pebbles flew into a panic. She didn't know what was wrong with her. She pulled out her cell phone and desperately dialed 911.

"Get here quick! Something's wrong! She passed out and she's pregnant," she hollered into the phone.

She continued to tend to Cartier and frantically cried out, "Hold on, Cartier! Help is coming."

EPILOGUE

artier was rushed to have an emergency C-section. Pebbles hung around until she knew Cartier's condition had been stabilized, but she had her own baby to tend to.

Dr. Smith was there to deliver Cartier's healthy baby boy. The moment they placed her newborn son into her arms to do the skin-to-skin, Cartier stared at him and knew that Caesar was the father. There was something about his eyes that spoke to her.

Damn! This complicated her feelings, which were still raw. Still, she would have the DNA test performed.

They ran toxicology on her to see what was wrong and deduced that she had been poisoned.

"Poisoned?" Cartier repeated in disbelief.

"Yes. You're lucky to be alive. If your friend hadn't called 911 when she did, you and your baby wouldn't be here today," Dr. Smith informed her.

Cartier sat there in silent shock.

"Do you know anyone that would want to hurt you?" Dr. Smith asked.

In fact, she did. She immediately knew of two people who would want to hurt her, and they both had the opportunity. Harlem and Pebbles. It was either one of them or both conspiring together.

She stared at Dr. Smith and replied, "No. I don't know."

"Well, the police have been notified, so try not to worry too much. It's up to the authorities to figure out who tried to hurt you. Okay?"

"I'm not worried," she said.

"Do you have a name for him?" the nurse asked her.

"Yes. Caviar . . . Caviar Timmons," she said proudly.

"Oh. Okay," was the nurse's response.

Cartier held her newborn son lovingly in her arms and beamed with joy. Once again, she was a mother, and Caviar Timmons would become a good kid. Not a thug.

Sana arrived shortly after the birth of her son. Cartier called her to bring her pre-packed hospital bag with her essentials to help get her through the next couple days like a nightgown, undergarments, and toiletries. Sana beamed as she walked in ecstatic for the new mother.

"Did you see him?" Cartier grinned.

"He's so precious. His little lips were poked out and I just wanted to gobble up his fat cheeks." Sana was a proud auntie. "I'm going to help out as much as possible when you're released. We can take shifts feeding him."

Cartier was grateful.

The small hospital room suddenly became crowded and loud when Majestic, Scooter, Lil Foe, and Roddy came through. They all called themselves "uncles" and couldn't wait for Caviar to be old enough to hang out with them.

Cartier thought about informing her triggermen that she was poisoned but felt that the news could wait a few hours. Right now she wanted it all to be about the birth of her son. She just couldn't stop grinning from joy.

The police eventually came to question her about the incident, asking who would have given her oleander, and Cartier didn't mumble a fuckin' word to them. She didn't want the police in her business. She would handle Harlem and Pebbles in her own way.

During her time in the hospital, Dr. Smith was there for her. He would sit by her bedside to talk, and like her conversations with Caesar, it flowed. Their chemistry was undeniable. During her second day after giving birth, he asked her out on a date again—when she was well enough. She agreed. Dr. Smith was a good man, and if things worked out, she knew he would become the perfect role model for her son. However, as soon as she said yes, Caesar entered the hospital room. For some reason, she felt his presence before he even stepped foot inside.

Caesar and Dr. Smith locked eyes briefly and then Dr. Smith left the room, giving the two some privacy.

Caesar stared at Cartier like he owned her but then broke into a wide smile. She smiled back.

"I saw your son," he said.

"You did?"

"Yes. He's so handsome."

Cartier grinned.

He then said cockily, "I told you that I only make sons."

It was confirmation that he knew it was his child. Within moments of his arrival, he had her room inundated with roses and lilies, balloons, teddy bears, and even armed security. She was now under his protection. There would be no second attempt on her life or his son's life.

"You will always be taken care of," Caesar assured her.

While they talked, Dr. Smith entered the room and loomed in the background. It felt like two angels were watching over her—one moral, the second immoral. Which one would she decide to be with?

While Cartier had a serious decision to make about her love life, she knew there was still a dark score to settle. She had tried to get out of the game and help others, but the attempted murder on her and her son pulled her back in.

The streets hadn't heard the last from the Cartier Cartel.

READING GROUP GUIDE

ABOUT THIS GUIDE

The suggested questions should enhance your group's reading and discussion of this book by Nisa Santiago.

1. Why do you think it was so important to Cartier that her relationship with Head work? Do you think that she truly loved him? Or was she in love with love?

2. Cartier and Head had a history together. In relationships, have you ever gone back to an ex knowing it wouldn't work out instead of taking a chance on a new love?

3. Pebbles invested three years of her life in Head by making jail visits, putting money on his books, and being supportive. He was home less than 72 hours when his ex shows up, apparently under the impression they would be together, and a fight ensues. Have you ever fought over a man/woman? Could you relate to either female's pain? And if so, who?

4. Head didn't show up to Pebbles' arraignment, yet when he was incarcerated, Pebbles held him down. Many female inmates complain that their men almost immediately abandon them once they're sentenced. Why do you think this abandonment happens to incarcerated women?

5.   Have you ever supported an incarcerated spouse and if so, for how long? When the inmate was released, did it work out? Both Cartier and Pebbles noticed a change in Head once he was released. Pebbles notes that Head had made her a lot of promises while he was locked down. Did your released spouse make promises while incarcerated that they didn't keep?

6.   Until the DNA test comes through for Cartier, at the time of Head's death, he had seven children by seven women. Rappers Future and Fetty Wap are alleged to have multiple children by multiple women. Do you think that all baby mamas/baby daddies should get along for the children's sake? And if so, how difficult do you think that could be? Should these blended families share holidays as Alicia Keys, Mashonda, and Swizz Beatz do? Or is that a bit much?

7.   Head couldn't seem to get over Cartier choosing Hector over him. So toward the end of his bid, he took up the teachings of Brother Kareem and set out to create a world where he would live his best life. Cartier and Pebbles would both agree that his actions were extreme. Have you ever discovered a secret of a loved one almost too shocking to believe? If so, did the secret make you love them less?

8.   Do you think Cartier was foolish to have two beautiful, young women living under her roof with her man living there too? If you had to place blame for the affair between Head and Harlem, who would you blame most? Cartier? Head? Harlem?

9. Have you ever had a friend sleep with your significant other? If so, were you able to forgive the friend or your mate?

10. Harlem accepted Cartier's benevolence with open arms and thanked her by stealing from her and sleeping with her man. Is the road to hell paved with good deeds? Is niceness treated as a weakness? Have you ever gone out of your way to help someone, only to have it backfire?

11. Cartier has only dated hustlers, so her getting into bed with Caesar was a no-brainer. However, with the arrival of her son, do you think that Dr. Smith has a chance? Who would you choose, and why?

12. Head was continually caught cheating as he went back and forth between Cartier and Pebbles. Have you ever forgiven a serial cheater? If so, what's your number? How many times can someone cheat on you before you call it quits?

13. If you have loved an unfaithful person, would you prefer that the cheater have one-night stands or repeatedly get caught cheating with the same person?

14. The premise of this book is head games. Have you ever played head games to get what you wanted in relationships?

OFF WITH HER HEAD

Even with South Beach in her rearview, Apple is still unable to settle down and focus on being a mom. Not when the streets keep talking about Queenie, an enigmatic sista who is calling herself the Queen of New York.

Queenie, a hardcore former drug mule, has seen and done it all in her young life. She doesn't scare easily, if at all. When it's time for her to step up to her newfound adversary, Apple, her heart skips no beats.

Apple refuses to give up her title after just reclaiming it. She's determined to snatch the crown from Queenie and see her bow down to the real queen.

GETTING LUCKY

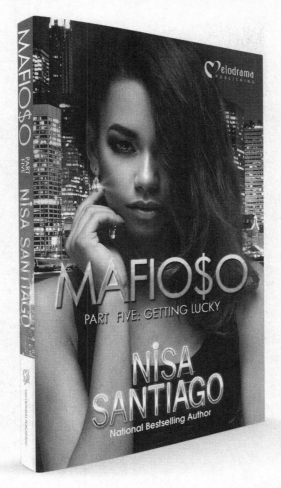

The stunning acquittals of Scott and Layla West resonate throughout the justice system, and the powerful cartels take notice.

The Wests were untouchable and their drug empire is still intact, but family ties begin to unravel.

New mom Lucky has a lot on her shoulders as she continues to deceive the head of the Juarez cartel. Partnering with her twin brothers, Lucky lines up the pieces on the chessboard, but she underestimates the king and queen.

BROOKLYN *Bombshells*

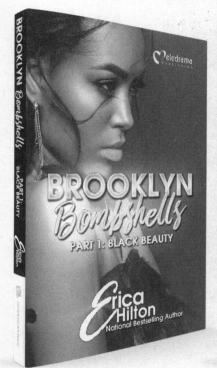

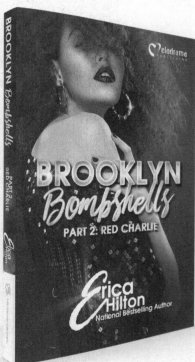

THE SERIES BY